Walks Away Woman

Books by Ki Longfellow

China Blues
Chasing Women
The Secret Magdalene
Flow Down Like Silver: Hypatia of Alexandria
Houdini Heart
Shadow Roll: A Sam Russo Mystery Case 1
Good Dog, Bad Dog: A Sam Russo Mystery Case 2
The Girl in the Next Room: A Sam Russo Mystery
Case 3
Walks Away Woman
Stinkfoot, a Comic Opera (with Vivian Stanshall)

Follow Ki Longfellow on the Internet:

Blog kilongfellow.wordpress.com
Facebook Ki Longfellow
Twitter @KiLongfellow
Official Website www.kilongfellow.com

Walks Away Woman www.eiobooks.com/waw

Sam Russo www.eiobooks.com/samrusso
www.thesecretmagdalene.com
www.flowdownlikesilver.com

Walks Away Woman

a Novel

Ki Longfellow

Eio Books

Published in the United States by

Eio Books
P.O. Box 1392
Port Orchard, Washington, 98366 U.S.A.

www.eiobooks.com

Library of Congress Cataloging-in-Publication Data

Longfellow, Ki
Walks Away Woman / Ki Longfellow.
    pages cm
ISBN 978-1-937819-90-3 (paperback)-- ISBN 978-1-937819-92-7 (ebook)
I. Title.
PS3562.O499W35 2013
813'.54--dc23
                2013040739

Cover designed by Shane Roberts
Book designed by Shane Roberts

Dedicated to
Ray Lynch

Who opened my heart

1

Ten minutes after ten in the morning and Mrs. Peter Warner is arranging her full bag of groceries in a trash barrel. A moment later she steps off the hot asphalt of a Safeway parking lot and into the Sonoran Desert.

Three silver cars, a rusted out pickup, and a white van away, there's a sunny moon-faced girl collecting shopping carts; she's made a train of them, is pushing it back to the market. Over by the ATM machine a pit bull grins in the heat. Dog's chained to a kid with a stud through his tongue; dog and kid hassle a hot woman in fat pink slacks out of her spare change. In wraparound shades and a sun hat, Mrs. Perez shakes a finger at a shrunken old man in a golf cart.

Not one of these see Mrs. Warner do what she's just done.

She's now picking her way through the broken glass and the barbed wire, the shotgun casings and the beer cans. Keeps clear of the thorns. Everything has thorns.

Place like this is full of pain. It's full of poison. It's full of snakes and spiders and centipedes. Not to mention the kissing bugs. Place like this is crawling with lizards and scorpions and toads. You remember the dog, Mrs. Warner?

Toad came and sat in his water bowl all night. In the morning, poor Buster drank from the bowl and died.

Her teeth are chattering. As if it's cold. It isn't cold. This is a desert. It's hot. She hugs her purse closer, keeps her elbows in.

The idea came in the jam and jelly section. One minute *Mrs. Robinson* played over the store PA — "... no matter how you look at it, you lose" — and Mrs. Warner was choosing peanut butter, chunky or smooth? The next minute she was charging five jars of peanut butter (smooth), a quart of nonfat milk, a roll of Certs, four rolls of single ply toilet paper, a copy of TV Guide, and a loaf of bread (it wasn't Safeway's fault she no longer needed these things, and she *had* put them in a cart). The minute after that, she was out in the shocking, bleach-boned light — walking away.

It was either that, or take the car in for a service. She could also go home. She's missing *All My Children*.

This isn't the Sahara; there are no soft white dunes of sculpted sand. It isn't the Great Basin of Nevada; nothing but an endless expanse of sagebrush and dirt. This is southern Arizona. Within seconds, she's disappeared into a jumble of brittlebush and palo verde, into cholla and ocotillo and greasewood and beavertail cactus. Mexico is sixty miles away — is it sixty? Could it be more? Less?

Forty. Fifty. Sixty. Any one of these was distance enough to get lost in, room enough to die in.

Avoiding the pale yellow spines of a teddy-bear cholla, stepping over a hard-baked pile of unidentified dung and already sheeted with sweat, Mrs. Warner wonders how long it would take someone to fall down and die out here. It couldn't be too long with no food and no water and no hat to keep off the worst of the sun.

Simple fact is, she has all the time she needs to kill herself. Peter isn't home. Peter won't be home until some time tomorrow. When he called, he said he was in Denver. He said if he could manage it, he'd catch the three P.M. flight into Tucson, but she didn't have to bother; he'd take a taxi home.

Peter isn't in Denver and he doesn't need a taxi. Peter is in "that" apartment on Dry River Street in the Dorado Hills

Estates. Turn round and look up, Mrs. Warner, you can see it from here.

Not going to. Too hot. Too much trouble.

As for Peter Jr., back in Southern California majoring in greed at Pepperdine, he might not call home for months, and only then because he needed money. As for Shelley, twenty-two going on fifteen, she's somewhere in East Los Angeles. In East L.A., Shelley could be doing anything — and usually is.

Peter can take care of it this time. It's his turn. From now on, it's always going to be his turn.

If she just keeps walking, sooner or later, she's bound to come to the end of the line. Her line. The one she's been walking all her life that ends out there somewhere, where nothing at all is waiting for her.

All it takes is one foot in front of the other. All it takes is the determination not to turn around, not to walk back to the house off the Calle de Flores mall, not to spend the rest of her life pretending the rest of her life means something. Or even the life she's already led.

Mrs. Warner kept walking. Past plastic bags pinned like torn flesh to tall whips of cruel ocotillo, past a lone red and white cow tenderly gumming buckhorn cactus fruit. You never know about animals, not even cows. They could bite you or kick you — give it room. Go around.

The ground was rising now, heading into the upper *bajadas* behind her housing estate. In every direction but back, rock upon rock reared up over her head in lipstick oranges and condiment yellows and haute couture reds.

This has to be like walking into the sea. Sooner or later the bottom is bound to drop out and you'll sink. Hope it's sooner — no place to sit down out here.

She saw a pair of hikers and avoided them. She heard someone calling his dog and veered away from the sound of his voice. A cottontail exploded out from under her feet. She shied in another direction. Barbed wire turned her this way or that. And as she went, plastic bags and plastic containers gave way to bullet shattered glass bottles giving way to old tin cans, deep red with rust, and the thought passed across what was left of her mind that the history of packaging was written on the wilderness.

It was one minute past high noon when she topped a rise and saw the little cross near the heat-dried ribs of a fallen saguaro cactus. She knew exactly what time it was because the Touch Time watch on her right wrist told her.

The cross was entwined with plastic roses, each shabby bloom sun-faded from waxy red to dirty pink. Crosses just like it marked roadsides all over America.

Mrs. Warner stooping by the cross. Wood, cheap. Stapled, not nailed. How sad. A season or two, it'll be gone. Like pop singers. Like airport books. Like actors in soap operas. Like first wives past their sell-by date.

Her mind filled with burning rubber, screaming metal, shattering glass, sudden ends, pathetic messes, traffic backed up for miles... and everyone trying to see, including Mrs. Warner.

But up here there was no road. There was no path. Here, there was nothing at all but rocks and things with thorns and things with stingers and things with teeth. And now, Mrs. Warner. Maybe someone else walked away just like you're doing. Maybe someone else decided it was time to wrap it up, call it a day, made up their mind it was time to just—stop.

She listened. Far now from the sounds of traffic, for this one moment, she became aware of birdsong. Birds sang all around her. Until she shut them out again.

Standing, surprised by dizziness, but still walking away.

She was descending rather steeply now, sliding a bit on the loose graveled side of a *bajada* punctuated with saguaro. Like pale green people, every cactus was different and every one of them was the same.

The young ones, the ones without arms, they're like exclamation points. What are they shouting about? Think about it, Mrs. Warner. They're young and they're restless. They're all your children, and they're shouting for attention. Just like everyone else.

When her hard-baked, hollowed-out husk of a body was found—and she supposed it would be found sooner or later — would Peter staple a couple of pieces of cheap wood together for her, throw in a few plastic roses?

Fat chance. If Peter ever got his hands on a staple gun, he'd staple his own foot to the floor.

In her big brown leather bag was a pair of sunglasses. About time she put them on.

She kept walking.

For the next hour or so, Mrs. Warner walked and worked on her epitaph. The best and the worst of them being: *Here Lies Mrs. Warner, Backed into a Coroner.*

She laughed. It wasn't a good laugh. It didn't feel like laughing. If it had felt like laughing, she would have turned on her heel and gone back—just like that.

It began to dawn on her that she was holding up surprisingly well for someone who was fifteen pounds overweight—well, all right, eighteen pounds overweight. That she was surprisingly spry for someone who'd let her gym membership lapse. It also dawned on Mrs. Warner that for her purposes, such as they were, she wasn't dressed for this. Coming out in good sturdy shoes, her favorite pair of well worn, if too tight, jeans, a white tee shirt under a faded denim jacket... it would have been much better, meaning been over much faster, if she'd worn her usual roomy shorts, silk shirt, and flip-flops.

But this morning, before Safeway, but after *Good Morning America* — slept on the couch again, didn't you? — Henri had done her hair. Who would have the nerve to present themselves in Chez Henri in flip-flops and shorts? Not you, Mrs. Warner. Never. Nope.

No going home to change. By now, she was too far in. Or out. And here was something else to consider: not having paid the slightest heed to where she'd walked — south? Have you been heading due south? — she wasn't altogether sure which way was "home."

That's when she saw her first rattlesnake.

Mrs. Peter Warner froze on the spot. Heat could kill her. So could starvation. And there was always some kind of accident. It suddenly occurred to her that none of these things sounded exactly comfortable. What she'd been hoping for was a silent slipping away. She'd thought she might find somewhere—go on, say it: somewhere "nice," preferably with a good view—where she could lie down and fall asleep and never wake up again.

Indians can do that. Indians... sorry... Native Americans can look out across a valley or up at a mountain, and say, "This is a good day to die." Then they'd arrange themselves for death, lie out under the sun or the moon on a nice soft rock and quietly pass away. Native Americans have dignity. Is death by snakebite dignified? Bet it isn't. Bet it's awful, so awful and so lingering, dignity would be the least of it—and misery the most.

As her favorite aunt would have said: "You're already in enough misery, dear—why make it worse?"

Holding her breath, Mrs. Warner tiptoed round the snake.

In her fourth hour, Henri would have hissed to see her hair. Worse, an overheated Mrs. Warner was suffering. Not only seriously hot, she was seriously hungry. She was also faint and dizzy as well as slightly nauseous—but worst of all, she was thirsty. Like no thirst she'd ever known, this thirst was no longer a desire; it was now a need. Like breathing.

But don't they always say nothing comes without effort? Besides, you're used to it; you've been starving for years. Either that or bingeing. Starved to lose weight. Binged out of a despair she never would. Not that Peter ever noticed. As for thirst... so? She had to die of something.

Mrs. Warner wiped the sweat off her sunglasses. Put them back on and kept walking.

Who was she fooling? Peter this and Peter that. She'd lost interest in Peter years ago... just about the time he lost interest in her. And she knew it wasn't Peter Jr. You're dying here Mrs. Warner, you can tell yourself the truth. Peter Jr. was turning out the kind of man she'd run a mile from if he wasn't her only son. He's like his grandfather, like Stan Warner, Peter's father. He has no heart. Worse than that, if he knew he had no heart, he'd think that made him strong. You love him, but you don't actually like Peter Jr., do you Mrs. Warner? So... was it Shelley? She adored Shelley, she'd always adore Shelley. But the way Shelley was going, her cherished daughter wasn't going to make it past her twenty-fifth birthday — and there wasn't a single thing anyone on earth could do about it. Heaven knows, Shelley'd been in and out of enough "programs" that took the money and tried.

Mrs. Warner quickened her pace, barely missing a fishhook cactus.

Bad as it is, it's not Shelley — it's you. It's because your gums are receding and your hair is thinning and your neckline is sagging. It's because all you ever had was your youth, and you spent that so long ago now it's hard to remember what you bought with it.

Mrs. Warner shuddered in her loosening skin, was almost running now.

It's because you're scared. Lately you're so scared and so aimless and so useless you sleep half the day and panic half the night. In between, you watch TV to ward off the evil of watching yourself.

So — if not death, then what? Let them lock her away?

When she tripped over a rock — and in tripping, plunged over the edge of a cliff — Mrs. Warner had forgotten the desert, the cacti, the heat, the hunger, the thirst, Shelley. All that was left was an ever increasing panic and an ever deepening desperation. And then there was the shock of falling and the screaming inside: Here we go, here we go — but don't hurt, don't hurt. Oh god, please! Don't hurt!

After that, there was nothing.

2

She came awake with her face pressed into coarse sand, staring directly at a line of ants. No more than two inches from her open mouth, each one carried a bit of brittle leaf. And they tugged and they pulled and they manhandled their leaves over pebble and twig and around a pair of sunglasses and the small pool of blood dripping from her nose.

She sat up so fast it made her head swim. Which made her put her hand to her head. Which made her head hurt. Her hand came away slick with red. Oh heck, it's not your nose that's bleeding; it's your head. You've hit your head on something — how bad is it? And with that, she laughed out loud. It was no more a laugh than a scream is a laugh.

How bad is it? Not bad enough. You're alive, aren't you, you fool.

She was alive and crumpled at the bottom of a wall of perpendicular rust-colored dirt. Just below the rim of the wall writhed a tangle of exposed ironwood roots big enough and hard enough and splintered enough to explain how she'd hurt her head. Snagged on a lone root was her Gucci leather bag.

Swaying, she rose to her feet.

Aside from your head, what else is wrong with you? That is, aside from your head and aside from you being suicidal?

She had the gash over her ear—hurts like three headaches at once—but the bleeding wasn't as bad as all · that. Tenderly touching her head again. Ouch. Lucky she hadn't torn off her ear, ear feels... flappy. The palm of her left hand was badly skinned. The ribs on her left side were sore. Breathing in too deeply made her cry out. Obviously, she'd hit more than her head on her way down.

But she'd landed on sand. The floor of the gully was soft yellow sand.

She was in an arroyo twenty or thirty feet wide, fifteen feet deep and who knew how long—a mile, two miles, a hundred miles? To the ants, it was the Grand Canyon. To Mrs. Peter Warner, it was way over her head. So it was either go up the arroyo or go down the arroyo. Where she stood, there was certainly no climbing out of the arroyo. The dirt would give way under her gripping hands and scrambling feet.

But why climb out? Or go up the arroyo? Or down it? Why do anything at all? And why, for god's sake, was it so hard to die?

People did it every day, millions of them. People crashed their cars. They took the wrong flight. They danced in the wrong disco. They drowned in lakes, in seas, in booze. They froze. They starved. They spontaneously combusted. They developed something there was no cure for. Their hearts gave way, or something in their brains snapped. They forgot to turn off the gas. They ate seafood even though it tasted funny. They were rubbed out, gunned down, nuked, whacked, or blown up for God. They choked on their gum. They hung themselves, poisoned themselves, swallowed all their sleeping pills at once, got in the way of someone else's war or someone else's anger. Or they climbed to the top of something and jumped off—and when those people landed, they died.

Mrs. Warner finally cried. Crying, she sank back to the sand and curled up like a woman curling up like a baby. And then, like a woman-baby, she bawled.

A big gray bee bumped into her cheek, bounced off and continued on its busy buzzing way. Startled, she noticed the air was full of gray bees — a thick wave of them, like a flag floating a few feet over the ground. One or two would drop away, landing and walking in circles on the sand, then fly up again into the flag made of bees. Her own head buzzing with pain, she watched a bee land and then begin to dig, throwing up sand in a fury of effort. A second bee dropped down to challenge for the hole. Buzzing with outrage, both bees wrestled in the dirt leaving a third bee to dive into the contested hole and dig like crazy. Suddenly, like a stripper in a stag party cake, a fourth bee came bursting out of the bottom of the hole in a sizzle of buzz. Quickly, the third bee mounted the fourth... then with a whirr of wings they took to the air, leaving the first two bees with a useless hole.

Mrs. Peter Warner lay where she'd fallen. Shut her eyes to the bees. From top to bottom, life was pointless. It was mindless, meaningless, pointless, endless, bee-less.

Her eyes shut, her hand stinging, her side aching, her ear throbbing, the sun sank into the sand and her arroyo sank into shadow. No glorious and lingering Sonoran desert sunset down here. Night was coming on, and with it, whatever went on in a desert after dark.

Mrs. Warner crept closer to the wall of dirt, fit herself into a deep red fold so that her back was protected, wriggled around until the worst of the pain in her side was favored, and waited. It was going to get dark, and when it did, it was going to get cold. Deserts get cold at night, even the mildest of them. And she was going to go to sleep. If all went well, if it was cold enough, her sleep should last forever.

But first she pulled her rings off her fingers. Engagement ring with its modest, but not too modest, diamond. Wedding ring, a plain band of good quality gold. Neither one had an inscription, not even a date or initials, but that didn't matter. They still marked her. They said she was somebody's wife. They claimed you for Peter Warner. They said you were Mrs. Peter Warner.

You're you, Molly Brock. At the end, be you.

Scooping out a hole in the folded dirt, she buried them both.

From one second to the next, she was awake to pitch black. No moon, no distant city lights, no planes flying by night, no passing satellites. But stars — my god, there were stars. You haven't noticed the stars in years. Look at all the stars. It was Van Gogh's Starry Night. The sky was a wheel of roaring stars.

And there was this — in the dark, she was too frightened to die. In the dark, there was nothing but a hot and primal desire to be safe. She was also bursting for a pee. But if she crawled away from her fold of comforting wall to find a place to piss on, she'd be exposed. There'd be nothing between her and whatever lives in the dark. And things lived in the dark; she could hear them all around her. Coyotes yipping each to each was nothing compared to what was down here in the arroyo with her.

Molly Anne Warner, once Molly Anne Brock, came alive all at once. Life brought hunger and thirst and cold. It brought the ridiculous demands of nature. It brought thick black fear. What was moving in the darkness? Spiders with bellies marked in red. Scorpions with stingers arched over their backs. Bats who supped on blood. Fat sluggish lizards like beaded bags of poison. Something worse? What could be worse than scorpions and black widows and vampire bats and Gila monsters? Tarantulas? She wriggled sideways, but only enough to clear the dirt and sand of her "bed," all the while pushing down her jeans over her hips just enough to keep from wetting herself.

Listen! What was that? Whatever it was, it was right in front of her, in the sand of the dry streambed. A slithering sound, a sort of a hiss, then a click! click! click!

She had her jeans up and was back in her fold with her spine pressed against the dirt no matter the pain in her head, in her hand, in her side. If she could have covered herself with sand, she would have. As it was, she tried.

Something exploded in her chest, and she knew it for the new enemy it was. A panic attack. Attacked by her own fear. Bone white nerve, yolk yellow nausea, a gagging, sagging loop into bodily chaos. And her mind, having no choice, followed... gibbering.

Oh my god, oh my god. You've done it. You've really done it. And now maybe you can't undo it. Maybe you've got yourself into something you can't get out of. No calling the AAA. No writing letters to your congresswoman. No whipping out a credit card, shutting the book, turning off the TV, walking out of the movie. Not even screaming at the top of your lungs is going to get you out of this. No one can hear you — except something that might... just... eat you.

Mercifully, along towards dawn, curled into a tight ball, she fell into the fitful sleep of nervous exhaustion.

She opened her eyes to a clean clear desert morning, and her ears to wind and the cooing of a mourning dove in a jojoba bush. Directly above — a good ten feet above — hung her soft brown expensive leather bag.

"Shoot," she said, which was the first word she'd spoken aloud since saying: "Fine," in dull response to the rote, "And how are you today?" from her Safeway cashier.

Mrs. Molly Warner always said she was fine. What else could you say? Who really wants to know? Who really cares? No one is fine. No one's okay. Life is one small misery after another. Life is like a sculptor. It chips away at you until all that's left is a headstone.

She also said things like "shoot" instead of shit. That was her mother's doing. Mom always said: "Only bad girls have potty mouths."

The second thing she said aloud since walking away was this: "Shelley has a mouth like a public toilet."

Her head throbbed with pain. Her side thrummed with it. From the wrist down, her left hand felt leaden. She was hungry and she was thirsty and she was chilled to the bone. Her legs were stiff with cramp. There was dirt in her socks and in the crotch of her peed-on panties, her bra straps had chaffed the skin of her shoulders, there was grit in her eyes and between her teeth. She was in a state of lingering shock from hours of panic and not enough sleep. Her armpits stank. The skin of her nose was badly sunburnt, her chin, her cheeks, the backs of her hands. Henri's latest creation was a matted mess. But she wasn't dead.

Dead? You still think that's such a great idea?

Gingerly pushing herself away from her protecting wall, the answer came rushing back: No! She was too miserable to seek death, too miserable to make the effort... and isn't this a laugh? Like everything else in life, death takes effort.

"Effort?"

Molly Brock looked straight up. Right over her head was a way out of here. In a side pocket of her brown leather bag — Christmas present from Peter, shopped for and chosen by her — was her cell phone.

Molly Brock looked to one side, to the other.

A stick. All you need is a stick. But the only thing that came close to a stick was a root, and the only root that might work was the one attached to more roots. So pull on it. Forget your side, forget your hand, they'll get fixed when you get home — pull! Wow, that hurts. Maybe twisting it until it breaks off? No. Wait. Rocks! The supply of rocks is endless. Throw a rock. You can throw a rock at it.

Molly Brock quickly gathering rocks.

Who could beat anyone she knew at tennis? But better, who was the star pitcher two years running on the girl's baseball team back in dear old Burbank High? Who pitched a no-hitter senior year to give Burbank High School the Coach Whitehead trophy? Who wasn't a southpaw? Molly Anne Brock, that's who!

Molly spitting on her hands, rubbing them on the seat of her pants.

Throw enough rocks and sooner or later, that bag's bound to work itself loose, and when it does, and when it does, it would fall right into her hands, and when that happens—praise cell phones, girl — she was home free. All she had to do then was punch in 911 and wait. In an hour, maybe even less, there'd be an emergency rescue chopper overhead, scaring the wildlife, whipping up sand as it threw her a lifeline.

Molly pitching her first rock.

Worry about explaining how you got here when the time comes, no use bothering your throbbing head about that now.

Forty-five minutes later, Mrs. Warner sat in the sand, dizzy and sick with the heat, tee shirt stuck to her back. Sunglasses back on her face, battered bag in her lap, cell phone in her hand, she was stunned into a stiff and perfect stillness. Her cell phone was dead. It was dead because she'd left the phone on. Lately, she always left her phone on. Just in case Shelley should call. Just in case Shelley wanted to come home.

Pitching a perfect sinker right across the plate, Molly threw the phone into the jojoba bush. Behind the jojoba was a rock as big as Peter was getting to be. As big as Peter Jr. Phone hit the rock with a sharp crack of snapping black plastic.

3

Since she was just sitting there, and since her bag was in her lap and the anxiety pills in her bag, and because she was pretty sure this was almost an emergency, Molly Brock shook two rather than one Valium into her hand. Tried working up enough spit to swallow them. Couldn't.

Chew them into dust, swallow them that way. Pah. Horrid. If it's this difficult to die, how hard could it be to live? The heck with it. If you can walk in this far, you can walk back out. On one of her soaps — which one? Can't remember, who cares? — a man walked away from a crashed and burning private plane. Had a gimpy leg, a briefcase manacled to his wrist, a haircut Henri would swoon for, didn't know where he was. If he could do it, she could do it. All she had to do first was be certain which way was "back."

Problem was, which way does the arroyo go?

Once more on her feet, she had two choices, and both could be wrong. So the best thing to do was get out of the arroyo. And the best way to do that was to follow it until she came to some part of it she could climb out of. Arroyos were carved by rivers, or seasonal floods; desert arroyos and desert rivers did not go on forever. They all petered out eventually. Once up where she could see the horizon, which way to go from there ought to become a whole lot clearer.

Rubbing dried blood from her chin, wincing at the sun-burnt sting, she squinted up at the sky. That was east. Probably. So over there was west. Probably. The arroyo probably went southeast one way, northwest the other. Northwest it was.

Whoa. No food and no water, a Valium can hit you like a five-pound sack of birdseed. Two Valiums feel more like a hundred pounds of sand.

One good thing about an arroyo in the desert— sometimes there's shade. Bad thing about Valium, you lost your will to move. But good thing about Valium was nothing hurt very much. Not whatever she'd done to her ribs, not the gash over her ear, or her scraped hand. As for her heart, she could barely feel it. She could barely feel.

She kept walking. It wasn't in a straight line but the red walls of the arroyo kept her from doing what lost people usually do: walking in circles.

Feel sick. Feel clammy. Got a new headache on top of my old headache. Lips are so chapped, they're bleeding. Keep going.

The sudden spasm in her left calf knocked her off her feet. Shrieking in agony, she grabbed her leg, squeezing and kneading and pounding—oh dear god, what in the world is the matter now? Thrashing in the streambed, sand in her mouth, her shoes, her hair, she was screaming at her own body. "Let go! Let go! You let go!" Just as suddenly as her calf had clenched into an iron fist, it unclenched. Panting, spitting out grit, she picked up her glasses again.

Won't cry. Won't whine. Will get up and keep walking.

Self pity washed over her like the flood that could rush down this arroyo, any arroyo, whenever it rained upstream. Can't. Won't. You need water. If you keep walking, you'll need it more than you already do. That was a heat cramp. You know it was. Peter had one the very month they moved here; all he was doing was trying to barbecue back of the house. Emergency doctor at the nearest hospital said,

"You ignore heat cramps, Mr. Warner, and you're headed for sunstroke—and make no mistake, sunstrokes can kill." So you won't keep walking. You'll lie here in the shade. You'll lie here until—

In her head, another voice. Not her voice, not the one that never stopped talking talking talking ever since forever. No, it was "that" voice. It said: "You keep up that crying and I'll give you something to cry about. You hear me, Crisco?"

Oh god. It's Norma. It's the mother who called her Crisco because Crisco was lard and lard was what Norma said her butt was made of.

Her mother always had so much to say to her. "Stop that fiddling. Can't you ever sit still?" "Shut that awful singing up. Who ever told you you knew how to sing?" "You wet your bed again; you're wearing a sign to school." Mother was in her head. She was in there somewhere, loud as life. "All you ever do is cry! How you ever got to be my daughter is beyond me. Look at me. Do I cry every time I hurt myself? Do I bawl when I don't get my way? No, I do not. I put something over my head to protect it from the sun and I move on."

Mrs. Warner rolled in the sand, ignoring the spines of dried jumping cholla stuck to her jeans, pushing herself up until she was crouched on one knee.

"Get up! Get up, you cry baby. Look at you down there, snot on your face. You make me sick. Stop that crying right this very minute and get up!"

She got up and she walked, not as well as she had in the morning and nothing like as well as she had the day before—but she walked. And as she walked, a terrible thought came to her: she had not done this one thing, this last thing, well. A second thought following after: when you were young, like everyone else ever born, you were the center of the universe. Now that you're older you are still the center of the universe.

Molly Brock was thinking about food in order not to think about heat and pain and thirst when a plane passed overhead. Sounded like one of those hotshot pilots in some hotshot jet out of the local airbase. It was so far overhead, even if anyone in it were looking down, they couldn't have seen her. No point in wasting energy waving; by the time she got her hand up all there'd be of the jet was its vapor trail.

Not bothering to wave, she didn't even bother looking up.

Just walking along down here, just out here walking and planning a dinner for eight. Got your tee shirt on your head, got sweat running down your back like a slow leak, got the shakes and the fries and the heebie jeebies and the chicken gumbo mumbo jumbo and you're just walking and dying and talking to yourself. This is what you're saying: a dinner for eight? And who would they be, these eight guests? Such as they are, your "friends" are all back in L.A. — who would come to dinner?

There were all the neighbors, including Mrs. Perez who had a house across the street but actually lived at the nearest golf course. All she knew of the rest of her neighbors was as much as they knew of her. And even if she had known her neighbors, why should they wonder if she hadn't come home? Mr. Warner didn't come home all the time. This wasn't the Age of Innocence, this was The Age of Indulgence — why not Mrs. Warner?

No friends? Peter was once her friend. Or she once thought he once was. But then, back at Santa Monica College, she had a lot of dumb ideas. She was going to be an actress... sorry, actor. Or a painter. Or she'd marry an actor or a painter. Or, if it came to that, even a musician. Or a poet. Or maybe just someone with a pot of money who didn't have to be anything other than rich. Then no one would have to be an actor or a painter or a poet.

She'd married Peter Warner who'd grown up in Hollywood which was only over the Hollywood Hills from Burbank but was half a world away. Peter wasn't an actor or a painter. He wasn't a musician or a poet. He was the son of a man who worked at Metro. Molly was never sure what Peter's father did, something in production — for one long and very interesting moment you thought Stan Warner might be one of those Warners, didn't you,

Molly Golightly? — but whatever it was, Peter grew up in a house that made her own house in the Valley look sad and shabby and small. Or maybe that was the Valley smog. Everything looked sad and shabby though not necessarily small through dirty brown air. And maybe it was the big white house behind the high white wall on a winding road in Laurel Canyon that made her desire Peter for a friend.

What day is this?

If yesterday was a Thursday, which it was, then today had to be Friday. What did she do on Fridays? Of course, that's right — every other Friday she did volunteer work at the Tohono Needlework Shop where most of the proceeds went to a home for battered women.

Is this a Friday?

She finally thought to look at her watch. A Touch Time didn't need batteries. It just kept working however it worked. Yes, it's Friday.

Wouldn't the women at the shop miss her? When they were short-handed, wouldn't they wonder why she hadn't at least called in? They certainly would when Edith got there. Edith had made a complete hash of her cross-stitching; she'd want Mrs. Warner to sort it out for her.

But Edith was eighty-eight years old, so who knows — maybe Edith hadn't called in either.

Basically, it all came down to this: since she obviously hadn't shown up on her usual Friday, and since she hadn't even called, did anyone leap to the conclusion that that nice Mrs. Peter Warner, a shoo-in for Miss Congeniality, was lost in the desert?

Nope. Don't think so. Not a chance. And you can forget a dinner for eight. You don't know, or even like, eight people in Tucson Arizona.

She woke up just in time to stop herself from stepping on a Gila monster out for a ponderous stroll.

Whoa. That thing bites you, not only will it make you sick, but to get it off you'll have to pry open its jaws with your eyelash curler.

"Will you look at that!"

Still in the arroyo, yet she was staring at a wall of rocks and broken chunks of cement that blocked her path. It wasn't a natural wall. It was a kind of a causeway, and the causeway was there so that a road could cross the arroyo. A road!

Amazing how fast life can turn you around. One minute your goose is cooked. Or at least cooking. The next minute, here come the Martians.

All she had to do now was climb up the rocks—much easier than climbing a perpendicular wall of crumbling dirt—and wave down the first passing pickup. Out here it was bound to be a pickup. Or an old van. Or a truck. Probably full of illegal aliens running from the Border Patrol. Who cares who's in the truck? The point was, she was saved!

Molly Brock licked her cracked lips. She had just enough spit left to do that. It took the last of her will to pick her way up the jumbled cement blocks and the rocks to the road.

True, it was only a dirt road. But like Gertrude Stein always said: a road is a road is a road is a rose.

Out of the arroyo, once again there was horizon. And on every horizon, north, east, south, and west, there were mountains pale in the heat. Stretching away: blue mountains, mauve mountains, salmon and lavender and pink and purple mountains. The Tucsons, the Baboquivaris, the Santa Ritas, the Sierritas, those whose names she didn't know... which were nearest? She'd come down out of the Tucsons, so those must be the way back. Which were the Tucsons?

She was almost home now. It was almost all over. This whole dumb idea, the one that seemed so right in the supermarket in front of the peanut butter, had come to its stupid end—and no one to tell her tale to.

She'd die before telling Shelley. Tell her beloved daughter she'd tried to kill herself when most of her precious conversations with Shelley were about Shelley surviving just one more day? As Shelley would say: no way, José. It would have to be her secret, the one that no one but she would ever know. Not even whoever it was in the truck or the old van which was on its way to pick her up.

You'll make up some kind of story. Hiking, got lost. Looking for your parrot, got lost. Too much to drink, got lost.

Shelley's favorite word: whatever. Did it matter? She was just some mad American woman out in the noonday sun.

Whatever.

Molly sat down. Carefully. No sitting on thorns. No sitting on spiders or snakes. No sitting on — to be blunt about it — dried shit.

But what about Peter? What about Stan, your loving father-in-law? What about their unloving plans for you?

Molly hugging her purse.

You'll deal with all that when the time comes. Right now, you're waiting for your ride.

4

Removing her shoes — ah, there is pleasure left in life — shaking the gritty sand from her sweat-damp and desert-dirty socks, Molly Brock's new idea was to sit by the side of the road until that someone came along. That could be a minute from now, an hour from now, it might not be until nightfall — but someone would come along. They always did. Nothing was really a wilderness anymore. People were not an endangered species. Or maybe they were. They might be breeding themselves into extinction or poisoning themselves into a worldwide cull, but they weren't going anytime soon. Not before she got back to her apricot colored house off the cantaloupe colored Calle de Flores mall. Not before she had a long hot bath and a whole wedge of extremely fattening room temperature Cambonzola cheese and at least half a bottle of chilled white wine.

God, what you'd give for a glass of chilled wine. No, wait a minute — not wine. Wine makes you thirsty. Water.

What she'd give anything for was water. Any kind of water.

Feel your heart, it's racing. You're breathing too quickly. Stop it. Look at your hands, they're shaking, they're burnt… oh, fudge — you forgot to dig up your rings.

No time to worry about that. She'd come back in the Jeep Cherokee, hike down the arroyo, find where she'd spent her hideous night. Her rings weren't going anywhere before then. Water was the important thing right now.

Behind her, in front of her, all around her, grew the usual cholla cactus. Miles and miles and miles of them. Every hundred feet or so there was a prickly pear cactus. To her right was a barrel cactus. There was moisture in any cactus, but in a barrel cactus there had to be actual water. Right? Why else was it shaped like a barrel? But how to get past its hooked and wicked spines?

She poked it with a tentative nail. Between the spines it was as smooth and hard and thick as pumpkin skin. Thicker. She'd need a machete to cut through that thing. She rummaged around in her Gucci bag. Hair brush and comb, lipstick (melted), eyeliner and mascara, both melted, mirror (broken, must be because of the rocks she'd heaved at it), Gucci wallet, a Reader's Digest that'd been in there since she and Peter'd flown out to L.A. — which is still what you think of as home, Molly Brock, no matter how bad you felt there, how bad you feel everywhere: bad is just how you feel — to spend Christmas at the Warner's (Peter Jr. practically lived on his Hollywood grandparents, but Shelley was lost again in East L.A., and what a hell of a Christmas that was), loose change, tweezers, motel pens... would a nail file do? Or fingernail clippers? Forget it. She wasn't getting into a barrel cactus, not before she croaked from the wasted effort.

Oh, good idea, you. Melted lipstick on chapped lips works a treat. Stick some on your nose, keep it from falling off.

Back to getting water. What about the cholla? The red and white cow was eating the fruit of the buckhorn cholla. If a cow could eat it, she could eat it. If it didn't kill the cow, why should it kill her? Truth was, she'd eat the iridescent beetle calmly crossing the road if she thought there was a chance it had water inside it.

Right there she knew how thirsty she was. Any other time she wouldn't touch something in her own refrigerator if it was more than two days old. Or offered by someone she didn't know. Or looked funny. Or smelled funny. Face it, Moll—as Peter always says —you're a world class weenie. The fruit came off the cholla cactus with ease. No problem there, except for the thousand and one sneaky spines so tiny they were all but invisible. In seconds, they were all over her hands, between every finger. Maddening. Especially her left hand which was not doing so well in the sun. But who had gloves? And who'd try and slip a glove over an abraded non-disinfected hand?

Inside the fruit—shaped a bit like a pineapple, though not much larger than a Bing cherry—were dozens of little brown seeds nestled in yellow flesh tinged with green. She sniffed. Not good, but not really bad. Smelled like wheatgrass. She licked the yellow flesh. Moist! At the first hint of food, her stomach did a barrel roll. Ignoring the irritating spines, she picked more, split them open with her nail file, bit out the flesh with her teeth. How much could she eat before she threw up? If it took bulk, then the answer had to be: hundreds.

"Don't eat that!"

In spite of Norma yelling, she ate nine.

Dried socks and shoes back on her feet, tee shirt rearranged on her head, sunglasses back in their case, mouth and nose and cheeks freshly smeared with Cover Girl's *French Toast*, Molly Brock cleared the thorny debris on a bit of desert pavement two feet from the edge of the road. While she waited, she would read.

Just you, Moll, out here sitting and reading something you've already read, but no doubt already forgotten. Just you, waiting for your ride as you gnaw the spines out of your knuckles and pretend you're not also waiting to die from whatever poison a cholla fruit is full of.

She began with an article on home improvement, something called "Loving a Crooked House." A little crooked house beside a crooked stile... something something something something—she walked a crooked mile. Perfect.

Two minutes later, she heard the crunching of gravel.

Is someone coming? Already?

Eagerly, she looked up from the magazine, wincing from the pain in her side. One way along the desert road, she could see for maybe a mile. The other way, more than that. No pickup truck. No van. No motorcycle. No roadrunner. Not even Wile E. Coyote. But what if there had been a pickup or a van? Suddenly, she was afraid. Who knew what kind of person — man, Molly, be honest, you mean what kind of *man* — lives out here? You're all alone. You're defenseless. No gun, no knife, not even some kind of woman's group martial art training. Nothing. You could scream, and what would it get you? You could bite and kick and scream — and all for nothing.

And with this, she saw something about life and herself she'd never had the need or nerve to see before. Spiders and snakes and food poisoning and the terrible, flat, black and white dark, none of these scared her like the greatest predator of them all: a man she didn't know. And she didn't know most men.

Knock it off. What are the odds?

She was in that house again. It looked nothing like the last house, or the house before that — it never looked like the same house twice — but she knew where she was. It was the Valley house she grew up in. By now, she even knew what the dreaming house meant. The house was her. Simple, really. But never comforting. This time it was as tall as a tower and as narrow as a chimney… and leaning precariously to one side. Each room was empty and each corridor bare as she made her way down and down and down the winding staircase, and the farther down she went, the darker it got, and the more rotten the walls and the stairwell until there were gaping holes through which she could see more and more dizzying descents of darkness and rot. But she kept going down and down, looking for a way out, until at last it seemed she'd come to the bottom. She opened the door she found there, hoping it led outside, but all she found was a lightless pit that went on and on into ever more labyrinthine blackened rot. Turning away, she saw four old people in a shabby alcove, sitting together in a booth like diners at a cancelled Denny's. And in the

wall above them, a small window. The window looked
out on a bright sunny street and in the street strollers and
bicyclists and flowers in window boxes. And light. With
her heart hammering in her chest, she asked the four if the
window was opened could she get out that way? One of
their number, gentle souls all, smiled up at her and gently
said, "Oh yes, you can get out. But not that way. To leave,
you have to sit here with us and join hands." And then
they held out their hands to her, held out their hands and
smiled and they were fine and she was fine and it was just
fine — that the only way out of herself was by dying.

   Rain woke her this time. Rain and cold. Her eyes
opened to dark.
   How could she do it? How could she lose consciousness
right out in the open where anyone or anything could come
along — and that, as they say, would be that. She'd fallen
asleep at the side of a dirt road in a desert. With nothing
to back into and nothing to hide under, she was a huddled
shape in the dark at the edge of a road. She was prey.
   Go back down into the arroyo. It's safe down there.
There's soft folded dirt and there's soft brown sand and
nobody is down there — but, oh god, she couldn't. What if a
car came along and she missed it?
   "What car?"
   Her own voice sounded flat and loud on her ear. It
felt hollow in her throat. But that didn't stop her. She was
talking now. Filling up the dark with herself. Whatever
rustled in the dry grasses, whatever chewed through the
cholla or came out of those little holes under every bush
and every cactus, whatever lurked down in the arroyo:
everything hushed to listen... probably as shocked at the
sound of her voice as she was.
   There is no car. There hasn't been a car. Go on, admit
it, say — there isn't going to be a car. Is there? If a car was
coming, you'd see the lights from miles away. You see any
lights? You know why you don't see any lights? Because
there aren't any. Not anywhere. Face it. You're screwed,
Molly Brock.

Hugging herself for the cold, Molly knew not only despair, but misery. Lost in the gathering dark and cold, she was sick with hunger and frantic with chilled fatigue and tormented by a hundred itching cholla spines. And now she'd burnt the skin on the back of her neck sleeping slumped over in the sun. She was wet with — wet? Water! Precious water fell all around her and she was wasting it? Molly turned her face up into the rain and opened her mouth. Not good enough. Quickly, she dumped the contents of her purse in her lap. Nothing, nothing, nothing — but this. A plastic bag from the Tohono Needlework shop, and in the bag, two needles and a dozen baby blue twists of pearl cotton thread. Dumping the needles and thread out of the bag, she held the plastic up to the rain. Might be silly, but it was all she had. The rain fell on the plastic, ran together into rivulets, and slowly she gathered a teaspoon full, a tablespoon full, half a cup. It was water and it wet her lips and her mouth, and she sat in the rain and sipped raindrops for as long as they fell. Then she wrung the water out of her tee shirt and drank that.

And when the rain lessened, when it had almost stopped, she stuffed everything back in her purse, even the wet magazine. Her damp tee shirt was back on her body. Her jean jacket had every snap snapped. No waiting for a pickup truck. It was clear by now, she could wait forever… and forever was much too long. In Arizona, some dirt roads were major thoroughfares, and some weren't. This one obviously wasn't. She had to get moving. Best to walk in the rain and the dark now that she had a road. With a road, there was purpose. No one made a road unless it was going somewhere. Exactly where no longer mattered. Anywhere but here. And in the dark, so long as she stuck to the road, there'd be no bumping into cacti or ocotillo. In the dark, there'd be no heat cramps. But most potently of all, if she didn't walk out of here now, she was beginning to understand with a clear and horrid clarity, she might never walk out of here.

Her side hurt her more than ever, but if she kept her spine straight and her shoulders back, it was bearable. Her head was better. The headache had gone. Her hand was

nothing really, a scrape. The Valium had worn off hours
ago. No doing that again, you. Seems to me, Molly Brock,
what with one thing and another, and no matter that all
three of them: Stan and Peter and Peter Jr. would laugh at
the thought, you need your wits about you.

Rain in the desert never lasts for long, not even the
monsoons of summer. But now that the rain was gone, she
endured the wind. By glittering starlight, she walked her
dirt road, kicking up rocks, and listened to the wind clatter
through the cacti. Funny, but of all she'd gone through
since setting out to die, wind spooked her the most. The
restlessness of it, the hiss and whisper in the dead grasses
and the greasewood leaves, the whistle past her aching ears,
the grit it blew in her raw burnt face, the way it smeared the
stars across the sky. Hate the wind, hate it. One foot in
front of the other, one breath in and one breath out, in and
out and out and in, hour after hour.

Phrases sometimes catch in the mind as if the mind
was a tape and the tape looped on itself, over and over and
over until it drove you crazy. This phrase had caught in
the mind of Molly Brock. "Yea! though I walk through the
Valley of My Shadow."

There were things on this earth that never saw the light
of day, creatures of the night. This world was their world.
In it, which was real: the shadow or that which cast the
shadow? Here, there was nothing but shadow, and all of it
monstrous. The cholla, the brittlebush, every rock, the road
itself – monstrous. What by day was warm and round and
understandable, was by starlight cold and thin and beyond
understanding... as if they had made a place for themselves
between one world and another. You've fallen between
two worlds, Molly Brock. You walk in some kind of edge-
land and things are different here. You are different here.
Which only goes to prove that even everyday housewives
go insane in the dark.

She held out a hand in front of her face, felt the thud of
her feet on the ground, smelled her own dry sweat trapped
under her jacket – and none of this comforted her. How

long before you are cold and thin and you too move beyond understanding?

She stumbled over nothing, felt her legs begin to buckle. Constantly frightened, now she was scaring herself, feeling the first feathery licks of looping panic between her breasts.

Time to look up. Look up, Molly Brock. Think of summers long ago, think of lying out under the stars, think of Aunt Evelyn and take comfort there.

Without meaning to, she walked faster. And faster. Until she found herself running. Pushed along by the wind, it seemed she'd never run faster, not even round bases back at old Burbank High or to reach a ball before she was aced at tennis.

She ran right up three rotten steps and onto a rotten porch before she even knew they were there.

5

Shack was too grand a name. Hut? Shed?

Whatever it was, it had a roof and a door and two windows. The glass of the windows, if there'd ever been glass in the windows, had long since shattered, but there were shutters. The walls were rough adobe, the floor more dirt than wood. Out front in the yard, there was an old iron cook stove. Next to the cook stove was a bathtub on claw feet. In a kind of ecstasy, Molly pushed open the tumbledown door. By the light of the stars, she saw a table, a chair, and a bed. A bed. Only a mattress on rusted springs, but it was a bed, a lovely bed. What she saw most clearly was the bed. By its side stood an empty oil lamp.

Molly eased the door shut behind her and walked across the room. The floor moved under her feet, loose planks, loose dirt, wind through the walls. Someone had lived here once, but not now. No one had lived here for a long time. How could they? No electricity, no water, no insulation, no glass in the windows. Maybe people used to live like this, but, really, no one would live like this now.

So no one would be here. She could climb into bed, she could cover herself with the army blanket tossed at the foot of the mattress. So what if the mattress was sagging and stained, so what if the blanket was shabby and rough, so what if the bed was no more a proper bed than the one she'd last seen Shelley sleep in? There was no pillow. It all smelled musty with an undertone of grease. So? As your mother liked to say: sew buttons on your underwear. Molly Brock fell asleep just as the first hot hints of morning touched the splintered windowsill.

She thought she was home. She thought she was in her own bed. She thought Peter was in bed with her, pulling off the covers. So she pulled back. And was blasted awake with the loudest most god-awful sound it almost stopped her heart.

Molly Brock snapped open her eyes to a huge hairy face hanging over hers. The thing had long pointed ears, both as hairy as its mournful face, a little white beard, a big white nose — muzzle, whatever — thick black eyelashes any woman would die for, and long bucked teeth as orange as a… well, an orange. And when it brayed at her again, it sprayed her with brown spit.

Clutching the stiff brown army blanket, unmindful of her ribs, her hand, the ache in her head, she was off the mattress and halfway across the one room in two jumps.

A donkey. It was only an ordinary brown donkey. With stripes. And a round white belly. Hadn't she shut the door? Door was shut all right — but in the dark what she hadn't noticed was the back wall. A good half of it was lying behind the cabin in a mess of tumbled adobe. No need to use the door. The donkey could walk in the back way. Anything could walk in the back way. It stood there looking at her, switching its short tail, a knot of dark hair at the end. Stood there and stared at her. She could smell the desert heat coming off its hide.

What does it want? Just for this one moment, she knew what she wanted. Food. And water more than food. But as soon as she moved, she knew what she wanted most. A chiropractor. Or a masseuse. From her scalp to her toes, every muscle in her body hurt.

Feels like you dug the Panama Canal single handed.

The stove was outside. The bathtub was outside. Inside there was nothing but a donkey and the humble bed and the Van Gogh table and the Wild West chair and a battered old hat on a peg near the door. There was a shelf nailed to one of the wooden beams that held up the adobe walls. On the shelf was a rusted iron skillet, a dented pot, a setting for one (enamel and plasticware), a jam jar, a coffee mug with Arizona Wildcats written on it, eighteen packages of chicken flavored Top Ramen soup mix, three of shrimp, nine boxes of Jiffy Corn Muffin Mix, six boxes of Hamburger Helper, and a can of Hills Brothers Coffee. Something had gnawed its way through most of the muffin mixes. Otherwise, everything looked fresh as most anything found in a miles-from-anywhere gas station convenience store.

So? So someone still lived here. They just weren't home right now.

The donkey said, "Aw-EE, aw-EE," and walked out the back wall.

Holding her side, Molly Brock made the bed with one hand. No sheets and no pillow, it was easy. She brushed her ruined hair, rubbed her teeth with her finger until they at least felt cleaner, smeared her mouth and nose with *French Toast*. Snorting at the irony of it, she noticed her jeans were looser. A woman who'd dieted as much as she'd dieted would notice the loss of ounces. This was at least a pound. Even if probably all water.

You can't lose water. You need your water. But heck — if you can't kill yourself, at least you can lose those unwanted pounds.

She was standing at the paneless window, breathing in the soft aromatic smell of greasewood, wondering what to do next and breathing away a whisper of fear — after all, Molly, you're lost in the desert and there's no electricity and no phone and no water, oh my god, no water, and you don't feel so good and you're all alone here — when the donkey walked back in again, and brayed. This time louder and longer and brassier than before.

"Stop that!"

In answer, the donkey brayed four times in succession, then turned and walked out the back wall again.

Molly went back to thinking about what to do next. She thought she might have a broken rib. But for the immediate future, she also had a roof over her head, a bed, a stove, and a lot of packaged soup. True, it all belonged to someone else, but there was cash in her wallet. She'd leave more than enough money to pay for what she took. What she didn't have was water. How does the guy who lives here make his Top Ramen chicken or shrimp flavored soup? Is there a spring? Are there springs in the Sonoran Desert?

Out the door, off the porch, and into the yard for a look. No wonder the iron cook stove was outside; inside, it would have taken up half the cabin. But what the bathtub was doing out here, she hadn't a clue.

Shaking her head. "Not even a planter."

Looking down towards the dirt road — last night, running, she'd veered off it; no point imagining what might have happened if she'd missed the cabin — she could see out across a desert basin.

Molly standing there, staring.

You'd think there'd be something out there, something to aim for when you were rested up and got to walking again. But there's nothing, not for as far as the eye can see — except more of the same nothing.

You can't believe it. Where have you walked to? You've driven into these mountains a dozen times. Early days with Peter before he wheezed just by collecting the morning paper on the drive. With Shelley, trying to lure her away from East L.A.. With Peter's parents, trying to please them. With Norma, which was merely trying.

Molly up on her toes... maybe with a little more height?

Arizona isn't this empty. Nevada's empty. There are places in California that define empty. For instance, Death Valley. But Arizona isn't that empty. There are roads everywhere. People everywhere. And there's more and more and more of them every day. People just like Peter and just like Mrs. Peter come away from the big cities. Come away from crowds and the cold and the wet and the snow and the bitter times. People just like Mrs. Perez and the women of the Tohono Needlework Shop and the un-needy kid cadging spare change in the parking lot. So where are the housing estates and the RV parks and the shopping malls and the playing fields and the swimming pools and the radio towers and the barbed wire fences? Come to think, where are the cattle ranches? If nothing else, she should be looking at cattle ranches.

Something gave her a nudge from behind, hard enough to make her bang her shin on the rim of the bathtub. Molly yowled with the pain of it.

"Heeee haw!" said the donkey, and shoved her again. Then trotted off a few feet, to look back over its shaggy shoulder, and repeat itself. "Awww EEE."

She got it. The beast wanted her to follow it. Like a dog, it was doing its best to tell her something. Off it went, disappearing around the tub and the cook stove. Molly Brock followed.

Behind the cabin rose a steep *bajada* armed with beavertail cactus and cholla and saguaro. Beyond the *bajada*, a wall of tortured rock rose up at least two hundred feet. Back here, looking in some essential way pretty much as it had the day it was parked, sat an ancient Ford sedan. Rusted a deep burnt red inside and out, the horsehair filling busted out of its rotted seats and the glass out of its windows, its tires were long since baked to tar by the sun. Better, it was riddled with bullet holes.

Molly Brock turned to look at the back of the cabin, at the collapsed wall.

You think they were holed up here, resting from their latest job. You think Bonny and Clyde sat out in the desert together enduring this terrible silent heat when all of a sudden they heard the cops coming. So they made a run for it. Couldn't go out the front way, cops were out there, so they busted right out of the cabin, machine gunning the back wall to smithereens, trying to make it to the car. And they did make it. They jumped in their brand new Ford and they started her up and Clyde was sweating with more than the heat. He was sweating with the wonderful horror of it all, and Bonnie was pounding on his arm and screaming,

Go, Clyde! Move it, honey bunny, move it! But the cops
came round the cabin, both sides, and were on 'em in a hot
flash. Ratta tat tat.

Creeping closer to the old car, she peered inside. Hot,
dusty, dead, a beer can in what was left of the passenger's
side of the front seat.

The donkey had trotted right past all this. It was going
around and behind the tangle of greasewood beyond the
rusted car, straight towards a small hump in the rapidly
rising ground. Molly scrambled to keep up.

The hump was an odd looking thing. Not natural.
Partly dug into the *bajada*, and partly made of a tumble of
fitted rocks, she saw it first as a tiny mausoleum, then as the
opening to a mine shaft, and then as a root cellar. Molly
Anne Brock knew a root cellar when she saw it—her Aunt
Evelyn had one. She still did, back of the old house on the
avocado farm in the hills behind Ojai, California.

The donkey'd stopped at the door, was turned around
waiting for her.

It really is waiting. Look at that eye. Last time you saw
an eye like that, your mother was using it. "Well, Molly,"
she'd say, "are you or are you not going to do what I asked
you to do?"

You always did what she asked you to do. Better that,
than the consequences.

Wincing, Molly ducked through the door—less than
five feet high by not more than two feet wide—and sure
enough, she found herself in what on Aunt Evelyn's farm
would be called a root cellar, though here, it was probably
called a cool-house. Dark and close and small, the drop in
temperature was delicious on the skin.

Oh, yes, very nice in here. Except for the spiders. This
has got to be Black Widow Heaven. And Brown Recluse
Retreat. Don't forget them.

Lined up against the back stone wall, were six five
gallon plastic jugs. In all six, there was water.

6

Sun's high. Must be past noon. Hot. Not as hot as it was going to be a month from now, but hot enough to dry her socks in fifteen minutes and her underwear in ten. No wind. Not a cloud in the sky. Far to the south — she thinks that's the south — a hawk circled an outcrop of spiky dun-colored rocks. A pair of big black butterflies bumbled about in a jojoba bush. Between her and the cook stove grew a buckhorn cholla like the desert's own Christmas tree. Purple and pink and as tall as she was, but much wider, its fruit was bright yellow and hung from every prickly branch. Right in front of her, the donkey was sucking up water from the bathtub.

Molly Brock was sitting on the top step of the rotten porch watching it drink, her stomach full of Top Ramen. Not a whole package, she couldn't manage — or abide — the whole thing, but more than enough to modify this moment's view of her world. To keep off the sun, she wore the old hat from the peg. Once a dark brown, most of it was faded to the color of vacant lot dirt.

Food — she supposed one could call Top Ramen "food" — and water and a hat, as well as a friend to count on, what more was there? In that case, Mrs. Warner, it's the friend to count on that's the problem. Out of nowhere, a mint green hummingbird came and hung a foot in front of her face — and was gone with a burr of invisible wings.

It's not that Peter's a bad man. Peter's not a bad man. He's just a bad husband. He's an even worse friend. And now he's gone off to be someone else's 'friend.'

Molly stared at her naked toes in the sun, didn't actually see them.

Unless, of course, the problem isn't Peter at all. Unless the problem is Peter and you together. And only made worse by Peter's job moving you here. In L.A., you had a life without Peter. You gave dinner parties, you went to the theater, you joined committees, you were never alone. Here, you have no life at all.

Molly leaned back on the sun-bleached railing, didn't actually feel it.

Or maybe — good golly Miss Molly, it's you. How about that? Maybe Peter's only a bad friend to you. Maybe Peter's a good and faithful friend to someone else.

Picking at a sliver of wood in the old railing, pulling it off with a small dry snap, twirling the sliver between her fingers, she never noticed the railing or the sliver or her restless fingers.

No one to count on and no one to talk to and nothing to say. Empty, that's what you are. Used up and empty. If you were home now, safe and alone—you're almost always alone, aren't you? In your pretty house on your pretty street of pretend adobe dwellings—what would you be doing? You'd be watching the soaps and panicking. You'd be waiting to be taken away.

Mother interrupting. "Stop whining. Pick up your room. Help me with the laundry. Set the table. And for heaven's sake, Little Miss Crisco, quit your moping right this minute. What do you think life is? Fair?"

The day before yesterday, she wanted to die. Yesterday, she wanted to live. Or at least survive. Today she didn't have the first idea what she wanted. Live? Die? Sit here until something happened that would decide for her? And if nothing happened — then what? Out here, what could happen? Out here, not only was there no water, there were no daytime soaps.

High over her head, a buzzard. Two buzzards. Out of nowhere, three buzzards.

No getting around it, this was her soap. Set in the heat and the silence, only Molly in the cast: what's the plot? Where's the bickering and the betrayals and the greed and the need and all the bad seeds?

No plot. No villain. Still, it was all she had. What should she call it? *As The World Burns.*

She suddenly realized she'd made an interesting discovery. To want something, whatever it was, had to be better than wanting nothing. If you don't want anything, what to do then?

Out from under the steps beneath her bare feet, walked a tarantula as big as a salad plate. Lifting one hairy articulated leg at a time, setting it slowly down with great care and precision, it crossed the patch of desert between the steps and the cook stove. Watching its progress, not breathing, not moving, every hair standing on end, and blood turned cold, was Mrs. Warner. When it disappeared under the stove, she gulped in air, then scrambled off the step and into the cabin.

Here's what you want. You want your shoes back on.

An hour later, she made another interesting discovery. If a person doesn't own anything, especially any labor saving devices, it was amazing how little there was to do. No dishes, no laundry, no scrubbing the toilet, no servicing the car, no getting put on hold and forced to listen to canned pop music trying to get through to some company you've bought an extended warranty from to fix something. No computer to fuss with until one day you yank the plug out of the wall, screaming, "You know what, Peter? I'm not even dusting this thing off anymore!"

No bills to open, deadlines to meet, groceries to buy — no shopping at all. In other words, now the kids were gone, most of the things she did was about taking care of the things she owned. Or about Peter.

But no coffee?

If she could wash her socks and her underwear, surely there was water enough to feel safe about making a cup of coffee. Can she stomach pre-ground coffee made in a dented pot without milk and without artificial sweeteners? You damn well can.

For one thing, making a cup of coffee was something to do. That, and finding a good place to take a dump. "Taking a dump" was what Peter called it. Until this moment, that'd always mildly offended her. Now it seemed exactly right.

Sipping coffee with the grounds still in it, she went poking about. Looked through everything. Behind and under and over, inside and out. Under a loose board in the floor by the table, she found treasure. Three fat candle stubs. A half full box of matches. Two bottles of lamp oil. An unloaded Smith & Wesson .22 caliber pistol. No bullets. But it would look good if the need arose. What kind of need? What are you thinking? Nothing. Forget it. Oh, look. An ancient sewing kit. A pair of men's work boots, the leather cracked and curled with age, the heels worn down to nothing. A tin box full of old poker chips and a newish deck of Bicycle playing cards. And books.

On her knees, butt in the air, and ignoring all the alarms of her body, Molly leaned into the hole under the house following the stash of books. Dozens of them under here, all paperback, all well thumbed — and every single one of them a Zane Grey.

Upside down with her head in a hole under the floor. Heard of Zane Gray, seen him in the library, in bookstores. But you've never read him, never wanted to read him, never even thought about picking up a 'western.' Shoot, look how many there are. Zane Grey wrote up a western storm. But who has time for books when they're keeping up with the soaps?

You see a TV anywhere, Mrs? No TV. And no power if there were a TV. Therefore, you will read a western now. You'd read anything now, anything. You'd hide in the pages of a computer manual if it could take you out of here, even for a moment.

Molly reaching for a book.

For the next three hours, Molly Brock read the first book out of the hidey hole: *Riders of the Purple Sage.* Lying on a stained mattress in a falling down adobe cabin in what was once Apache country, someone who was once Mrs. Peter Warner, once of Burbank, California, lost herself in the tale of Jane Withersteen — a proud woman, alone, without issue or husband, standing against the creed of the Mormons. And this in the person of one man, an Elder called Tull. Tall, dark, and arrogant, as well as downright rude, Elder Tull wanted not only her land and her body, he wanted her soul.

Scant pages in, Molly found herself — or at least found an interesting part of herself — when Jane met the strange rider, the man in black leather. Lassiter. "Jane Withersteen wheeled and saw a horseman, silhouetted against the western sky, coming riding out of the sage... An answer to her prayer!"

Just before it got dark, Molly filled and lit the oil lamp, placed the gun on the floor near her head — in case of what? In case of Mormons, of course, and kept on reading.

To Jane Withersteen, the gunman's face, " ... had all the characteristics of the range rider's — the leanness, the red burn of the sun, and the set changelessness that came with years of silence and solitude. But it was not these which held her; rather the intensity of his gaze, a strained weariness, a piercing wistfulness of keen, gray sight, as if the man was forever looking for that which he never found. Jane's subtle woman's intuition, even in that brief instant, felt a sadness, a hungering, a secret."

Somewhere close, a coyote bayed at the stars... and Molly scooped up the gun. Think you can face down a ravening pack of wild coyotes with an empty gun? No. But you feel better just holding it.

A little later, the donkey walked though the back wall again, settled down in a corner, and went to sleep.

First thing the next day she gathered dried bits of cholla trunk, dragging armfuls of feather-light tubes of fibrous mesh to the edge of the dirt road. Got to do more than read about strange riders, Molly Brock. God helps those who help themselves. In dead cholla trunk letters almost as wide as the road was wide, she spelled out the single word: HELP. Then made a cholla trunk arrow on the desert pavement pointing to the cabin. When that was done, she spent an hour tweezing tiny cholla spines out of her fingers.

That same day, she named the donkey after the man her dad had called the biggest ass he ever knew — Mark Millard Brewster. M.M. Brewster owned the Hotel Encino Grande. From bellboy to manager, Lindsay Ray Brock worked in Mr. Brewster's hotel until the month before he died. She also discovered that besides Brewster the donkey, she shared the cabin with an owl as small as her diaphragm.

The day after that, in a borrowed hat but her own sunglasses, she hiked a little way up the road to see what lay on the far side of the ridge it climbed. On the far side of the ridge was another, higher, ridge, and a higher one after that. The road behind her dropped down and disappeared into the shimmering distance.

And so, for the moment, it went. It was spring, the heat was still bearable, but not for long — getting hotter every day. She could eat, but not for long. She could drink, but not for long. She could read herself to sleep at night, but only until she ran out of Zane Greys and lamp oil. Or matches. She could be pretty sure of sleeping alone if she shook out the blanket and punched the mattress before use. She was entirely sure she'd never run out of dead cholla fuel for the cook stove. If she grew anxious, she had her Valium, although, oddly enough, she did not grow anxious. The gash in her scalp was healing up nicely, her side was on the mend... no broken rib after all, though her bruise was as purple and yellow and green as the sky over the desert before a summer squall. And her nose and her chin and her neck and her hands had peeled. Underneath the hot pink, it was now hot red. If she got ill? Then it was grimace and bear it.

But she could play Solitaire for the rest of her life.

If only the larder were larger, if only there were a well or a spring, you'd never have to do another thing, Molly Brock, you'd never have to go home again. If you didn't go home, you wouldn't have to decide how to live — you could just eat and read and count the cacti. How would that feel?

Sitting on a rock with a good view of the shot-up Ford sedan as well as down the hill to the dirt road below, she was surprised to hear herself answer, "Actually, that might not feel too bad at all."

One thing about a life without stuff, she didn't have to feel like a fool when she couldn't work the computer or adjust the multiple choice shower head. She didn't have to watch Peter get that look on his face whenever he had to reboot her laptop or when she'd made a mess of the microwave programming. And she never had to hear her own son calling her a ditz ever again.

She watched Brewster who did nothing but eat whatever he could find, drink whatever water Molly allowed him, and stand around under his favorite nine-armed saguaro, snoozing. Sometimes he gnawed on his hide; sometimes he sneezed. At night, he varied all this by sleeping in his corner in the cabin and farting now and then. She herself ate what there was to eat, drank only as much as she was sure she needed, and lay around reading Zane Grey or sitting on the front porch waiting for someone to come home, or for someone to drive by on the road to who knew where, or for someone to fly over low enough to notice her message. Out here, life was really nothing more than getting through the day. And waiting.

Though I can't just sit here. I can't just drink all the water or use up every package of Top Ramen and Hamburger Helper until there's nothing left to eat. Can I?

Moving slowly through her fourth day at the cabin—though her sixth since walking away—Molly Brock had a series of insights. Beyond simple survival, everything else was nothing more than desire. The desire to impress. The desire to control. The desire to have. The desire to have more of whatever one already had. The desire to feel more or the desire to feel less.

Now that she no longer wanted to die, what did she desire? To change her clothes would be nice. Second best: to wash them.

7

Late in the afternoon of the seventh day, her purse in her lap, she was sitting on the porch with Brewster dozing under his cactus. Already spent an hour playing with her Time Touch, changing the display face, fiddling with its strap—she'd chosen pink. Expensive thing, useless thing... who cared what time it was? Donkey knew it was either time to eat, time to sleep, time to piss, or time to wake up. In her life it was always the same time which was no time at all. Who cared what the date was. She didn't have anything planned. Now she was looking through her wallet. Credit cards, driver's license, library card, a membership in Safeway's discount club, an AAA card. A photo of Peter Jr. when he was three and still held promise. Three photos of Shelley, the last one taken only a month ago.

Photos of Shelley lie. In them, Shelley always looks wonderful: healthy, alive, happy. And here's a photo of you. You look terrible. Fat, dull-eyed, dead. Nice hair though. Henri is a genius.

She turned the photo over. Christmas. At the Warners. Last year.

Last two days she'd gone around hitching up her jeans... until she remembered the laces of the boots she'd seen in the hidey hole. Tying both together, they were now her belt. This morning she'd shortened her bra straps.

How simple fat is. Maybe not in cause, but in effect. People get fat because they eat too much and do too little. People get sick because the food they eat is all processed sugars and fats, because it's more poison than food. You, Molly Brock, got fat like anyone gets fat. But you're getting thinner by the day. You could write a book about it. You could call it *The Lost in the Desert Miracle Diet Plan*.

The tarantula walked out from under the bottom step again. It did that at least twice a day, crossing from the cook stove to the step, from the step to the cook stove. Molly sat there and watched it. On the third day, she'd named it Puppet. Puppet was like a hand with too many fingers. It was like an eight fingered hand in a handsome fur glove. Soft and glossy brown with a golden back and golden knuckles. Puppet was actually rather splendid, but it gave her the total heebie jeebies. Though it no longer made her leap up and run. For one thing, she was never barefoot. And for another, it was obviously more afraid of Molly than Molly was of it. The one time she'd been going down the steps when the huge spider was coming out, it was Puppet who'd cringed and flattened itself against the ground, and stayed there until Molly climbed the steps.

What could it feel like to be a spider, to see life through a spider's eyes? Wouldn't be the least surprised to learn you give it the chittering creeps.

The photos of Shelley, of herself, slide from her lap. Like Brewster under his cacti, Molly is dreaming. She's fallen asleep on the wooden steps of the adobe cabin but she dreams she's back with Aunt Evelyn again. It's summer. One of those faraway summers when she'd be sent to the farm near Ojai in California. To visit, they said. For her health. To clear her lungs of the Valley smog. But it was really for her mother, so that her mother could play nonstop bridge or golf or bingo or whatever it was her mother did every summer when Molly was gone and Lindsay would work round-the-clock at the Hotel Encino Grande. Sometimes her mother would come along for a day, two days, sometimes her father would rush in for a few hours, then rush away. She doesn't remember them there. She only remembers Aunt Evelyn and the avocado trees. She remembers the windfall fruit, burst open on the ground — acts of green plenty, nature's instant guacamole. There were books in Aunt Evelyn's house. There were pictures. Aunt Evelyn is why she thought she might be a painter, an artist. Aunt Evelyn is why she never really believed she was a bad girl or that she couldn't sing. Aunt Evelyn, who lived alone, who had always lived alone on her farm on the side of a mountain at the edge of the world, and beyond the edge, the sea—Evelyn is why she stopped wetting the bed.

She's dreaming about the books lying open on the tables, on the chairs, open and scattered over the floor like avocados. And the wind is riffling their pages, slowly at first, then faster and faster.

Molly woke up. There was a tremendous whirr of black feathers and black beak and black eye — and out of the sky dropped something so big and so black and so loud and so sudden, for one timeless moment she was lost in the frozen surprise of it. If Brewster hadn't chosen just that moment to shake his scrub brush of a mane, and snort down the pink skin of his white nose, Puppet would have been snapped up as he — she? — scurried for the cook stove. As it was, she lost the tip of a dragging back leg.

Brewster, meanwhile, had kicked up his own hind legs, then bolted round the back of the cabin.

The huge black bird came down in a turmoil of racket and fuss, crash landing at the foot of the buckhorn cholla. It flipped over, wings outspread like black rags in the dirt, legs stuck up like black twigs, black head thrust forward in outrage and surprise. Molly Brock laughed. It was the first real laugh she'd laughed in months. And the crow — crow? Very very big blackbird? Was it an actual raven? Was it Poe's *Nevermore?* — slowly turned its hard black eye her way, opened its curved black beak, and said a very definite: "Tock!" Then righted itself. It wasn't a graceful effort, but it was effective. With a shudder — like a cardsharp ruffling cards — it organized its gloss of feathers, then strutted towards the cook stove.

Molly was on her feet without thought. "No! Leave it alone!"

Good grief, Molly Brock, you're concerned about a tarantula, a tarantula! Last week you would have sprayed it. "Don't move, Puppet. Lie low. I'm a comin'. Scat!" she said, standing up on the top step and waving her borrowed hat. "G'way!"

The big black bird ignored her. Instead, it thrust its huge beak under the iron stove.

Alarmed, Molly jumped down all three steps at once and dashed across the small yard. "G'way! G'way!"

By now, the black bird was tugging at something. Oh heck, not Puppet.

"Stop that. Stop it!"

Slapping at the bird with her hat, kicking at it, bird dropped what it held in its beak, came out from under the stove with a huge squawk of indignant surprise. The thing it dropped wasn't Puppet. It was nothing like Puppet. What it was was not much more than a foot long and no thicker than a pencil. There were no legs, no stiff irritating fur, no bulging abdomen. But there were scales, and the scales were banded with the deepest black and the bloodiest red and the sunniest yellow—and she felt the blood drain from her heart at the sight of it.

"What's that? Is that a—?"

Can't remember its name. Poisonous. Very bad. Alone out here. Wouldn't know what to do. Can't be bit by a deadly snake. Can't be bit by a giant desert centipede. Or a brown spider. Or a cone-nosed bug. Or a Gila monster. Can't be bit by anything.

Loose on the ground, exposed to the light, the snake buried its blunt black head in its coils and raised its red and yellow tail. Lord, what next! Everting what she was sure was its cloaca or its anus—spit it out, Moll; that's an asshole—it made a loud pop, then another. Pop! Pop! Good grief.

Both she and the bird backed up.

Got to get out of here. Got to go home. Intended to die here, not to live here. Not with all this! Thorns and spines

and stingers and fangs and claws and popping assholes.
Even the toads can make you sick.

She grabbed up her bag, ran inside the cabin, and
slammed the door. Do that again, the rusted hinges will
snap, and then where will you be? With another hole in
the wall.

She curled up in the clothes she'd worn for a week and
cried herself into silence. Then into sleep.

Waking just before sundown, Molly Brock knew there'd
be no more waiting. No one was ever coming home. No
one was ever driving by. No one was going to read the
cholla sign she'd made on a dirt road to nowhere. She was
back where she'd been days ago. She had to walk out of
here on her own. Though at least now she had the rest of
the water — little enough, and no more washing socks with
it — and what was left of the Top Ramen and the muffin mix.
She even had a beast of burden to bear it. She and Brewster
would follow the road. Which way could be a toss of the
coin. But having seen the way over the ridge, she favored
the way she'd come.

There. That's settled. One more night of Zane Grey —
got to finish *The Rainbow Trail*, can't leave before the earnest
white man John Shefford and the noble Navajo Nas Ta Bega
find Surprise Valley, before they save Jane and Lassiter —
and you're gone from here, Molly Brock. You're walking
home.

The thought made her sick to her stomach. Sick enough
to stand by a window and gulp in desert air. Overhead, the
sky was salmon with sunset, the clouds puffed like pastry.
Molly threw up. Leaning over the cracked beam of the
window sill, she vomited out into the dirt and the sand and
the ants and the centipedes and the scorpions and whatever
else crept or crawled or slithered or lurked or crouched
outside her adobe walls.

Long after dark, she lay in bed trembling with shock,
coming to the end of *The Rainbow Trail*, fighting off panic
as she read: "The moon had long since crossed the streak of
star-fired blue above and the canyon was black in shadow.

At times, a current of wind, with all the strangeness of that strange country in its hollow moan, rushed through the great stone arch. At other times there was silence such as Shefford imagined dwelt deep under this rocky world. At still other times an owl hooted, and the sound was nameless. But it had a mocking echo that never ended. An echo of night, silence, gloom, melancholy death, age."

She closed her eyes. Found herself slipping towards a bodily fear she could not bear to bear.

Please, Molly, not all alone out here, don't panic here, in the desert, in the dark. Opened her eyes and kept reading: "There was a spirit in the canyon, and whether or not it was what the Navajo embodied in the great Nonnezoshe, or the life of the present, or the death of the ages, or the nature so magnificently manifested in those silent, dreaming, waiting walls — the truth for Shefford was that this spirit was God."

A fingernail moon climbed through the arms of Brewster's pleated saguaro and sailed halfway across the sky before Molly gave up and took three Valium.

8

A week and a day since walking away. This was the day she was going back home. It was early on a Friday morning and she was walking away again.

Molly Brock lifted her head. And immediately let it fall back. Whump.

Oh lordy, going home but not yet, not yet—too sick to get up, too sick to walk, too sick to do anything more than lie here and endure. What is it? What's got into you? Feels bad. Feels so bad. Snake didn't bite you. Didn't. You'd remember if it did. Wouldn't you?

She gripped the edge of the blanket hard enough to whiten her knuckles.

You will endure. You always endure. That's what you do. Whatever it is, whatever poison is in you, remember: this too shall pass. Like panic passes. As everything passes. All the bad things. And all the good.

Brewster was already up and about. She could hear him outside kicking at the tin tub.

Wants his water. Wants you to get up and give him his water. Can't get up.

A sudden itch on her leg. A furious itch. Molly reaching down to scratch it.

Going to be sick again. Both hands, holding her stomach, tightened belly muscles, tightened sphincter. No. Won't. You'll lose your fluids, Moll. Precious bodily fluids. You will not throw up. You will lie here until this passes. Can't lie here. Bed feels like a cork on a choppy sea. Brewster needs water. You need water.

The water was in the cool-house. The cool-house was up a hill behind the cabin. The remaining water jugs were a million miles away. But Molly tried. First crawling, then up into a stumbling bent-double lurch—and all the while her head swimming and her stomach cramping and all over her body, an insane itch.

She made it as far as the rusted out Ford before passing out.

Coming round, the first thing she sees is a hoof. Brewster. It's Brewster. Wants his water.

"What you doin' down there, woman? You got no sense? Get off the ground."

A human voice. Is it a real human voice?

"You hear what I said? Get up. You sick?"

With a supreme effort, Molly turns her scraped and gritted face away from the hoof, sees a booted foot, tries to look up—is blinded by the burning sun. Voice comes from up there somewhere.

"Say, you Meryl Streep? Hot damn, if you don't look just like Meryl Streep. What's Meryl Streep droolin' around my place for?"

In answer, Molly Brock goes into a convulsion, flailing away on the hot and stony ground—and then there are hands on her, hands under her armpits, strong hands lifting her up, pulling at her. Don't care. Don't give a damn. Let me die. G'way. Give Brewster his water.

No. No. No! Someone was stripping off her jeans, pulling her tee shirt over her head, unhooking her bra. Someone was pinching her arms and her legs, rubbing their rough hands down her bare back and over her bare buttocks. Molly fought back with all the strength that was in her. Couldn't beat back a First Grader. But she tried.

Someone prodded the soft inner skin of her thighs. She tried breaking their fingers.

"Stop fussin'. I got to know if you're bad bit, don't I?"

Then everything went black again.

A long time later, someone said, "You ain't Streep. You ain't govn'mint either."

Molly turned her head towards the voice. She was back in bed. By the shade and the slant of the light, she thought it might be late afternoon. On the table there was a whole lot more chicken and shrimp flavored Top Ramen and ground coffee and packaged muffin mix. On the floor there were full bottles of lamp oil. The air smelled of ammonia. The one chair was pulled up to the bed, and on the chair sat someone in a Dallas Cowboys jacket. Jacket wasn't new, but it wasn't old either. Is it a woman? Might be a woman. Or a man. Don't think it's a man. Not sure it's a woman. Almost moves like a woman... or some sort of man. It's a woman. Isn't it?

"You been eatin' my food an' drinkin' my water— you a golfer?"

I'm Goldilocks and you're Momma Bear.

Did you say that, Molly Brock? Out loud?

One eye opened, and the other eye closed, sicker than she'd ever been in her life, Molly studied the woman in the chair. Her bones were good and her teeth were perfect and her skin was stretched over her face like brown canvas on a needlework frame. Aside from that, she had no earlobes, her head was shaved, and she was chewing on a huge piece of jerky. Or maybe it's tobacco. Hope it's not tobacco. Going to be sick again. The woman was seventy if she was a day. Probably a lot older than that.

"Golfer?"

Old woman swallowed whatever she'd been chewing. "Golfer's one of them comes down here to make green grass in the desert, then uses all the water to water it until he kills everything needs it, including his stupid self."

Thick gold wedding ring on her finger. Is there a Poppa Bear?

"Them saggy baggies're suckin' up the aquifer into their saggy baggy bellies so they can piss out their saggy baggy Golfer pee. You one of them?"

"Peter is."

"That your man?"

"Was."

"What he do, run off an' leave you out here?"

"No. Yes. No. In a way." It was all she could do to talk. Mouth dry. Trembling. Dizzy. Dizzy was the worst. No. Not dizzy. The itch was the worst. "Could I have some water?"

"How'm I gonna get back what you already used?"

"Money in my wallet."

"Already took that. But I figure you bein' in my bed an' drinkin' my water an' readin' my books an' makin' trash for me to pack out, you ain't calling me charity. Put that ammonia pack back on your leg."

After that, Molly Brock was delirious. Either that, or there really was a cocktail party for spiders and scorpions and birds dressed like Dracula out on the front porch.

The old woman was as strong as ironwood root. She was lifting up the bottom of the mattress with Molly still on it, all the while saying, "Before the world, there was electricity, you understand?"

Too ill to talk, too ill even to nod her head, Molly lifted a finger, then dropped it. That seemed enough for… for—hadn't she said to call her Charity? By now, Charity'd disappeared behind the uplifted mattress, holding it steady with one hand, using the other to pry up a floorboard, one Molly never found that was obviously under the bed.

"Before everything, we were all electricity, but one tiny spark became Mr. Hate. You understand?"

Bent as the mattress was bent, she didn't understand, but how to say that with only a finger?

Charity lowered the mattress, and when Moll saw all of her again, there was a notebook in her hand, a fat blue one, spiraled and new. "Keep my thoughts in here. Always keep hold of your thoughts, woman. Thoughts power the world."

Blue notebook under her arm, a stub of a chewed pencil behind her ear, Charity dragged the chair back to the side of the bed. Molly couldn't remember it being dragged away. Must have been asleep, nothing more blessed than sleep. In sleep, chairs move and old women with bald heads water your donkey.

"From the very first, there's always been two kinds of people in the world. First is them who come from Mr. Hate who are demons clothed in flesh. And the second is them who come from Mother Light who are angels clothed in flesh. So, I figure it this way. Your man was a saggy baggy Golfer demon, so you're a saggy baggy Golfer demon's wife. This means you got to feeling bad 'bout the mess you an' he was makin' in the desert, so you volunteered. Am I right?"

Was she right? Your every-other-Friday at the Tohono Needleworks Shop was for saggy baggy guilt? Don't think so — think you did it out of complete boredom. And for company.

"So you're out doing some volunteer work in the desert, an' you got lost. Am I right? For someone like you, it's the only reason to be out here alone — unless you was aiming to kill yourself. Don't figure you for a suicide. I seen a whole lot of suicides in my time, seen murders too, seen accidents peel back your skin. But nope an' nada chance, you're too vain by half for any of that crap. So that means you're lost, an' that means they're bound to be out huntin' for a Mrs. G. M. Warner of 2586 Burning Jail Road. An' if that ain't one, ripe, round, pain in the ass, I'm a rubber spoolie."

You don't know what the heck she's talking about, do you, Molly Brock? But you know why she knows your married name and your address — been in your wallet, hasn't she?

Mercifully, Molly passed out.

It was night when she woke again. Out the open window, half a moon rode on a raft of a cloud. Below it, the teddy-bear chollas were as blonde and as numinous as... Marilyn Monroe. The old woman was pushing her way into bed, taking most of the blanket. Against Molly's hip, she was all bones.

Old woman's bald head shines by the light of the moon. Old woman breathes like a dog in a locked car. She's awake. You can feel how awake she is. Ask her, Molly. Ask her what you want to know.

"What's wrong with me?"

"Hoopedy-do if I know."

People, when they talk in the dark, almost always whisper. Not the old woman. Old woman sounds like a coyote pack. Ask her the other question — the big one.

"Am I going to die?"

"Who isn't? Woman and man born of woman, by'n'by, everybody kicks it. You, maybe sooner'n me. Figure you got an allergy to somethin'. Centipede? Fiddle spider? Scorpion, could be — one of those liddle bark ones. But most pro'bly a kissing bug. What with the rash. Worse reaction I ever saw."

Well, there you go. Maybe you killed yourself after all.

Later, when Brewster tried walking through the back wall, he got no farther than the table. Old woman shouted at him. "Get the holy hell out of here! What you think this is?"

Brewster flicked up his tufted tail, spun on a deft hoof — and ran.

Old woman pinched her arm. "Useless critter, that one. Wanders off. You been lettin' him sleep in my house?"

Ouch. Thought it was his house. Thought you were sleeping in Brewster's house.

"Don't matter. You're leavin'. Unless you die in the night. Tell you what, you die in the night, you do it quiet. I got a long day tomorrow."

Old woman was asleep in five seconds flat.

Molly was awake. Awake and staring at a big dark blotch on the moonstruck wall.

Funny, now you might really be dying, the things that go through your head. Not Shelley. Shelley has to take care of herself, time she took care of herself. And not your wasted life — but was it wasted? How can you waste a life?

You were alive, weren't you? Minute by minute, no one but you lived the life of Molly Brock. There's never been another life in all of time and space like your life. And if you live through one more night, you'll ask Charity for a page of her notebook, take a pen out of your bag, and you'll write a letter to Shelley and tell her so. Only gift you have left to give her.

Molly scratching. Itched everywhere.

What was really going through her mind was the dream. The dream she dreams about the little stucco house on a street in Burbank when she was young. No matter what form the house takes, and it takes many forms, she wanders the rooms looking for something. What is she looking for night after night, year after year?

Now that you're halfway dead — will you find it?

9

Molly Brock lived through the night. Came awake with a jump start. Eyes flying open to brighter color, stronger color, more color. The rest of her not moving, afraid to move.

What is it now? What's happening now? You still itch. You still have the maddening itch. But only in one place. You want something. What do you want?

Out the cabin's rear window, the rocky ground rose as it had risen the day before: straight up into a cliff wall jumbled with fabulous shapes. There were trolls of stone up there, root vegetables, chess pieces... and one huge bearded head, its face eternal with stony wonder. On the *bajada* grew what had grown the day before: an otherworldly landscape fantastic with crazed cacti and tortured thornscrub. And just as it had the day before, cupping it all in blue, curved the electrical snap of the sky.

But today it had all changed. Today she saw it.

Molly sat up in bed and clutched her head. You're dead. That explains it. You are dead and the afterlife looks remarkably like a tumbledown adobe cabin in the Sonoran Desert. No old woman lying beside her. No pistol under the bed. But the supplies were stacked away on the shelf:

cans of sardines and tuna fish, a box of sugar cubes, kitchen matches. Under the army blanket, she was naked, but her clothes were thrown over the chair. Her leg itched, her eyes stung, she had to, well, basically, take a dump. All right, so you're not dead. Physically, you feel better. Weak at the knees and light in the head — and the itch! But better.

Don't lie here. Get dressed. And do it while you have the time. No telling where Charity is. Or if a Mr. Charity is around somewhere.

Crawling out of bed, using the crumbling adobe wall to steady herself, Molly dragged on her clothes.

Except the bra. No point wearing the bra — not your size anymore. As for the dirt, didn't you read somewhere that after a week without bathing you couldn't actually get any dirtier? That, as a matter of fact, your own oils would begin to cleanse your skin naturally?

She ran her fingers through her lank and tangled hair. Shampoos and conditioners were like "refined" white flour. Just as refinement stripped the wheat of its nutrients, shampoos stripped hair of its natural oils, and then conditioners replaced them with chemicals. When she combed her hair back, it stayed back. Think of it all this way: another month of this, and your hair will either shine like a well fed cat's — or it'll fall out.

Meanwhile her head itched like hives. But not as badly as her leg itched. She was alive. And she liked it.

Now there's a feeling. You hold on to it.

Outside, Brewster stood under his saguaro. But not alone. Two other donkeys stood under it with him. Both of these were larger than Brewster, and darker, though their ears were smaller. And both wore rope halters. Noses to the ground, the two new donkeys slept on, but Brewster opened his eyes, gave her a resounding bray, and shook all over in a kind of peristaltic wave from rump to ears.

"Morning, Brewster. See you have friends."

Amidst a tangle of leather straps, four large Mexican panniers woven of some sort of soft yellow fiber lay on the ground near the bathtub. Donkey harness or burro tack or whatever. Like a good guest, she'd put it away if there was somewhere to put it.

Starving, she ate what was left in the skillet of Charity's breakfast: sun-dried sardines and Top Ramen. Thirsty, she discovered the cool-house was full of water in more five gallon plastic jugs. Curious, and looking in the Zane Grey hidey hole, she found a dozen packs of Big Red gum, a Zane Grey that hadn't been there before, and three boxes of .22 caliber shells. But no .22 caliber pistol. She opened a box. Six bullets missing.

Must get all this from somewhere. Water may come in desert springs, but Top Ramen doesn't grow on cactus. Old lady will tell you which way, and off you'll go. That is, soon as you find the old lady. Has to be around here someplace.

She waited all morning and all afternoon but no Charity. Where could an old woman go? And what could an old woman get up to out here?

She'd been lost a week, and what had she done? What would Robinson Crusoe have done? By now there'd be hammocks woven of yucca leaves. There'd be umbrellas made of kangaroo rat skin stretched over saguaro ribs. There'd be water brought in from a high mountain spring through an ingenious system of hollowed out bones. If necessary, thirty miles of them. That's what Crusoe would do. But Molly Brock? She'd eaten Top Ramen soup, read five Zane Greys, and lost a little weight.

But what in the world does that old woman do?

Along towards evening, she had a peek at Charity's notebook in its own hidey hole.

Old woman not only wrote down her thoughts, she drew them: odd little cactus angels, disturbing little cactus demons, Mr. Hate like Peter Pain, Mother Light like the Statue of Liberty, demonic battles raging in a crowded pink sky.

Under the notebook was a sizable leather bag, and in the bag, rocks. But Molly knew gold when she saw it: Peter's little brother Andrew was a goldsmith.

Must be three or four ounces mixed up in here. Had to be a fortune to Charity.

Bag back under the floor, notebook back where she'd found it.

So there it is. I know what she does. Old woman's up behind me somewhere, probably in some old played-out mine, gouging for gold.

Molly went back to what she'd been doing most of the day. Aside from waiting.

Sitting on the top step reading the new Zane Grey, *The Light of Western Stars*, she found herself looking up, and in looking up, traced the usual jet high in the sky. Jet reminded her of what Charity had said. "They're bound to be hunting for you."

Is that true? You've been gone for over a week. No you in the house for over a week, and only you ever clean the place, Mrs. Saggy Baggy Servant. Must be dust everywhere. Spiders have moved in, mice, scorpions, maybe even a snake. Sure to be junk mail spilling out of the mailbox, newspapers piling up in the shade of the entryway.

Getting dark. Molly up off the step and inside.

Last week, when Peter came home to collect you — what did he do? When he found your clothes in the walk-in closet, your jewelry in the bottom of the cedar chest, your new e-book reader — the one his mom and dad gave you for your birthday — doing nothing on the shelf over the bathtub, the open jar of peanut butter on the kitchen counter doing something interesting all by itself — did he think you'd heard something about Shelley and rushed off to East L.A.? How? The Jeep Cherokee's still in the garage. So he must have called his dad. What did he say? Did he say: "Dad — I've got good news and bad news. Molly's disappeared." And did Stan fly out from the coast to help him find you? Or did he say: "Son — do what I do when a movie goes in the toilet. Flush."

Shadows falling. Time to light the lamp, to sit at the table.

Or does he think you've left him? Taking nothing? Don't think so. He might believe you'd leave him, but he wouldn't believe you'd take nothing. It wouldn't be like you. Not the Molly Brock he knew. So? Has he called the police? The heck with it. Not your problem. Your problem is walking out of here — and doing it well. Borrow some paper, find a pen, write that letter to Shelley like you promised.

Last time she saw Shelley, Shelley was sleeping. One room in the back of an empty store off Vermont Avenue, stained mattress on the floor, no sheets, cigarette slowly melting another hole in the worn and torn linoleum. Window was shut and no air conditioning. Molly, come to provide cheer, purpose, hope, which always seemed to look like money, knelt by her side, gazed down at her sleeping daughter with a vast, deep, despairing love. Make-up from the night before owling Shelley's eyes, smearing her cheeks. And under it all the face of a child.

She stank of drink.

Molly'd poured out a glass of stale beer on the cigarette. Tucked two hundred dollars under her sleeping body. And tiptoed away.

Now she stared at the paper. Blank. Her mind was a total blank. She'd said it all. She'd said it a hundred times: "Stop hurting yourself. Stop hurting me. Please. Promise me. I love you. You're precious. Take care of yourself. Come home."

Molly shoved the paper away. Not dying here. You'll tell her in person. Maybe now you'll find something new to say.

She opened the newest book. Stepped off the train with Madeline Hammond, a New York society girl come west to buy a ranch.

She was still waiting for Charity.

10

"I see you ain't dead an' I see you ain't gone."

Molly jerked upright. Seated at the table, she'd fallen asleep over the book.

Old woman looks exactly like she looked the day before. Except a lot dirtier.

"You know what's really stupid? Sleepin' with a lit lamp." Old woman grabbed the coffee can off the shelf, took down the dented pot. "You supposed to be gone, one way or the other. Wasn't lookin' forward to buryin' you, though. Do enough digging. Why ain't you gone?"

"I needed to ask you which way to go."

"You think I'm the Cheshire Cat? You think I'm gonna say that all depends on where you want to get to? I ain't tellin' you scat. You got yourself here, you can get yourself out."

"You're serious?"

"Course, I'm serious. You got some idea I like people? Shit, what you think I'm doin' out here?" Using the jam jar, the old woman measured out the coffee, dumped it in the pot. "You bein' mebbe an angel, don't mean I got to like you. An' it sure don't mean I got to let you write 'help' all over my road. Though writin' it tells me you don't know where you are an' you not knowin' where you are, means you won't be leadin' anyone back."

"Why would I lead anyone back?"

Old woman got a gleam in her hard blue eye. "That cooks it. I want you out of here. An' I want it now."

"Now?"

"Can't feed you. Don't want to feed you. Only got so much food and so much water. Even if you was to offer me one of them cards of yours, plastic don't cut it out here. You hear me? I said to get out."

Mrs. Warner would have left on the instant. Mrs. Peter Warner might even have apologized for the inconvenience. But not Molly Brock. It's dark out there. Night creatures are out. You've done your walking in the dark. You've done your falling down in the dark and your panic-stricken running in the dark. Not to mention you've just been ill. You're weak. You need a little more rest. So you'll go when you're going. But whenever that is, it isn't right now.

"I'll leave in the morning. If I feel better."

Old woman stared her in the eye. Molly stared back. Brewster walked in and looked at both of them. When neither looked at him, he curled back his hairy lips in a buck-toothed yawn, then settled in his corner.

Old woman turned away first. "One more night." Old woman walked out the door. "Water's boilin'.' I'll make the coffee. You find you somethin' for a cup."

Molly and the old woman sat out under the moon and all the stars. Charity said, "I am the wind, the alpha and the omega. I made the world and all things in the world. I am she who was prophesied, the Daughter of Zion."

Staring up into the unspeakable cosmos, Molly said nothing. But her mind talked back, saying: *We are all the wind, the first and the last. We all made the world and all things in the world.*

Hearing herself, Molly raised her eyebrows in the dark. No telling where that came from. Certainly wasn't Norma.

Charity was saying, "Was a time, I came in out of the Wilderness to call up the angels. Make your head spin I told you how often I got thrown in the pokey for that.

Last time was El Paso, Texas. Right in the lobby of the Camino Real, biggest, oldest, an' the best hotel in town, got a window over the bar in there like to pop your eye out. Saggy baggies come in from all over the country, come from the Hawaii they already ruined, come from Alaska they're tryin' to ruin, all of 'em converging on the hotel for a Governor's Conference. A gaggle of governors. A gag of 'em. A pollution of politicians. No angels there, I can tell you." Reaching deep down inside her shirt, she pulled out a small leather pouch on a long rawhide thong around her neck. "Keep my possibles in here. Lookit. Here's a calling card from the Governor of Nevada. Here's one from the Governor of California. Here's a bullet almost killed me. I got more than one of those."

Molly looked at the bullet, at the scar on the old woman's shoulder, at the cards dog-eared and soiled. Old woman was warm to a foot out from her skin. Molly warmed herself by the old woman's skin. Old woman's no crazier than anyone else she'd ever met. No crazier than your average zealot. No crazier than she was. Angels are those she likes. Angels are those who agree with her. Devils are everyone else. And God is the Daddy people yell for in need. And right there, maybe, is all there is to say about revealed religion.

Over by the saguaro, Charity's donkeys suddenly stamped their feet, snorting down their noses and wagging their ears. Old woman had her gun in her hand on the instant, was off the steps and standing. "I got me a gun. Who goes there?"

Molly was up and standing too, trying to see everywhere at once.

"Why now, lookit that. Not too often you see somethin' like that."

Charity was pointing at the cook stove. Bobcat on the griddle, dancing on the cooling metal. Bobcat was licking up the last of the old woman's supper. Licks, shakes its head from the heat, licks, shakes its head. Old woman put her gun away, sat down again — but Molly walked forward a few feet, the better to see the cat.

Never seen a bobcat before, got to see the cat. Cat sees you too. Cat's turning your way. Forward another two steps, holding out her hand, palm up. Aunt Evelyn taught you that. Like you've got something to feed them, Molly — the other way they think you might hurt them. Don't look in their eyes. If you look in their eyes, you're challenging them.

Smiling now, one more step.

The report of a small gun rang out behind her, small bullet whizzing past on her left. Followed by a big ping of the bullet hitting metal and a bobcat hissing in alarm. Cat sprang off the griddle to bound away into the night.

Molly spun on her heel. "Why'd you do that?"

Old woman still sitting there, gun in her hand. "Ever had a cat attached to your face? Sooner you get out of this desert, angel, better for all concerned."

A little while later, under the blanket and out of the chill of the night, the old woman arranged her bones better, saying, "For someone takin' up half my bed, you sure don't have much to say for yourself."

Molly had nothing to say to that. Seems like you lost your apologies out in the desert somewhere. Probably find them again, but not now. Now... you're too used up.

"You do any readin'?"

"I used to. Not so much any more. I've been reading your—"

"More fool, you. Most folks are liddle bitty rumpled notebooks with nuthin' written in 'em. Most folks are just as empty as all these fuckin' plastic bags you see everywhere you look. Bein' empty is what help's 'em be pure demons out of Mr. Hate. I mean, somethin's got to fill 'em up."

Old woman's knee bone knocked into Molly's bug bite. Scratching, Molly moved her leg.

"But some of 'em's already filled and what fills 'em comes pouring out worth all the gold in the ground and all the stars in the sky. Take Mr. Zane Grey. All you ever need to know is in his books. Tell you what I know. Won't cost you another penny. At three, my father taught me sorrow. At five, he took my innocence. At sixteen, I married a devil.

Them's his boots under the floor but where the rest of him is, I ain't tellin'. An' all I've known is devils since. But all of that's nothin' compared to what you're doin' to the desert, all you saggy baggy golfers. You and yours. Killin' Mother Light for ever and ever. Got no doubt Mr. Hate is stampin' his feet an' laughin' up his sleeve."

Not a golfer. Peter's a golfer. Mrs. Perez is a golfer. You're a... you're not a — my god, Molly. What are you?

Long after, she lay awake watching the moon grow fat. Old woman at her side snorts in her sleep, digs a horny old toenail into her ankle. Ouch!. Old woman bucks and grabs at the blanket, throws herself onto her back, flapping her wrinkled lips. The moon hits her face, turning it waxy and white. From a foot away, Molly stares at her, bony old face glowing in the moonlight.

Child this old woman was, breaks your heart. Bride this old woman was, boils your blood. The old woman this old woman is, scares the hell out of you. Tell you one thing you are, Molly Brock. Compared to this old woman, you're a quitter.

Worse, you haven't even got started.

11

In the cool of first light, Molly Brock packed her purse, since her brown Gucci bag was all she had. And Charity, the alpha and the omega, the Daughter of Zion, and no friend of Mr. Hate, sat at the table watching her do it, her notebook open in front of her, tapping her pencil on her perfect teeth, occasionally scratching her smooth pink head.

Molly shoving her things in the bag, cramming them in.

Old woman's going to let you walk out of here. Old woman's not going to offer you water. Not going to tell you where the road goes. Who knows who owns this land? Could be part of the National Forest. Could be a military installation. Could be private. Could be anything since nothing's wild anymore. Know what you think? You think the old woman's squatting here, working an abandoned mine, digging out just enough gold to keep her in Zane Greys and Top Ramen. And she thinks you're going to tell someone. Or get her chased off.

"I'm leaving now."

"How do you spell association?"

"ASSOCIATION."

"Those around Mr. Hate he made into demons. But it wasn't their fault; it was by association. As it says in the Bible: 'Beware bad association.'"

Swear to god, Molly, you ever get to be an old woman, maybe you'll understand the saggy baggy old bitch—but right now, what chance she'll shoot you if you just help yourself to the water?

"Go up."

"Excuse me?"

"You hard of hearin'? Go on down from here to the road. Turn right. That'll be the climbing road. Three miles, mebbe a little more, you'll come on an old paved road. Hardly used. Turn left. By an' by, you'll see a gas station. No gas there anymore. Nothing there anymore but Rupert. I know, who calls a kid Rupert? Damn stupid name. But Rupert lives down to it. He's a natural born asshole, and honey, I ought to know, but usually one or the other of his trucks'll work, and if not, maybe one of his cars. Drives whatever he can start, goes in for supplies most every other week, and the kind of supplies Rupert needs, sometimes it's every week. You catch him near to sober, he'll give you a ride."

"All along, it was that close?"

"What was that close?"

"A ride back."

"For cryin' out loud—you think you're in Oz?"

Molly tied her denim jacket around her waist, put on her sunglasses, slung the strap of her bag over her shoulder, checked out how her head felt, her body, stomach, her itch. Not bad. Not great. But not bad. She could walk.

She nodded at Charity. "Thank you."

"Take the hat. An' next time you think to take a stroll in the desert?"

"Yes?"

"Don't."

One foot out the door, the other just about to follow, Molly turned back. "And the other way? Where does that go?"

Old woman looked up from her notebook. "That one just goes. Until it don't go no more. Then it's all Injun. Nothin' out there for a golfer angel like you."

She was a quarter of the way back down to the road when she heard Charity call out, "Remember what Teddy Roosevelt said!"

Who can resist hearing what Teddy Roosevelt said? Molly Brock stopped to listen.

"Don't turn your back on Rupert. Find a big stick first. Now fuck off."

She made it to the paved road and turned left. Once, maybe fifty years ago, a two lane blacktop, now it was more desert than road, and it humped and it dipped through wash after wash — but it looked like Route 66 to Molly. Rusted five-strand barbed wire fencing both sides of the road. A rusted metal sign on a rusted metal post, post and sign shot full of rusted holes, sign said: **State Trust Land. No Trespassing. Enter Only With Valid Lease or Permit.**

What kind of trust is that? But you're walking on the shoulder here. Chin up, steady stride. It's just you, that nice Mrs. Warner, out for a morning's walk. And now you're not killing yourself, you wouldn't dream of entering private property without a valid lease or permit.

This time, walking the road was like an outing, a stroll. It was like exercise — knowing where she was going, knowing where the old road went, knowing she'd be asking for a ride from a natural born asshole called Rupert at the once gas station, but also certain she knew that assholes love money. We all love money, don't we, Mrs. Big White House in Laurel Canyon Warner?

No big stick, but cash for Rupert at the end of the ride.

This time, having every intention of living, and no expectation of being out here much longer, she heard the birdsong, tried not to step on the beetles and the ants, clucked her tongue at the trash strewn on the roadside.

Walking's good for the cardiovascular system, great for the leg muscles — and speaking of muscles, Mrs. Warner, have you noticed how trim you're getting? Get home, you'll have to go through your closets, rummage through all your drawers. A bundle of things for the Salvation Army, a bundle of things for the women at the needleworks shop. All of it dry-cleaned first, of course. And then you'll go shopping. Now, there's a lovely thought. Shopping.

She was in the lingerie department of Macy's when the pickup truck bounced by. Doing at least sixty down the middle of the roller coaster road, there were two men inside, the passenger holding on to the dash, the driver gripping the steering wheel, a big brown dog in the pickup bed. Long ears flapping in the hot wind, only the dog paid her the slightest bit of mind as the pickup disappeared around a crumble of rock.

Not men. Boys. No older than Shelley, those two. Both look stupid enough to do something really stupid. Thing about stupid, Molly, is that stupid people are too stupid to know they're stupid. It takes brains to know you don't know much.

Poor dog, though. Bounce high enough, dog's going to pop right out of that truck.

A minute later, a cop car careened by. Cop gave her a startled look, but that could be due to the potholes. He kept on going, cop car shuddering and shaking, to disappear round the same crumble of rock.

Never met a cop professionally. Never ran from one. Never committed a crime. Unless it's a crime to ignore those signs telling you to turn on your headlights for the next umpty doodle miles. Or attempted suicide—don't forget that one, Missus. So much you haven't done. Oh, shoot. Sorry. Forgot about the summer you were thirteen. That summer your best friend Laura and you discovered make-up—but what teenage girl doesn't steal make-up from the Burbank Walgreens? It may be wrong, but it's almost a rite.

On foot, she too made it round the crumble of rock, humps and dips flattened out a bit here, and—oh lord, what's that on the side of the road? Looks like a lacquer box, like more than one smashed lacquer box.

Seconds later, she was looking down at what was left of three desert tortoises. One was still alive. Its shell surely damaged beyond all hope of repair, still it stretched out a stumpy back leg hopelessly trying to right itself.

Don't want to see this, can't see this. Against the law to take tortoises, against the federal law. So they got rid of the evidence. Threw them out of the pickup truck. Tossed them out like beer cans.

Face tight with a sick helpless anger, Molly looked up. Maybe only an eighth of a mile down the road, there was Charity's gas station. One wall left. Like a Buster Keaton movie, the other three walls were flat on the ground on three sides of the building. No pickup, no cop car, but out back the carcasses of a dozen old cars and trucks littered the desert. Next to the one-walled gas station, a sagging mobile home stained with who-knew-what, windblown with trash. Cardboard in the windows, flapping plastic for a door. Half a once enormous saguaro leaning into a chain link fence, the rest of it shot to pieces. Instead of Keaton, a fat man sat on an upturned red plastic pail collapsing in the middle of a once garage. In one fat hand, an overlarge bottle of beer, in the other fat hand an overlarge bag of something as orange as nuclear fallout.

Oh, good. There's Rupert.

Molly watched him for a time. Seemed a long time, though perhaps it wasn't. Long enough to see the rifle across his knees. Long enough to see him shoot another hole in the cactus. Long enough to watch him lean forward and barf between his feet. Great steaming fallout of nuclear yuck. Wipe his mouth with the back of his hand. Shove the same hand back in the bag.

Eventually she untied her denim jacket from around her waist. Took a step towards the surviving tortoise.

"Don't touch it, Molly!"

Jesus wept. There she is. Mom in your head.

"You touch that, I'll make you wash your hands with Clorox. Nasty. Nasty."

"Not nasty, Norma. It's dying." Then she leaned down, carefully gathered up the smashed tortoise, and wrapped it in the jacket. "Do you feel pain? I do. Are you frightened? I'm frightened too."

Tortoise did nothing but blink, wag its legs.

She began walking back the way she'd come.

Old woman's cooking up a mess of Top Ramen and canned tuna. No doubt spots Molly when she tops the last rise in the dirt road below her cabin. Doesn't look up when the wife of the golfer demon walks back into what she considers her yard. But Brewster under his cactus, goes, "Awww EEEE, Awww EEEE."

Molly says, "Hello, Brewster." Then stands there, watching Charity stir tuna fish into her chicken and noodles.

"What you got there?" old woman finally says.

"Tortoise. Kids threw it out of a pickup. I think it's going to die."

"Prolly. Let's have a look. Hell yeah, sure as shit it's gonna die. What you gonna do with it?"

"Don't know. I just couldn't leave it like that at the side of the road. The other two are already dead."

"Demons found 'em three of the critters? Not bad for a day's evil doin'." Charity looks up from the shattered tortoise to stare at Molly.

Know what you're thinking, old woman. You're thinking I think I'm coming back here. You're thinking you might have to run me off with your pistol. But you're wrong. Watch this.

"Decided I'll skip Rupert and just walk home."

Old woman's surprised. Then pleased. Then, begrudgingly, concerned. "S'hot. Road's bad. Bad people on it."

"I'll stay off the road."

"Could do that. Still pretty far on foot. You could kill yourself."

"Not that easy."

At that, the old woman lifts her bald head. Stares at Molly a long time. "I see. You ain't a volunteer an' you wasn't exactly lost, was you?"

Molly shakes her head. "Not a saggy baggy golfer either."

Old woman laughs. "Should of known all along. Should of known you was shaded by the wings of an angel of death." Then she laughs some more. "Gimme that tortoise. I got me some duct tape. You never know what'll happen. Might even make it, s'long as it sticks around here."

Molly turns to go, but in turning, catches Brewster's fringed eye. "How much you want for the little donkey?"

Old woman's eyes narrow with calculation. Stares at her three donkeys, Brewster the smallest by far. "That un's cut. He's worth more."

"Cut?"

"No balls. Plus, I already got all your money."

"You want my Touch Time?"

"What's it do?"

"It tells time."

"I know the time. Don't care. Anyhoot, time is always now."

Molly heard that. She even understood it.

"OK. How about this? Just a touch on the dial, you can play with the design."

"I ain't got money for them saggy baggy batteries."

"No batteries."

"Let's see."

In the end, Molly Brock was walking away with a hat and Brewster. Brewster had a pair of old panniers strapped round his belly. In them were her packed Gucci bag and two five-gallon plastic water jugs. Old woman's army blanket was in a tight roll over his rump.

"Got me another one," old woman said.

No point in asking for *The Light of the Western Stars.* Old woman wouldn't let her have it. But, heck, you can check a Zane Grey out of any library anywhere. At the last minute, Charity threw in some matches, five packages of Top Ramen, an empty Hills Brother coffee can to heat it in, and a pack of Big Red.

Old woman was left with the Touch Time, the sunglasses, and a five month old Reader's Digest.

12

Molly's five years old and she wakes up one morning in the hush, already scared of her mother. Her mom and her dad are still asleep in their bedroom across the hall. Nothing's moving, not even outside on the street. Her blanket covers her nose. No sister, no brother—Mommy said: "Catch me having another kid, hah!" But Teddy's with her. If she lies in her own bed long enough, Daddy's going to work and Norma's going to start yelling at her. No matter how good she is, Norma yells at her.

"Get out of the way." "Put that down." "Go out in the yard and play." "Not now." "Go to your room." "Stop that whining."

All Molly wants is to be who she is, and who she is is a little kid. Little kids want to know things. Little kids want to be picked up, they want to be tucked in, they want a story, an apple, gum. What they don't want is Mommy yelling at them. Or Mommy smacking them.

So Molly decides to run away.

Quiet. Quiet. Quiet. She leaves on her pajamas because she'll need her pajamas. Over her pajamas she wears her favorite dress, the one the color of tomato soup. Over her favorite dress, she pulls on the big blue sweater Mommy's older sister, Aunt Evelyn, knit for her. She wears her patent leather Mary Janes because this is a special moment and they are her special shoes. She takes Teddy.

Molly is running away to Aunt Evelyn's farm. If she can get to the farm, then she can get away from Mommy.

She'll need food for the walk to Aunt Evelyn's. Quiet. Quiet. Pushing a kitchen stool over to the kitchen counter, she climbs up and finds a bag of chocolate chips in the cabinet. She takes those. Molly wraps them up in a piece of yellow cloth she finds in a wooden box in the living room. She ties the yellow bundle on the end of a stick like hobos do. Quiet. She opens the front door and walks away.

Molly and Teddy get to the front gate. They get past the gate. They get almost to the dusty oleander hedge that separates her house from the house next door. And then Mommy yells: "Where do you think you're going!"

Molly's curls flying as her head whips around. Mommy on the stoop. Mommy with that look on her face. Uh. Oh. You're in for it now.

Molly had to stand in a corner for an hour. To a little kid, that was forever. Her arm hurt where Norma pinched her.

When night came down, Molly Brock made camp in a shallow wash. Washes had less cacti and rocks and thorny things, more bare sand which meant fewer places for biting, stinging, crawling creepies to hide under. Making camp meant a small fire of dead cholla bits and pieces, a supper of a little warmed over Top Ramen, and getting wrapped up in Charity's blanket. For Brewster, it meant having her take the itchy panniers off his back, then a good roll in the stony sand and then chewing on palo verde leaves.

Later when the fire was out, fat white belly to the ground, Brewster slept resting his white bearded chin on a knobby brown knee. Molly sat up for a bit watching the stars, sat remembering what Aunt Evelyn once told her about the stars one summer on the avocado farm when she was twelve years old.

"Up there, that's the Big Dipper, Moll. Like a scoop serving up stars. If you draw a line between the two bright stars in the bowl of the Dipper, that'll be an arrow pointing to the pole star. Over there. The faint one. Polaris is due north. True north. And around the north star wheel the heavens. Around and around and where they stop no one knows."

Still looking up, Molly jumped in her skin. Oh, god—listen to that.

Up through the saguaros came a fattening moon as yellow as butter. Out came the coyotes. Yip yip yipping. This time not on a distant hilltop or from out of a far arroyo—but from practically underfoot. Even in sleep, Brewster cocked both ears forward, spun them this way and that. More barks, a high broken-barked yowling. Eyes snapping open, Brue heaved himself to his feet.

He's backing into me for protection, the big baby. Get off.

Down the wash, shoulder to shoulder, trotted two coyotes.

Must be young, they're both so small. Don't move. Keep quiet. Say to yourself: coyotes can't harm you. True, they'll eat anything, but usually the largest things they eat are lizards—did Zane Grey say that? Or was it in the Sunday section of the *Arizona Star*? Wherever—and every now and again they'll eat a fat juicy house cat. They got this close to making a meal of Mrs. Perez's dog. But what's a pussy cat more or less when cats are eating all the songbirds? What's a yapping snapping dog more or less? Cats and Mrs. Perez's dog are smaller than you are, Molly Brock. But you keep still anyway—better safe than sorry.

Sudden thought: are they rabid?

Fur shining in the moonlight, one coyote began leaping into the air snapping its sharp little teeth at bugs. Caught one, and chewed it up on the spot. Gah. Horrid crunching sound. The other was circling a cholla, nipping at its fruit. Knows something I don't know. Or it doesn't mind its tongue getting stuck through with a thousand tiny spines.

Either the coyotes didn't see her, or saw her and didn't care... both sat down where they found themselves, both lifted their scruffy little muzzles straight up towards the buttery moon, and they both howled aye-aye-aye-eeeiooow!

Ay-yipyap-iiieeee-ip! came the answer... and down the wash trotted three more coyotes, one as small as the first two, but the last pair much bigger.

It's Mr. and Mrs. Wile E. Coyote with three little ones... no one has rabies, no one's going to get rabies — and they've all come to sing me to sleep.

Later, resettling Brue and drifting off to a quintet of midnight coyotes singing in the distance, it occurred to Molly Brock that she was alone with only a donkey in a dark and crowded desert, and that she was more tired than afraid.

Molly walking along behind Brewster. Narrow little donkey hips, odd little donkey tail, Molly finding herself just naturally holding on to his tail.

Back at Charity's cabin, life was sitting and standing and lying about and reading. It was a time of small insights. Out here, life was just walking and holding onto Brewster's tail and stopping to rest and stopping to drink and stopping to look at strange and unusual things. But mostly, life was a hot walk and a long talk to Brewster.

"Guess what, Brue?"

Brewster rotated a furry ear. What if he's really listening?

"Never did dig up my rings. Lassiter would say: reckon I shore did fergit 'em. Which, by the way, is the only thing about Lassiter that gets up my nose — the way he talks. Fortunately, he's a mostly silent gunman. But we're not going off to look for those lil trinkets, oh no. Come git 'em some other day. Today, we head for the hills. And speaking of coffee, we can't have any. But we can have us a sip of water."

Molly letting go long enough to share out the water.

"Digging up those rings reminds me of one new thing I've learned about surviving in a desert. Learned it just this morning, Brewster. Don't bury your toilet paper. Burn your toilet paper. You bury your toilet paper, and something's bound to come along in the middle of the night and dig it up. Not only is that disgusting, and not only is it unsightly in the midst of all this beauty, it's a sure way of letting something with teeth and claws, and an appetite, know exactly where you are."

High noon now. Hot. Getting hotter. Molly getting used to the heat… but even with water and a hat, she could take only so much of it, and only for so long. Got to get out of this desert. Road's over there. Somewhere. Been following the road. Always keeping near the road. When's the last time you actually saw the road?

Molly stopped. Held on to Brewster's tail which made him stop too. Brewster looking round, curling his lip, snorting down his nose.

You last saw the road this morning. Very early this morning. But it's right over there just where you think it ought to be. Of course it is. Where else would it be? Keep moving.

Some time later, Brewster, passing a brittlebush, reached out with long orange teeth to snatch at the tiny leaves — and out crackled some sort of bug as big as a golf ball and stung him on a soft furry lip. Brewster reared up, came down, shook his head, then humped his back and went huckety bucking off through the cacti.

In the midst of all this, Molly lost her grip on his tail.

Last thing she saw of Brewster was a scurry of grit and a flurry of yellow dust as he raced round a big yellow rock. But she could still hear him.

"Awww EEEE! Awwww EEEE!"

In the half hour it took to find him, to calm him down, and to rearrange the Mexican panniers, Molly was scratched by cholla spines, scraped her ankle on a ledge of hard rock, went in this direction and that, and came close to passing out in the heat. She'd also had another small insight. Or perhaps not so small. Perhaps this one was large.

"Don't do that again, Brue," she said when both of them were bedded down for a rest from the afternoon heat and the glare and bad tempered bugs. "You scared the heck out of me. You're my best friend. In all the world, the very best."

And what does that say about you, Molly Brock?

13

Molly and Brue later that day, toiling up a ravine.
Nothing looks right. Nothing seems right. Ought to
be getting closer and closer to home. Should be there by
now. Should be coming over the hump of the last ridge and
looking down the last *bajada* into the city. Should be able
to count the sun-faded cars in the parking lot of a mall, any
mall. Ought to hear the trains and the cars and the dogs
and the gunshots and the screams and the stomach-turning
thump-thump-thump of defiant kids in musical cars. Where
the hell are they? Where the hell is anything? Lost our way,
haven't we? Chasing Brue made us lose our way.

Walls of rock on either side, interesting cacti growing
out of every chink and crack. No matter where she might
place a foot or a hand, there were holes for hiding in and
crevices for lurking. Behind her, she could hear Brewster's
hoofs tapping on stones.

"What day is this, Brewster? No Time Touch to tell.
So where are we? You think we're lost in time as well as
space? Tell you what. I don't think anyone's looking for
me. But *why* aren't they looking? Your everyday housewife
has to be worth *some* sort of manhunt. When Peter called
the cops — by now, he's sure to have called the cops — would

they think I was lost? Heck, no. They'd think I'd left him. Wives are always leaving their husbands, and the husband the last to know. But what would they think when they saw I took nothing, when they found my car still in the Safeway parking lot? So then they'd check into everything and when they did, they'd see I hadn't used my credit cards. So maybe not the women cops, but the men cops, they'd say to themselves: a woman who isn't using her credit cards? Unthinkable. And then they'd wonder what else could have happened. Kidnapped? But if I was kidnapped, where's the ransom note?"

Molly deciding not to put her hand near a suspicious hole, gripping a root instead to steady herself.

Good thing Brewster seems just naturally steady. We fell here, we'd die here.

Bits and pieces of dirt breaking away, getting up her nose.

So—someone murdered me. But who? And what for? Holy cow! I just bet they think Peter killed me. I just bet they think I'm dead and he did it. The nearest and dearest almost always does it—whatever it is. Who else would bother? Bet they've been round to see his mistress on Dry River Street. Does *she* think he killed me? Is she frightened? Or flattered? And what about the people he works for? Think of the office gossip. And what about his dad? Stan was bound to ask: Where's your wife, son? Stan would say: Man goes to all the trouble of having a wife, he ought to know where she is. Would he also say: You know I'll understand, boy, you know it won't go any further, and you know I'm behind you one hundred percent, but—did you get rid of her, son? Did you kill her?

Poor Peter. Must be going through hell. Poor you. No search party.

Sudden crash behind her, sudden shaking of the earth, sudden grit in the eyes, dust caught in the back of the throat—Moll, even Brewster, almost jumping out of their skins. Heart hammering, Molly swinging round to find an entire rock wall fallen away. Whole thing, rocks as big as Brewster, blocking the path they'd come up by.

And for no earthly reason at all, far as you can see.

"We were ten feet back, we'd be under that, Brue."

Molly hurrying forward, Brewster leaping along like a goat—and with a last grunting effort and a hard tug on Brewster's halter, they were up and out of the ravine and looking at a big concrete and brick building that had seen much better days. Faded paint on the side of the building said: Copper Crown Mining Co. 1881.

A huge thing, impressive even now, the building was set back into a wall of blasted rock. Three stories tall, sectioned into four wings, the fourth and farthest wing leaning at a rakish angle. Built on a steep hillside dug out and scraped flat long ago, the rest of the Copper Crown Mining Company sagged here and humped there like Charity's paved road, but most of its bricks were set firm, most of its wooden siding held fast, most of its concrete was solid. The roof looked intact, and two of the five doors fit straight in their frames.

Molly led Brewster across a wide gravel road towards what had to be the main entrance, and as she went, she saw more and more of what lay beyond the wall of rock on the far side of the building.

Stopped short to stare. Maybe you can't find a city to save your life, but you found a real live ghost town.

Straggling up one baked hill and down another, strung along an old rutted road and hanging off rocks, everywhere there were ramble-shamble buildings of flapping tin and crumbling adobe and splintered wood—and everywhere else pits and slagheaps and bits of rusted this and chunks of rusted that, these last no doubt once mighty machinery to wrest copper from the mountain. Up the side of a steep *bajada*, and built one on top of the other, were miner's cabins, most gutted now and open to the sky, but one or two still roofed, their chimneys still standing. To her right, one half a railroad trestle spanned a much bigger ravine than the one she and Brewster had just come up, and one half lay jumbled at the bottom in a mess more confused than a collapsed cholla.

Once upon a time, it fell as suddenly as the rock wall fell. And who saw it tumble?

That was surely Main Street, and those were without doubt the remnants of a dozen once imposing storefronts. And way up there, away from the slag and the pits and the miner's huts — that was the right side of the tracks. Up there were mansions, and one — weathered to bare wood — almost as fine as the day it was built.

Old woman would cry to see this. Old woman would pack up her Zane Greys and her Top Ramen and her bathtub, choose her a cabin or a store or that mansion — a Norman Bates of a house, a Hill House of a house — and move right in.

Gravel road she stood on, wide and flat where it ended in front of the Copper Crown building, narrowed as it went winding on down through the town as its main street. From town, it hair-pinned back and forth across the side of the mountain until it reached the desert flats far below — then curved away towards the east.

"Look, Brewster, way down there. Car's coming."

Late afternoon sun glinting off its windshield, kicking up a half mile of white dust and yellow grit, sure enough — a car was coming. Or a van. Molly, walking to the very edge of the gravel road before it fell off into a hair-raising drop into a desert basin, gripped Brewster's mane for balance.

"No, not a car. Or a van. It's an old VW bus. What do you bet? PEACE on one side and LOVE on the other?"

Just like the one Antonio once had. Prettiest boy you ever knew. Breaks your heart to remember. Where's he now, you wonder? Long ago, run off from the Burbank Burger King to New York City, gone to be a folk singer. And you, still going to Burbank High, almost ran off with him. Last thing he ever said to you was, "Come with me, Moll, and we'll live in the East Village and I'll sing in a coffee house and you can paint in a loft." And your Aunt Evelyn said, "Just think of it, Moll. New York City!" But your mother said, "Over my dead body." And your father said, "Do what's in your heart… but, oh dear, I've worked so hard to send you through college." So Antonio went on without you, and he promised to write and you promised to write, and he did and you did, and then you didn't, and after that you never heard another note. By now he could be dead. He could even be a folk singer who knows Bob Dylan personally. Miracles do happen. But you, you'll just sit right here on your saggy baggy Crisco butt and wait for whoever that is acomin' round the mountain. Chew a stick of Big Red and pray for salvation.

"Going home, Brue. We're going home."

And for the first time, she wondered what to do about Brewster. Could he live in the garage, graze tethered out back of the house? Graze on what? Out back of the house was nothing but sand and a mess of prickly pear and a barbecue pit. Also, if Brue lived in the garage, she'd have to park the Jeep Cherokee in the driveway, get a car-cover to keep its dark blue paint from fading to a powdery blue in the Arizona sun. And what would the neighbors say?

Heck with the neighbors. They don't like an ass in the garage, they can kiss my ass. Or move. If they won't move, you can move. Somewhere. Else. But where? No time to think about that now. Now it's time to sit down and wait.

Brewster wandered off to eat the top off a brittlebush growing out of a large crack in the Copper Crown wall. But Molly selected a spot where she could see the whole of the Copper Crown ghost town, then sat cross-legged in the dirt at the edge of the road on the edge of the cliff. From there she could see every stutter and rattle of her valiant rescuer. Wind practically blew off her hat. Got so bad, she took it off and sat on it.

Love weather, but hate wind. Hate it.

It took what seemed forever for that old bus to chug its way to the top.

14

Molly stood up when the VW bus jolted to a halt in front of the big brick and plank building. No PEACE on one side, no LOVE on the other, just dull brown paint all over and dull black bumpers. Slapping the dust off the seat of her jeans, stamping the dust off her shoes, planting a big dusty smile on her dirty face, she walked forward, one hand shading her unmade-up eyes from the glare of the setting sun, the other held out in greeting.

Door of the bus opened and out he came.

Lassiter!

Silhouetted against the sky, golden in the sun: it's a desert angel, Molly Brock, a mote in the eye of Mother Light.

One of Zane Grey's lonesome strangers, one of his restless riders: "...tall, lean, wide at the shoulder and narrow at the hip, his boots were down at the heel and his clothes were shabby."

From under the brim of a sweat stained cowboy hat, the stranger looked from Molly to Brewster to Molly again. Touched the brim of his hat. Gave a curt nod. "Can I help you?"

Even has a slight drawl. If you could see his eyes, would they be Newman *Cool Hand Luke* blue eyes? A Kurt Russell *Tombstone* blue?

"God, yes. I seem to be turned around. Where's the city? I was sure if I just kept going north, I was bound to find the city — but I haven't. All I've found is you."

Big smile. High voltage. Give him your True Grit and your good heart, show him a blossom in the desert, a damsel in distress — maybe he won't care you're not twenty. Or thirty. Or even, oh hell... maybe if he *does* care, he's still a natural born gentleman. Even housewives need directions. Water. A ride.

Cowboy nodded his head towards a ridge of pink rock half a world away from the way she'd been heading. "City's over there."

"Guess I wasn't going north then."

"Guess not."

Molly stood there, horribly aware of her unbrushed teeth, the dark roots in her filthy blonde hair. Only god and the cowboy knew what her face looked like. But at least she was thinner. Over five pounds thinner, maybe even six. By now, her jeans hung off her like pants hung off a teenaged boy. Be serious, Molly. Not that thin. If you were that thin, your pants would have fallen round your ankles and you'd be standing here in your boxer shorts.

"Could I use your phone?"

"No phone."

"Ah. Well, then... when you leave, could I go with you? I can't pay for the gas, old woman took all my — forget that. I can pay at the other end, when I'm home."

"Not leaving."

Cowboy was moving by now, opening the side door on the bus, pulling out two huge sacks of groceries, at the sight of which, Molly's stomach clenched into a mournful knot. She couldn't help herself, she followed him like a starving coyote pup.

Striding towards the side of the big building, the cowboy said, "If you're still here, take you when I go down again."

"Thank you. Thank you. When's that?"

"Whenever."

Cowboy didn't slam the door after himself, which Molly took as an invitation. Checking quickly to see where Brewster had gotten to—off to the side, eating another bush—she followed the cowboy into the old Copper Crown Mining Co. building. Took her eyes a minute to adjust to the light. Been outside so long hardly remember a proper inside.

But, oh my, look at this! It's an art gallery. Or it's a studio. Or it's a huge room full of huge paintings and sculptures and constructions of one sort or another. He's an artist. The cowboy is a painter. He's a sculptor. He's a model maker.

"Did you do all this?"

"Didn't do any of it."

"Oh."

Cowboy kept moving, so she kept moving, through the first enormous room into a smaller one beyond it. This room had smaller paintings, smaller sculptures, in entirely different styles. Then into a room beyond that. Here, there were kilns and tables covered with wire frames and blibs and blubs of dried white plaster and white glue and spattered paint of all colors. On the floor there were huge tubs of plaster and clay. Out the door and into the back of the building. A yard out here, walled in by the building itself and by the sheer rock wall behind it. In the deeply shadowed yard, a wood shop. In front of the wood shop, furniture. Mostly dining tables and chairs. Made out of a wood she'd never seen before. Deep and glossy golden brown wood, with a lovely pinkish red running through. Nothing was straight, no right angles—it was all curved and coiled. Tables and chairs looked alive.

Always wanted furniture like this, but Peter would take one look at the price and turn green. Besides that, it wasn't "normal." He'd hate it.

Cowboy kept going through another door back into the building.

The kitchen. Lights powered by a generator she heard before she saw. Wiring and switches out of the 1920s. Refrigerator also out of the 1920s, the kind with the motor on top. Big lima bean green Hamilton Beach mixer out of the 1950s. Cabinets and shelves and cast-iron range out of the Nineteenth Century. Stacked by the double-ovened range: stove wood and kindling. One window, four feet wide and twice as tall, looked out over the long dead town. Window could have used a good scrub way before the town around Copper Crown died. Tin ceiling high over her head. Crook her neck far enough, she could just make out that the ceiling fan was covered in fly blow. Fan went round and round with a lazy shrieking creak.

Cowboy dumped the groceries on the table. Table, which could seat twelve and then some, was an example of those in the yard with the wood shop.

Cowboy said, "You cook?"

"Why yes, I do... I—"

"You cook, you can have something to eat. Don't get fancy."

Then he walked through another door—and this time he slammed it.

After washing her face down to her collarbone and her hands up to her elbows, Molly made a spinach and egg salad. Made her own special dressing. She grilled two steaks. And when she was done and the food was on the table, somehow the cowboy knew exactly when to walk back into the kitchen, wash his hands under the hand-pump in the sink, then sit himself down, and tuck in.

Smelling faintly of paint and gasoline, he'd left his hat somewhere.

Good face. Strong. Shrewd. Beaten up some by time and the sun, but all the better for it. Only wish you could say the same for yours. Hair flattened in back by the hat. Dark brown hair, almost black. Never much liked a moustache, unless it was growing on the face of Tom Selleck. Or Sam Elliot. Or Mark Twain. But you like his. And no, his eyes aren't blue. They're gray. Like smoke. Or maybe it is smoke. Cowboy smokes like the Marlboro man. Damn, you're hungry.

Two weeks of Top Ramen and a boiled turnip would be something. Steak and spinach salad was like chateaubriand at what used to be Granitas in Malibu, like lobster in that little fishing village in Maine, like anything at Aunt Evelyn's farm, was almost like a four-course Molly Brock meal when she was really trying—and to think, two weeks ago it was all you could do to eat peanut butter off a spoon.

No talking at the table. This wasn't her mother's rule and it wasn't Molly's, this was the cowboy. At the end farthest from her, he ate in silence, pushed back his empty plate in silence, shook out a Camel in silence and lit it. Then he smoked three of them back to back while she did the dishes. To wash the dishes, she had to fill a large black kettle with water from the hand-pump, then put it on to boil. Hot water went into a tin sink no doubt hauled overland by a Prairie Schooner. Or a mule train. Compared to the old woman's mining cabin, it was the kitchen in the house on Laurel Canyon Drive.

And what does a mule train remind you of? Go see to Brewster. Get those panniers off his back. Make sure he has water. And maybe a treat. Do donkey's like hard boiled eggs?

Back again—Brewster's bedded down with the furniture (didn't want an egg but inhaled the leftover spinach, even with dressing)—cowboy's gone. But his smoke still hung in the air. Hooking the strap of her soft brown bag over a chair, she dried the dishes, humming a little tune to herself and watching a little movie in her mind.

This is you and it's the year 1888. You're a miner's wife—no! Heck with that. Not a miner's wife—a miner. Wait. Better yet, you're your own Jane Withersteen and you're the female owner of the new Copper Crown Mine. You've given the Mexican woman the night off and, for the pure devil-may-care of it, you're doing your own dishes in your own huge kitchen and all the while, over at the mine, your miners are digging more and more copper out of the mountain—millions of dollars worth. You can hear the train rattle over the trestle taking another load of ore off to do whatever they do with ore. Got Lassiter in your kitchen. Lassiter just rode hard to bring you news of an Apache raid, or yet another Mexican stand-off with yet another passel of Mexicans, and he's sitting at your table now, not even winded, but dusty as all outdoors, and looking at you with smoke in his smoky eyes — and he's dark as a mystery and as mysterious as God. And you, you're stirred to your — well, to be nice about it — your "quick," wherever that is, but you're laughing it off. Ha ha! After all, who are mere Mexican bandidos or Apache savages to mess with Mad Moll, the Arizona Copper Queen? Or Lassiter himself to stir Mad Moll's quick?

Drying the forks and knives and spoons, she stuck them in jars with the others. Flatware around here was kept upright in jars, a jar for each type.

When she's rich enough — but who can ever be rich enough? — Mad Moll will go to San Francisco. Maybe she'll take Lassiter. Maybe she won't. Though she probably will. After all, how many broad-shouldered, slim-hipped mysterious strangers in black leather does she know? She'll live at the Palace Hotel. She'll have a carriage drawn by a matching pair of pure black horses. She won't call them Night and Black Star, she'll...

"You can wear something of Paula's."

Molly dropped a fork. Cowboy's back. "Sorry. Who's Paula?"

"Sculptor."

"I couldn't wear another woman's clothes, not without asking. Besides, I haven't had a bath in, uh — I'd need a bath."

"Use the kitchen sink."

Stubbing out his smoke, cowboy was off again. Molly cleaned out the ashtray and boiled another kettle.

Boy oh boy, could you use a Lady Gillette right about now. Had no idea how much hair you could grow under your arms. As for your legs — jeezus.

Hair wet and combed straight back from her scrubbed face, a hint of eyeliner and mascara and a slick of *French Toast* (on her mouth, not her nose), Molly went looking for Paula's clothes. Funny how you think you're someone who couldn't wear another woman's clothes, not without asking, and find out you're a woman, now she was clean, who couldn't wear her own clothes another minute.

To find Paula's clothes, first she had to find the cowboy.

This place is bigger than the Calle de Flores mall. Half the corridors dip up and the other half dip down. Like the road to Rupert and his Buster Keaton gas station—only no dying tortoises and no trash and nobody's shot up the cacti. But there are bedrooms. Six or seven of them. People live here. By the look of things, every one an artist. But not full-time or someone should be in at least one of them.

So far as you can tell, only people here now are—

Molly says it out loud. She says in a deep smoky voice.

"Me and Lassiter."

15

She found the cowboy in a large, high-ceilinged, slant-floored room on the second floor in the third section—which is somehow still attached to the fourth section, and if you think the third floor slants, the entire fourth section leans so far over, anything loose on the floors would need roping down. Whatever the room in this third section once was, now it was a studio: three easels, three paintings in progress, two paint stained armchairs to rest in, ashtrays and coffee cups on the floor, cartoons pinned on two of the walls, canvas on stretchers stacked against a third, and the big windows on the fourth wall clean inside and out.

Cowboy had his hat off and his boots off, one paintbrush in his hand and one between his teeth. High on a wooden scaffolding in his socks—clean socks, you'll note—he was painting the roiling boiling clouds massed over the desert during a summer monsoon.

Turned out, cowboy was a painter after all and his paintings were as enormous as all outdoors, which was his subject—all outdoors. Cowboy was a landscape painter and he painted the Sonoran Desert like the Hudson River School once painted nineteenth century America: romantically, lyrically, mystically, and very very large.

Molly in the doorway, smiling. "I was looking for Paula's room — do you sell these?"

No pause in his painting, cowboy spoke around his brush, "You buyin' one?"

"I would. But there's not a wall in my house it would fit."

No response.

"I took art courses in college."

No response.

"I thought I would be an artist."

No response.

Getting embarrassing here. You being pathetically eager and obvious, him being — at best — hard of hearing. But more like unimpressed and uninterested. As well as too obviously busy.

How to back out without looking rejected? How to slink away? Oh, for rollers on the soles of your feet, silent and swift.

Smile back in her pocket, Molly edging out the door.

He hasn't asked you, he won't ask you, but you will. Why aren't you an artist?

Molly turning away.

Here are some answers. Choose one. Choose two. You wanted to paint portraits and couldn't relate to everyone else's conceptionalist painting, confrontational theater, installationist sculpture, experimental fiction. You secretly believed you had too little talent so were too frightened of failure. How about — no money in it? And no heart for the hard times, and unless a person got lucky, they told you in your Santa Monica College art classes they were all hard times. An artist was supposed to "say something" — and you had nothing to say. Although your mother did. Your mother said you couldn't draw a straight line if your life depended on it. Your father said, "Leave the kid alone, Norma, nobody can draw a straight line." And then he said, "You sure you want to be an artist, sweetie pie? Wouldn't you rather you did something useful in the world?"

Last and final answer: you got knocked up by Peter the jock and Peter the jock lived in a big white house in Laurel Canyon.

Cowboy used a brush to point at the distant ceiling.
"Third floor. Behind the tapestry."
"Yes?"
"Paula's room."
"Right."

Something out of Paula's wardrobe would never have
fit her a month ago, but now everything in it fit her fairly
well. Another week or so on her Miracle Desert Diet Plan
and they'd fit very well. Whoever Paula was, she favored
frontier clothes. Cotton twill pants with button-up flies
and more buttons on the waist band for forked suspenders.
Fringed shirts with a lot more buttons, opening not in the
middle, but down one side. Long pants like wide skirts.
Little jackets with tidy tucked-in waists and padded
shoulders.
    Molly holding up this, posing in that.
    Great stuff. Always wanted to wear stuff like this.
Didn't though. Felt foolish. Felt like a fake. What does
Paula feel like? What does Paula look like? No photos on
the dresser, none in her top drawer — stop snooping. How
you'd hate some woman looking through your drawers —
which is ironic when you stop and think about it. By now,
if Peter's called the police, and he's sure to have called the
police, the cops have gone through everything you own.
    Molly selected buckskin pants and a buckskin shirt.
    Holding the shirt up to her chest, she took one look in the
cracked and mottled glass over an old bureau—these were
in a Fifth Avenue shop, they'd be pricey antiques, bureau
as well as mirror, not to mention the terrific wardrobe—and
hello, Annie Oakley!

Paula had a bed. Not like Charity's bed, Paula's bed
was high up off the floor of loose, whitewashed planks.
It had pillows in soft white pillowcases, it had soft white
sheets and there was a real goose down quilt in a quilt cover
of violets and sweet peas. It all smelled of soap.
    Maybe if she could just lie down for a minute or two?
Maybe if she could have a little nap?

Where's the harm? Paula isn't here. If Paula didn't come home for dinner, she probably won't be coming home until bedtime. And by then you'll be out of her bed and sleeping on the floor somewhere all rolled up in your own blanket, won't you, saggy baggy Molly Brock, you failed wannabe artist, you?
You bet your life you will.

"Nine o'clock!"
Molly threw herself out of bed and across the room. Woke up standing there in her clean, rested, thinning, firming, bruised and partly tanned, partly peeled body. And nothing else. Woke up flinging her arms around her bare breasts, lifting a coy stubbly leg to cover the delicate dirty blonde triangle of her crotch, and bending forward from the waist. Woke up feeling flushed and foolish and exposed.
Cowboy said, "Your ass is kicking in the door."
He looked at Paula's bureau — middle drawer open. At Paula's wardrobe — long black culotted skirt on a hanger hanging from the door. At Paula's buckskin pants and shirt — still laid out over a chair. And then he looked at Molly. And only then did he do what he seemed born to do. He pushed aside the tapestry, and walked out of the room.
Molly flung herself on Paula's clothes.
Nine in the morning, he means nine in the morning. You slept here all night. Did Paula come home? Did she find you in her bed? Is she furious? I'd be furious. But here I am — Goldilocks again. Oh shoot, if Paula's home, I can't wear her clothes.
Back in her own clothes — rags, you might as well call a spade a spade; clothes you've worn in a desert for two weeks straight night and day without washing are rags — holding on to the walls of the third section to keep upright on the slant, she tracked down the kitchen in the upright second section by the smell of coffee. Walked in: don't mind me, I'm nobody. Only passing through on my way out to my ass. Soot blackened enamel coffee pot was on the stove, but no cowboy in the kitchen. And no Paula.

Just as well. Don't know about her, but don't want to see him right now. Don't want to see him at all. "Solemn monosyllabic shit."

Surprised by the way that came out, she opened the door—and the sound of Brewster hee-hawing his head off out in the yard ramped up a decibel. She spun on her heel. Back to the sink. Forgot the water, didn't you, you wee timid beastie you.

Behind her back, the cowboy'd appeared. Corner of her eye, there he was now, newspaper in his hand, pouring himself a cup of coffee. Tempted, she resisted spinning on her heel again—but instead took out a basin from under the counter and pumped water into it. Looking up from his paper, cowboy watched every move she made. Yesterday, he never looked at her. Today, she felt like a target. Already nervous, it made her as jumpy as a bobcat on Charity's cook stove.

"I'm so sorry. If Paula's angry I slept in—"

"Isn't here."

Oh sheesh, no Paula. "Oh, good. I'd have hated for her to find someone... I mean, honestly, I never meant to stay there, I meant to—"

"Nobody's angry."

"Oh. Right. Well, then. I'm just taking Brewster his water. He'll shut up when he's had his water."

Ducking out the kitchen door, Molly slopped water all the way across the yard.

You're out here all alone with this man. You were sound asleep, and he walked right in on you. How long was he there before he yelled the time? Not "Good morning" but "Nine o'clock!" Then he watched you leap about naked. Would an angel walk in on someone? Wouldn't an angel knock? Would Lassiter walk in on Jane? True, there's only tapestry for a door, but there's also a perfectly good door frame. Maybe he's not a perfect stranger. Maybe he's an imperfect stranger. So maybe you can't wait for him to get around to driving you out of here. Maybe it's Rupert all over again, and you're back to walking home.

Trying to get out the door and into the yard with a basin of water, Brewster was pushing at her, butting her in the hip with his hard boned head.

"Stop that, you idiot. You're spilling it."

Pushing him out of her way, she set the basin down, and then got out of his way.

"How'd you get out here?"

Molly spun round. Cowboy was leaning in the doorway, smiling. First smile she'd seen on his face. First expression. Was it an angel's smile—or a demon's? Old woman would know; old woman would have her gun out and aimed for the heart. Halt! Who goes there?

"Sorry. You scared me. You mean out here? With Brewster?"

"I mean out here in the desert."

"I was... I—got lost. But you mean, what was I doing when I got lost?"

"That's what I mean."

"I guess you could say I was taking a walk."

Taking a walk? Better think of something else, Molly Brock, better think of something better. When you get back, they're all going to ask you what you thought you were doing. Peter. Peter's parents. Your neighbors. Shelley. The police. You're certainly not going to tell a single soul you tried to kill yourself. Because, aside from the embarrassment... isn't attempted suicide a crime?

Hands balled into fists, blood drained from her face.

What if the police want to lock you up too? Evaluate you? Drug you? Force feed you therapy? Like Shelley. Oh, dear god. Run away, Molly. Run.

"Long walk, Mrs. Warner."

16

There she was, on the front page of last week's *Arizona Star*.

Pardon me, but—good god shit! It's *that* picture. The one Peter Jr. took when he found you hiding in a big stuffed chair in the lobby of the Regent Beverly Wiltshire Hotel. Everyone else was still in the dining room, singing *Happy Birthday* to Peter's dad, blowing paper whistles, snapping snappers, ignoring the fact that, as usual, Stan sat at the head of the table like something carved out of Mount Rushmore.

Thought he promised he'd delete it before anyone saw it. He lied.

Overwrought, overwhelmed, overweight, and completely undone, a very UnPretty Woman, you'd taken one look at that image, and felt like throwing up in a flower vase. But—oh, no—here it is, large as life.

Going to cry.

Sitting at the kitchen table, chin propped in a cupped hand, she was reading about the mysterious disappearance of one Molly Anne Warner, formerly Molly Anne Brock of Burbank, California, wife of Peter J. Warner of Hollywood, California, mother of Peter Jr. and Shelley Warner, daughter of the late Lindsay Brock & wife, Norma Brock, deceased, daughter-in-law of Mr. and Mrs. Stanley Warner. The newspaper said that Stanley Warner was well-known as the executive producer of a number of successful movies, most of them action-adventures, the latest opening soon in a theater near you. "Mrs. Warner was last seen at the checkout counter of the Safeway Supermarket in the Calle de Flores mall in residential Tucson. As of this date, neither her husband, Mr. Warner, nor the Tucson police can offer anything substantial in the way of explanation, and there are as yet no leads on the present whereabouts of Mrs. Warner. With nothing else to go on, the police are still treating it as a missing person's case, although suicide has not been ruled out."

Cowboy sat down across from her. Lit up a Camel. Studied her through its pale blue smoke. Something different about his eyes? More light? Her face no doubt a deep unhappy red, Molly kept her head down.

Suicide has not been ruled out? Never thought what that might look like in black and white for anyone to read. For Shelley to read. Her mother killed herself? That's your legacy to Shelley? Good grief, Molly Brock—what were you thinking? But of course, you weren't thinking.

Story continued on page three. "But, as an informed spokesperson within the Tucson Police Department informed us, 'The status of this case could change at any moment.' The family is said to be deeply concerned. Mr. Warner offers a reward of $10,000 for any information leading to the whereabouts of his missing wife, dead or alive."

Dead or alive! Dramatic old Pete. The Mysterious Case of the Missing Mrs. Warner could "change at any moment"? That was said last week. "Any moment" must have come and gone.

Poor Peter. Really must get home and save his ass.

Cowboy finally spoke—and Molly froze. But instead of saying: Think I'll mosey on down and collect me that reeward, he said, "I think you need to paint."

"Paint?"

"What else would you do?"

Big blank canvas, nothing like as big as the cowboy's epic landscape, not by an epic long shot, but plenty big enough for Molly Brock who hadn't faced a canvas since college. In charcoal, she made a little squiggle towards the bottom and off to one side.

Cowboy took hold of her wrist. "Start in the middle. Make great... big... gestures. Like this." Then almost pulled her arm out of its socket drawing a large emphatic curve up the middle of her canvas.

"You don't like that, make something else. But give it heart, give it passion. It's like dancing. Screw the small steps, leap around the room."

Bouquet of cowboy in her nose: warm leather, hot skin, Camels, coffee, moustache wax, Molly made a big bold line.

"Go for it. I'll be back later, see how you're doing."

"Later" was four hours later, and by then Molly had covered the canvas with big bold lines and the big bold lines with bright bold paint, yellows and reds and oranges.

"Lunch."

"Can't eat. Busy."

"Crap. Even Van Gogh ate."

For the rest of the day, and for the next three days, other than scrubbing her clothes in a galvanized tub in the yard and sewing a patch on the sleeve of her denim jacket, Molly Brock did nothing but paint. Cowboy gave her a small whitewashed sleeping room all to herself on the third floor. She wore her own tee shirt and an old kitchen apron to paint in. She ate most of her simple meals with the cowboy who liked simple meals, took Brewster for walks so that he could eat the scenery, at night before going to sleep she worked on a letter to Shelley—and she painted. Absorbed in his own work, the cowboy said little, Molly said little, Brewster said a lot but not to them, and Molly painted.

On the evening of the fourth day, Molly Brock stood back from what she had done, squinting at it.

Not a Picasso. Thank god for that. Know those who "know" think Pablo's the cat's meow, but for you Picasso's stuff is like the Emperor's new clothes. And even if he is a master for the ages, and you're only an idiot, you still don't like his stuff. Except his goat. You love his goat. And it's not a Matisse. Matisse looks like your shower curtains. And it's not avant-garde neo-now. Too bad. But it's not a Van Gogh or a Folon or a Georgia O'Keefe, and for that you grieve.

Even so—it felt good, Molly Brock. It felt like something. Not passion, exactly, but quite a bit of enthusiasm.

"Paint again."

"Jeeesus. You're always scaring me."

"Fear keeps you moving."

"Fear scares me."

"Paint again. You want to be an artist, you paint again."

Surprised, Molly looked at him. "I don't want to be an artist."

"Crap. Paint again."

Molly painted again.

On the twenty-first day since Molly Brock walked away into the Sonoran Desert, she finished her second painting, which was an improvement on her first, and began her third. She wrote her letter to Shelley, which would never say enough, and standing in front of Paula's mirror using scissors she'd found in Paula's top dresser drawer, she cut her hair.

Not bad. Not too bad. Better than not cutting your hair. As for the style, what would you call it? Henri would call it Le Absolute Mistake. Trying to see the back of her head, Molly turned and twisted in Paula's room. Henri would change his mind. He'd call it Le Crap. But it's off your neck. In this heat, that's heaven.

And then, on the evening of her twenty-first day, she made love to the cowboy, which was so much better than she remembered it ever being with anyone.

Probably because it's been so long you thought you might never do it again. It's also because it wasn't too hard to pretend you were making love to Lassiter.

The cowboy hadn't said he loved her. He hadn't said he liked her. He hadn't even told her his name, and she hadn't asked. Who pesters Lassiter with a lot of nosy questions? Would he answer? Not if he's a real silent stranger. And the cowboy's real silent. So, of course, the cowboy hadn't said anything, had only touched her waist while she was working, and when she'd turned to see what he wanted, had taken her on an armchair in front of her painting.

When they were spent and were sprawled on the armchair and the chair in a puddle of moonlight, he'd whispered, "Talent is sexy."

You know what he means, Molly Brock, and you didn't learn it in a book of Zane Grey's.

Lying back on the stained and musty rose velvet, arms up over her head, fingers slightly curled, and with an artist soft inside her, she looked out at the waning moon over Copper Crown town and wept silently that a talented man would think she might have talent.

Why else are you crying, Brock? Because a young man thought you were still young enough and tender enough to fuck?

Yes. And no.

You're crying because you still fucking care that a fucking young man would fuck you.

17

Molly was wearing Paula's buckskin pants and buckskin shirt as she held a twitchy Brewster by his halter. He thinks we're heading out, going somewhere, going anywhere, silly thing wants to go. She and Brue and the cowboy standing at the edge of the road looking down into the town that had risen up out of the desert around the Copper Crown Mine. And then faded away under the sun when the mine played out.

"Town's called Chappell Bell after the man who staked the first claim. Copper Crown Mining bought him out." Cowboy pointed up the mountain and he pointed down it. Swept his hand across all they could see. "Place is private. Paula's people own the mine, the town, and all the land around."

"Paula's people are rich."

"Paula's why me and some others can work here."

Ask him who Paula is, Molly. Ask him if Paula's his woman. No you don't. No you won't. None of your business. Not going to pry. He'll tell you what he wants to tell you, just as you're telling him only what you want to tell him. Brewster leaned on her buckskin thigh, shoving her towards the edge of the drop at the edge of the road. She leaned back. Oh, for god's sake. Here's the flat out truth. You very sincerely, deeply and profoundly, don't want to know who Paula is. Not knowing is like Schroedinger's cat. Cat's in a box. Box is closed. Cat could be dead. Cat could be alive. If you don't open the box and look, you'll never know for certain which it is. Therefore, the cat is alive if you want it to be—or dead if you want it to be. Put it more simply: what you don't know can't come alive and hiss at you.

"Boy once disappeared north of here." Cowboy tightened the strap holding Brewster's panniers. Brewster grunted, then sneezed. "Kid wandered off forever. Guess you could say he was taking a walk."

Can't miss that one, Molly Brock. But like an itchy moustache at the height of passion, you ignore it.

Molly loosened Brewster's strap. "Hates it too tight. He won't walk. They never found the boy?"

"Found his donkeys, found he'd etched the word Nemo into a sandstone cliff face."

"Nemo like Captain Nemo?"

"I figure Nemo like 'nobody' in Latin."

"If they never found him, he could be still alive."

"Doubt it. Walked off in 1934."

"Ah."

"Before he got lost, or whatever, he wrote a lot of letters to his folks. You make it back, I'll read some of 'em to you."

Typical of the cowboy to disappear back into the building before she could say whatever she might think to say before walking away for the day.

Tugging on Brewster's rope, Molly jogged him on down the road towards Chappell Bell. When the road ran through town, it was called Deanna Street. When it entered or left town, it was just the Chappell Bell road. Molly was carrying nothing, but Brewster had his panniers, and in the panniers a big bottle of water, a tin pie dish for a donkey to suck his water from, a peanut butter and rosehip jelly sandwich for Molly, an apple for whoever wanted it most, and two sketch pads, thick paper and thin. Under these things, and wrapped in a soft cloth, a collection of sketch pencils and charcoal sticks.

On the morning of the twenty-third day, Molly had decided to look for her "subject."

"All very well," the cowboy had said in bed last night (*his* bed, Molly Brock, which you've shared two nights in a row), "to paint great colors—your color sense is very good—now it's time to find the thing that moves you, that makes you want to paint it over and over." And she'd said, "Like you and your vast and mystical desert landscapes?" And he'd said, "Like Georgia O'Keefe and her flowers like vulvas. Like David Hockney and his one-dimensional swimming pools and two-dimensional boys. Maybe even like Jackson Pollack whose medium was the subject."

Walking along behind Brewster, her hand on his comforting brown rump, all she could hear other than the soft crunch crunch crunch of their footsteps and the tick tick tick of the little brown grasshoppers in the greasewood bushes either side of the road, was her own voice in her head.

So here you are looking for what moves you. Moves you? Something you want to paint over and over again? Oh yes. And you are also going to write the great American novel even though Mark Twain already wrote it. Or maybe that was Margaret Mitchell. Or maybe even Ross Lockridge Jr.'s *Raintree County.* Heck, it could even be Zane Grey. And then you'll sit down and compose an American opera. Hasn't someone already done that? Of course they have. *Porgy and Bess* is the Great American Opera. Or maybe *West Side Story.*

Tumbleweed on their left as wide as it was tall.

One minute, nothing but tumbleweed and Brue's rump. The next a memory, clear as ice in iced tea. There was Aunt Evelyn saying, "The Spanish called tumbleweed a Flying Bush, Molly, but I call it a Wind Witch."

Out from under the Wind Witch dashed five little quail, sprinting madly across the road by going straight through her feet, then Brewster's. Donkey lifted one hoof, then another, then another. Gambels quail wove in and out, one to five.

Fellow bringing up the rear looks like a Twenties flapper. Feather in his headband, beads around his neck. Wow. Getting hotter by the day. Bless the old woman's old brown hat.

"Hey, Brue, would you look at that? There's the wagon the kitchen sink came in."

Prairie schooner sitting in a sandy lot on their right, ribs and canvas twill long gone, wooden wheels and side boards splintered in the sun, prickly pear growing up through a hole in its floorboards.

Gutted two story frame buildings on both sides of them now. Empty eyed. Only voice left was the wind through the walls. Boardwalks of warped planks, rabbitbush and burro-weed squeezing through. Corrugated tin sides peeling away. Porch roofs sagging on rotted posts. Faded signs over missing doors. U.S. Post Office, Chappell Bell, Arizona. The Rose of the Desert Hotel, M. B. Lawrence, prop. 1882. Wheelock Mercantile, Purveyors of Fine Goods.

Molly stopped. Though Brewster walked on, nosing out a small palo verde rooted under a cracked cement step.

Why do I think I love this so?

Back at the Copper Crown Mining Company, on the walls of what was once the main office, hung old photographs of Chappell Bell when it was young. Young Chappell Bell had telegraph wires and oil lamps and indoor toilets. Its shop windows were full of New York elegance and Paris finery. There were saloons and restaurants and gaming houses. The splendid Deanna Theater stood like a clapboard temple at the end of Deanna street.

Looking at the photos, you could smell it. Town must have stunk of pine pitch and horse crap and lamp oil and whiskey and wood stoves and a hundred different body odors and over it all—hot copper and French perfume. But what you looked at the longest were the people. Their faces, their hands.

Men and women caught in a moment in time, forever strolling the new boardwalks, stepping out of The Rose of the Desert Hotel into the dust of Deanna Street, big brimmed hats and ruffled parasols small help in the relentless Arizona heat of long long ago.

In black wool and stays, how did they live here before air conditioning? How did they breathe? You can barely breathe now.

There were men hitching their horses to rails, men leaning back in rockers on second-story porches overhanging the boardwalks, a boy caught as a blur as he chased the small blur of a dog in the street.

But there was one photograph you looked at over and over.

Brown like old photos are brown, this one was warmer, more alive, as if any minute it could shake loose what held it and walk again, talk again, breathe again—and in it a woman stood facing the camera, staring straight into the vanished lens. Feathered hat on her head, bright curls escaping the hat, bold mouth, she looked out through a hundred and forty summers come and gone right into Molly's eyes. Molly stared back.

Who were you, young woman? Where did you come from? Where were you going? Were you all alone? Did you come out west to make your fortune? Did you think you were walking into a brave new world—or out of it?

Far end of town and up a steep hill stood two tall pillars made of rounded stones. Remnants of a lacy iron sign curved from one stony pillar to the other. Under the old iron sign walked Molly and Brewster. This was the Chappell Bell graveyard, and in it, Chappell Bell graves. Letting Brewster loose to wander, leaving his panniers by a pillar but taking her sandwich and the bottle of water, Molly walked the rows of boards once stuck upright in the thorny ground. Slabs of split wood so dried by the sun no names remained, half fallen flat, most leaning like dead drunks. But here a natural boulder with a name carved in its side, and there a "real" headstone. Off by itself, a misshapen lump of cement. Molly standing over it, looking down. Who in the world was Old Profanity? Man or woman—or? And here and there, something more ornate. A big stone enclosed by a fence, a small tomb. Oh my god, look at this. Did Dorothy Parker's family go west? *Sun's*

too hot. Bugs are fatal. Spines can kill. Life's no cradle. Down
a dip into a small ravine, cholla and brittlebush and prickly
pear obscuring something that looked like a mass burial.
Over there a cross made of rusted iron. And who would
have used a Franklin stove to mark a grave? But here it is.
A lizard popped out of the rusted flue, scurried down to the
ground, and then ran off into the prickly pear, its striped
tail straight up in the air.

To eat her peanut butter and jelly sandwich, Molly
chose a smooth rock to sit on. Stared at teddy-bear cholla.
In the golden cholla, a raucous cactus wren flew in and out
of a nest as big as the wasp's nest that used to hang in Aunt
Evelyn's garden shed. The garden shed was down at the
end of the garden and the end of the garden was well away
from the house.

"Nothing doing, Norma," said Aunt Evelyn, when her
sister—who was also Molly's mom—wanted her to gas it.
"I don't kill things just because I don't like them."

From her rock, Molly could look back up the road,
could clearly see the Copper Crown Mining Company
building. But she couldn't see the cowboy. He's in there.
He's painting. That's what he does. He paints. He paints
and he smokes and he makes love to me. Who's Paula?

Molly toed the sand with the toe of Paula's shoes. Even
Paula's shoes fit her.

If you'd died that first day, Molly Brock, and if someone
found you and buried you, you might have ended up
somewhere like this—but with an eighth the charm and
none of the wit. As for the rest of the world, the one you
walked away from, you'd be three weeks gone, and who
would really care beyond the first flush of vague loss? Not
Peter. Maybe Peter Jr. But not for long. Not after his first
million and all that came with it. He'd be much too busy.
And not your own father since your father's been dead and
gone somewhere else—where?—for nine years.

Molly wiping peanut butter off her cheek.

Shelley would care. That is, if she'd made it past you.
You don't know, do you? Shelley could be dead on a rank
mattress in a rank room in a rank homeless squat and how
would you know? Shelley would feel something. She'd

feel betrayed and abandoned. Shelley would feel angry. And nothing you could do about it. As for Aunt Evelyn? Aunt Evelyn would plant you an avocado tree and call it Molly. By now there must be a whole grove of trees with names on Evelyn's farm.

Of course you know what your mother would have said about you. Your mother would have said, "Served her right, for being so stupid."

No tree called Norma at Aunt Evelyn's.

But you didn't die—not that day or the next day or the next. You lived and you're living still. Matter of fact, you don't know about the cowboy, but you, you're living in sin. Another matter of fact, you love how you're living.

Life. As Mehitabel the alley cat used to say: Life is just one damn kitten after another.

Retrieving her sketch pads and pencils from the panniers, Molly sat down on her hot stone and began drawing the hot graveyard. Don't know about painting it over and over—but I shore do want to paint it once.

A graceful marker taking shape under her hand, the sad rust of the iron fence that boxed it in, the way the light hit the once white stone like... what's it say, Brock? Whose grave are you drawing? On her feet and walking towards the old marker under an overhang of amber rock.

Hilma Jane Withersteen. Born 1869. Died sudden 1909.

18

Late in the evening of the twenty-fourth day, the
cowboy sated and sleeping by her side, Molly Brock took
stock of her situation.

What are you waiting for, Mrs. Robinson Warner? You
waiting for a ride home? Or for the cowboy to tell you he
loves you? Why do you need the cowboy to love you? Do
you love him?

Half moon over Chappell Bell. Far down the hill,
coyotes in and out of the shadowed husks of long ago.
Mice in the kitchen, bats in the eaves, scorpions under the
bed. Windows open to catch the slightest breeze up from
the cooling desert basin below. Sweat under her breasts,
trickling down her ribs. Cowboy's tribute between her
legs.

Love the cowboy? You don't even know if you like the
cowboy. It's hard to like a Lassiter, so hidden from view
he may not even like—or know—himself. But you found
out his name. Had a peek in his sock drawer, didn't you?
Looked in his wallet. He's not from Arizona. Not even
from Texas. He's a New York City cowboy and his name
is Thomas Lucero. Too old to be a Tommy, he's a Tom.
Cat. Picture in his wallet, only one. A woman. Couldn't

be Paula. Couldn't be some other lover or an ex-wife. The photo was in black and white; its edges were scalloped. In it, the woman was standing in a room somewhere, her arms crossed over her breasts. She looked dazed, as if where she was and who she was wasn't what she had in mind at all. Was she his mother? Norma was never dazed. Norma would look out of a photograph like a woman selling Tupperware.

After making love, before falling asleep, New York Cowboy Tom had read her a few of the letters left behind by the long lost boy. Boy's name was—maybe even is—Everett Ruess.

One passage, written when Everett was no more than twenty, she would remember forever. Not the exact words perhaps, but the meaning. "The absorbing passion of any highly sensitive person is to forget himself, whether by drinking or by agonized love, by furious work or play, or by submerging himself in the creative arts. Sometimes, if his will is powerful, he can pretend to himself that he does not know what he knows, and can act a part as one of the rest. But the pretense cannot endure, and unless he can find another as highly strung as himself with whom to share the murderous pain of living, he will surely go insane."

Molly saying this low, whispering it to the shadows. "Murderous pain of living." And the cowboy rolled over, grunted in his sleep.

Like the cat in a box, is the boy alive? Or is he dead? You chose alive, and so—he lives. You chose that somewhere, the boy, no longer a boy, has lived out a life under the blue cup of the sky unlike any life you know. At this very moment, he sits looking up at the waning moon, himself waning, waning—have you gone insane, Molly Brock? Have you murdered yourself to escape the pain of living? You might have loved the boy if you'd only known him. Can you love the cowboy? You love that he's an artist and you love his art. You love how his body makes your body feel. You adore being fucked by someone Zane Grey would have invented if he hadn't come out from the wilds of New York City to invent himself.

You need to get out of here.

Up now, and walking out of the room. No point in tippy-toeing, this old building already sings like a saw.

Down to the kitchen in the dark to light the fire and brew up a pot of tea. No air conditioning, no microwave, no washer and drier, but Paula had a teapot and a whistling tea kettle and a tea cozy. Paula liked good tea.

All this is Paula's, everything is Paula's. The cowboy told you so. Tom Lucero is Paula's. Cowboy gets a look on his cowboy face when he mentions the woman who owns the Copper Crown and all the ghosts in Chappell Bell. It's the same look I bet my mother wanted to slap off mine back whenever I mentioned Antonio, gone to be a folksinger so long ago. What does all this feel like? What does it mean to make love to a man in his woman's home?

Depends on the man.

Molly taking her tea, walking the roller-coaster corridors of the Copper Crown Mining Co., looking out windows when she came to them, her reflection in black looking back.

This is what you think. You think silence isn't always golden. You think the limits of a woman's role, east or west, can be killing, but the limits of a man's role anywhere at all—strength and silence and control—can be death in life. You think Paula must be someone to meet. You think you'd better not meet her.

So heck yes, Molly Brock, it's time to go.

But first you'll wait until morning, and right now you'll drink your tea.

It was the little house in Burbank again, three blocks from Burbank High, but this time it was deep underwater. No fish, no air bubbles, yet she knew it was on the bottom of the sea. As she wandered the rooms like coral, like caves, like the Titanic blue with deep water pressure, she knew what she was looking for. She was looking for Shelley. And that could only mean she was looking for the self she used to be. And as she looked for what she could not find, she wept salty tears into the salty seawater.

Whatever sense woke her, she knew he was there, watching. Molly'd fallen asleep in the rose velvet armchair before her last painting—the Chappell Bell graveyard and all its pale brown ghosts like old photographs faded and curled.

Cowboy drank a cup of coffee, smoked a Camel, said nothing. But he smiles, there's a smile on his cowboy face. And you know it's for you. Gather ye cowboys while ye may.

She said, "I thought I'd leave today."

Nothing around his mouth, but a small movement in his eyes, down and to the left. He won't protest. He won't try and hold me. Cowboy's going to let me go, open his hand and release me like a bird with a mended wing. She stood up, stretched the sleep out of her shoulders. Trembled with the pain. It hurts, Molly Brock, freedom and grace and integrity—hurts.

He said, "I'll give you a ride home."

"No need. I have Brewster. I can walk."

"Crap. Look, I need to go to the airport anyway. Paula's coming in tonight from New York. Plus some of the others."

It took all she had, right down to the bone, but Molly finished her stretch, gave him back his smile. And when was he going to tell me this? And if I weren't leaving on my own, what then?

"I'll walk. It's only over the hill."

"Not quite over the hill."

"It can't be farther than I've already come."

"Still a bit of a walk."

"I'll make it."

"Suit yourself."

"I'm getting there."

Right after eating the last dinner Molly Brock would cook at the Copper Crown, cowboy sits in the Sixties VW bus, gently gunning its Sixties engine. Molly, come out on the road to watch him go, hands him an envelope. "I'm sorry. I don't have a stamp, but would you mail this for me?"

Cowboy glances at the address. General delivery in East L.A. somewhere.

It's for Shelley. It's the letter I wrote to Shelley.

Tucking Shelley's letter into a clip on the visor, cowboy shifts into reverse. "First thing," he says, "I won't forget." He backs up the bus, turns it so that it heads downhill, leans out the window which makes her take a step back. He says, "Take anything you need."

Stop it, Molly Brock. Where's the pride in this? Kiss the cowboy goodbye.

She watched until the bus disappeared in the dust of the desert far below.

Molly alone in the vast echoing Copper Crown. Hours before Tom could get back from the airport, she had hours to prepare to walk out of Paula's town. But there were only three hours before full dark.

First: pack. Second: a good guest erases all trace of herself from the building. Third: she also removes all trace of her donkey. Fourth: walk off in the right direction, which is... that way. Unfortunately, as the crow flies, "that way," rather than following the dirt road down into the basin, goes over the top of the biggest thorniest lump of sheer rock-on-rock mountain for miles around. But without the luxury of traveling in an old VW bus the much longer way can't be your way. On the other hand, how many people can boast transport like Brewster who can travel straight up and over a mountain on palo verde leaves alone?

Molly set about packing the panniers with the same efficiency she'd brought to running her pretty apricot house. Food for two days, at least. Maybe best to bring enough for three? Four? But even better to bring much more water than food because in the desert food runs a very poor second to water. She'd take as much water as Brewster could carry without pissing him off. Brewster got pissed off, Brewster sat down. No Top Ramen. Nothing in cans. Food in cans weighed too much, and then there were all the empties to carry out. A few condiments to make whatever she brought palatable. Where did these come from? Big bag of sunflower seeds. These would be good for the salt. You can lose too much salt from too much sweating. You lose too much salt, you get sick. Take the sunflower seeds.

Matches. Three thick candles. Knife too. A good one. You'd leave a check for it, but how would Tom explain the check? One enameled cup with a handle. One enameled plate. A fork and a spoon. To atone for the good knife: the oldest skillet on the shelf, the most beat-up pot.

Bedding. Charity's blanket smelled. It itched. Brewster could have the old woman's blanket all to himself. But if Brewster had the army blanket, what would she use? Way in the back of the big wardrobe in the cowboy's room, she found a mummy bag, dark green outside, orange inside.

Hate mummy bags, hate being swaddled, hate it more than the wind. On the other hand, snakes with and without rattles can't crawl in for a midnight cuddle.

Stuffing the bag into its cover, she quickly looked round his room. Should she? Shouldn't she? She should. Molly took the cowboy's pillow. But she left the case.

In a storage room off the kitchen, she found a length of good rope and a fat ball of string. She took those. Ah. Black plastic garbage bags. Take one of those. Remember the water trick? Take two. Take lots. You can use them for ground cover, for packing out garbage, for covering the panniers, for a rain slicker if the monsoons come early. Which, you read in the book you once bought at the Desert Museum, they never do. Well, hardly ever. And here's one of those little flashlights. You might need a flashlight. They must have the right size batteries in here somewhere.

She emptied her leather bag onto the kitchen table. Big Red chewing gum wrappers go in the trash, as well as these movie stubs — what was the last movie you saw? Can't even remember. When life's a movie, who needs movies? Throw away your old Needleworks volunteer work schedule. Throw away Safeway's receipt. Molly picked up the small bottle of Valium, had a squint at it. Half full, maybe more than half full. Throw the pills away too, Molly, you don't need them anymore. How long has it been since you panicked? A week, two weeks? Is it three weeks? You see? You can't remember. It's over. You've beat fear.

Tossing the crumpled-up paper, stubs, and wrappers in the pail, she looked at the Valium again. Quickly shoved the bottle to the bottom of her bag. She also took a handful of aspirin from a cabinet in the bathroom, a roll of toilet paper, a little bottle of baby oil, and a tube of toothpaste. She took the toothbrush the cowboy said was hers.

Last, she went looking for clothes. Not Paula's clothes. Old clothes. Took a faded black sweatshirt. In dull red stitching on the back, it said: *Nature is a revelation of God; art a revelation of man.* —Henry Wadsworth Longfellow. Took the pink canvas overalls she'd used to paint in. But no more bras and no more panties. Though you'll have to pack them—impossible to explain if they were found in the trash. Took a parka with paint stains. Very artistic.

"Oh, shoot. Your paintings. What will you do with your paintings?"

None of the pictures were dry. If she took them, she'd have to roll them up. If they were rolled, they'd be ruined. If she left them to dry, there'd they'd be. Not good. Only thing to do was to carry them over to the dangerous third story of the risky fourth section where no one ever went, and shut them in a tipsy room no one would ever see.

Then she took a nap curled up in the rose red chair. Best to travel when it's cooler, and in a desert it was always cooler in the evening.

19

Like ghosts or old photographs, Molly and Brewster walked through Chappell Bell in the dark, heading up rather than down.

You and Brue are not the only ghosts walking here, Brock. Move along, move along.

By midnight, they'd reached the top of the last *bajada* before climbing a ravine that had seemed, when still light, to lead to the best pass over the mountain. Moon almost gone, but the stars as bright as ever.

And here, on a bit of sandy flat near a grouping of twisted star-struck saguaro, they bedded down for the night. Black plastic bag ground cover, a careful unrolling of the cowboy's green mummy bag, a careful getting in, and a careful zipping up. She smacked the pillow around a bit, made sure nothing was already sleeping in it.

Smells like the cowboy. Goodbye Cowboy Tom.

No fire. No food. If she wasn't hungry, why eat? But drink a lot of your water. Then perhaps a sit up and a look at the heavens. Yawning so hard she thought she'd crack her jaw. Nope, no sitting up, no stars, no thinking, no feeling. Go to sleep.

Molly plucked away whatever was crawling on the back of her neck, snapped it between her nails, wriggled around a bit, and was gone.

At the first flush of dawn on her twenty-sixth day, Molly Brock awoke to the sight of Brue's warm brown ass. Donkey'd bedded himself down on the edge of her ground cover, was still asleep and breathing out clouds of donkey breath. Fortunately, all that was going on at the other end and nothing at all was going on this end. Over her head, no more than a foot away, a thicket of palo verde branches with their tender green bark, and crawling along against the green, a bright orange fly, big as a bumblebee. Rolling her eyes to the right, there was a spider's web, spread like a sail, golden in the firstborn light.

Where's the spider? Over there, tucked under a leaf. Big one. Gray.

Right about then, a little yellow butterfly cradled down from a higher green branch, bounced in the air over her nose for a moment, and then blundered straight into the web. Gray spider up and running on the instant.

Poor little butterfly. Hurry up! Free it.

Hand almost to the web, Molly stopped. But if you free the butterfly from the web, won't you be disturbing the natural way of things? Even a spider has to eat.

One spider leg at a time, the spider advanced on the struggling butterfly.

Must not interfere. This is their world and if you are anything at all, you are merely a distant goddess and a goddess lets them get on with it. Think of those TV nature shows. Wounded animals, lost babies, followed around and filmed for days as they die. You watch, and you think, why don't they save them? It would be so easy. For pity's sake, take the baby to its mother across the valley, who, desperate and calling, endlessly searches for it. Drive back the hyenas from the valiant zebra with the broken leg. But no — nature is nature and science is science and it is not for us to interfere.

One more inch, and the spider would be close enough to leap on the butterfly.

But hold on a minute. Here is a hungry gray spider and here is a lemon yellow butterfly about to die in a sticky golden web and here you are, Molly Brock. A foot away and aware. So you, too, are part of this. And if you are conscious of it, you share in it, and this must surely mean you can do what the spider is doing and what the butterfly is doing. You can do what your heart inclines you to do.

Reaching up, Molly gently released the butterfly. Which fluttered up and fluttered down, then flew right back into the web.

The heck with it. A goddess can only do so much. If a butterfly intends to be breakfast, then it's breakfast.

Molly slapped Brewster's butt. "Wake up! Time to be moving."

Brewster scrambled to his feet, shook all over like a big wet dog, and then pointedly stared at her as she pulled on her painter's pink overalls.

"Walk first, water later."

Silent strangers traveled at dusk and they traveled before dawn. They ate little, they rested ten minutes out of every hour, they kept their mouths shut not only because they were silent strangers, but because keeping their mouths shut conserved water. They watched where they put their hands and their feet, and they kept on moving. When the heat of a desert did its worst, which was between high noon and three o'clock, they shaded themselves as best they could, and they waited it out.

"You and I, Brue, are silent strangers. So shut up."

By the end of this day, or sometime in the morning, they ought to be hitting the Trash Line. Trash meant people. In twenty-four hours, or even less, Mrs. Peter Warner and her ass should be walking out of the Sonoran desert and into a mall or a self-storage complex or an airbase or an RV resort or a lone trailer spread out over the desert like an exploded dumpster—or something.

But first they had to get up this ravine and over this mountain. Breaking camp was easy, looking back was hard.

So don't look back.

She looked back. Chappell Bell and the Copper Crown were far below her, a good long walk away, but both were clear and rosy in the rising sun. In the wide space at the end of the dirt road curving up to the mining company, Tom Lucero's old VW bus sat where it always sat.

All righty. Paula's home.

An hour of climbing, and Chappell Bell was gone. Another ten minutes, and so was the Copper Crown. From where she and Brewster now stood, there wasn't one thing in all her world that looked other than natural. Another hour, and Molly was sheathed in sweat. In the hours that followed, a little more of the fat that still coated her body burned away in the heat and the struggle to climb this steep and spiky ravine.

Molly and Brewster exhausted at noon and lying in the shade of a jutting rock shaped like a pink pepper grinder, Molly using Brewster as a bolster. Brewster sneezed. Molly sneezed. Brewster dropped one ear forward, held the other ear back. Molly scratched an itch. Brewster fell asleep. Molly laced her fingers over her belly and stared up at the sky. Pink sky. Pink clouds.

She closed her eyes.

Molly's not asleep but she's in the house again. The little house like all the other little houses on a suburban street in Burbank, California. She's sitting in the dark at the top of the stairs. Norma and Lindsay are watching TV down in the living room. She can't see them. But she can see almost all of the TV. They're watching *Bonanza*. *Bonanza* is her father's favorite television show. It's why he's gone out and bought a brand new color TV even though Norma says they can't afford it. It's Molly's favorite TV show too, but it always comes on past her bedtime. Not that she's missed a single show. She watches most of her TV in the dark at the top of the stairs. It would be nice if she could get closer so she could see Little Joe better. But this is the best she can do. Any closer, and Norma might see her.

Over the sound of the TV, she can hear her mother's cards snapping on the coffee table. While Lindsay watches what's happening on the Ponderosa, Norma is playing solitaire. Snap. Snap. Snap.

Norma is playing her cards and talking through Hoss. Hoss has just ridden hell-for-leather to warn his father and his brothers that trouble is coming to the Ponderosa. Molly wishes her mother would shut up so she can hear what the trouble is.

She can hear what her mother is saying though. Her mother is saying that they need a new car. Now that they have a new TV, which they didn't need in the first place, they could buy a new car, which they do need.

Molly is only nine years old but she thinks she knows why her father loves *Bonanza*. It's certainly why she loves *Bonanza*. It's because there's a father on the Ponderosa. And there are sons. Three sons. But there's no mother.

Molly suddenly sitting up. Brewster suddenly opened his eyes. "Good grief, what's that smell? Pigs!"

From a small side ravine, a kind of a tiny box canyon, came a snuffling noise, a wuffle and sniff. Then a short bark and a snort and a grunt. Out from behind an outcrop of red and yellow rock, came a herd of javelinas, babies as small as guinea pigs under their mother's bellies, one old male as big as a trash can, the rest anywhere in between and as alike as one barrel cactus is to another.

Molly clamped her hands round Brewster's jawbone to keep him quiet, held on to his lead rope to stop him from getting up. If we don't move and we don't bray, they won't see us, and if they don't see us, they won't run away—look at that. Babies' legs are so thin, they're like tent pegs. Tent peg legs.

Big pigs chuckled and grumbled, rooting up whatever they could find with their big piggy snouts. But the little pigs bounced about, bumping into each other with squeals and tiny yips of irritated joy.

If it weren't so hot, Molly Brock, you could stay out here. You could be a wanderer like the boy, the vanished Edward Ruess. Mix a little Charity with a lot of Ruess, add a pinch of Kerouac... you'd be an Old Woman On The Road. Or off the road. And armed, of course. But happy. What else do you need? You've got a friend in Brewster and a home in Brewster's baskets. You've got something to do which is walk. Does it really matter where, when you've got beauty everywhere you look? And now you've got pigs. Those who know say they're not really pigs, but those who know aren't sitting here enjoying pigs.

Two babies, both leaping and twisting and squealing, one fell into a cholla. Whole branch of the cholla came away stuck to its head. Baby with the cactus on its head, ran bleating for its mother, ran right under her belly. Now most of the cholla was stuck to her, but what remained with the baby hung from its snout. Much jumping about and whoofing and complaint until they all ran off down the ravine.

Molly stood up, shook herself off in case of stinging, biting, spitting bugs, and walked on. Brewster, freed at last, walked with her.

20

Scrambling out of the ravine at last, panting with the heat, Molly and Brewster startling a chuckwalla clamped to the side of a hot rock. As fast as it could, dirt red and dirt brown lizard crammed itself into the closest crevice, then inflated its already fat tummy so that Molly, if she'd a mind to, could not pull it out. Or at least not easily.

Molly standing there, sweat in her eye, looking at it. Well, what do you know? Fat does have its uses.

So thinking, Molly felt her own tummy, her thighs, her butt. Not gone, but almost all gone, soon all gone, melted off in the heat.

She and Brewster had reached a high basin, nothing like as large a basin in which the city sprawled — city must be around here somewhere — but large enough. Up here, it was flatter and hotter and drier and, if possible, spinier.

Got to walk across all of this in order to reach that last little mountain range before the drop into Tucson.

"How you feeling, Brue?"

"Aw-Eee, aw."

"That good, eh? Come on. Miles to go before we drop."

Another hour of nothing but the comforting sound of Brewster's hooves sparking off stones, of a Harris hawk's heavy flapping as it came to land on the top of a towering saguaro, of a striped lizard running like a mad thing straight up a sheer vertical rock, then over it, and straight down the other side into a tangle of creosote, of Brewster taking a dump on an ant's nest. Hate to be the clean-up crew on that one. Another hour of nothing at all but desert and sky and her own thoughts—and the heat.

They walked on into the dark as a million bats, like fine black netting, streamed out from somewhere darker and captured the cold white moon.

Moon's cold. Desert's hot. Even now with the sun fallen over the side of the world. And every day it's getting hotter. Soon, just breathing the air will hurt your lungs. The sand will burn through the soles of your shoes. Already, the rocks are almost too hot to touch. Was a time, people used to cross this desert on Butterfield's Overland Mail. The woman who drove you half batty at Tohono Needleworks, Edith, old as a bristlecone pine and just as spiky, told you her people came here on the Mail. Said it was so awful a ride, one poor fellow snapped. He leapt off the juttering, jolting, bone-cracking stage and ran shrieking into the wilderness, never to be seen again. But that's all right, Molly Brock. That's just fine. Home's right around the corner, right over the hill, right up there at the end of the rainbow. Not that you think there are any rainbows in the desert.

"Although Zeno was full of paradoxes, Brue—you wanna hear one of them?"

Nothing from Brewster. But he didn't say no.

"Zeno wondered if you walked halfway to something, for instance, home, and then you walked halfway there again, and then half the way, and half the way, and so on and so forth—would you ever get home again?"

If Brewster had the foggiest idea, he still wasn't saying.

"This looks good. We'll spend the rest of the night here."

Molly woke in the shushed half-dark of the very early morning desperate for a pee. But to pee, first she had to get out of the cowboy's mummy bag. Hate mummy bags, hate them, what if there were an emergency? What if the zipper stuck! Molly now twice as desperate to get out of the mummy bag.

Brewster already up and scratching his rump by rolling onto his back on the soon-to-be-hot and ever thorny sand, then twisting his spine from side to side in a sort of belly-ass dance. And Molly, naked and shivering and clutching four sheets of toilet paper — waste not, want not — crouched under a mesquite tree, mesquite branches low to the ground, mesquite beans hanging down like stiff hair ribbons.

Don't know why you still hide. Who's to see you? Brewster can piss walking — you think he cares? This keeps up, maybe you can learn to piss walking too. Oh my lord, what in the world's that?

Not enough light to see clearly, wouldn't be light enough for awhile yet. But she could see one particular thing well enough. Deeper under the mesquite tree and lying on its side near the trunk—isn't that a skull? It certainly looks like a skull.

In the desert, bones are bleached white by the sun. Texans find one, they mount it on the grill of their Cadillacs. Golfers in Arizona's spreading saggy baggy suburbia find one, they put it in cactus gardens as a "feature."

Molly quickly standing up — this bone isn't bleached white, hasn't been here long enough — only to hunch over again on her way to the skull. Mesquite branches laden with their heavy beans, mesquite and bean pods dragging along her bare back.

And it's not a cow's head or a bull's head. Not even the poor dead head of a chuckwalla or a coyote or a pig — and it won't be going home with a Texan or a saggy baggy. This one's human. And over there, that's the body.

"What happened here, Brue?"

Dead man under here. Dead for months.

Brewster, nibbling a bean, closed his eyes and sighed.

Brewster doesn't care. But you care, Molly, you certainly do. You care a lot. And why? Out of a terrible pity, yes. And from horror, yes. But mostly you care because if he could die, you could die. Was he murdered? Was he dumped here?

Molly's heart turned over.

By his clothes, by the crumpled letter in his pocket, by the photo in the letter, the man was a Mexican. It's miles and miles and miles to the border. How did he get this far? By truck? Don't think so. Think he walked in. Don't really think he was murdered. He must have died walking. Sometimes people who take on the desert go crazy in the heat. Sometimes they stare at the sun until they burn out their eyes, stuff their mouths with sand thinking it's water. They call out to Tata Dios or to the Lady of Guadalupe. Happens all the time. You read about it in the papers and then you turn the page and read about something else. They try it and they die. In their hundreds. Every year. But why did he die under here?

"What do we do, Brue?"

Brewster under the mesquite with her now, nudging a dead leg with his nose. Leg bones moved under the sun-rotted pants, foot bones slipped out of the sun-cracked shoe. Brue snorting and pulling away.

"We'll tell someone. They'll come back here and get him. What we need to do is, we need to mark the spot."

Molly searching in her bag for the baby blue cotton thread, tying her first bow on a branch of the mesquite tree. Intending to tie at least two more.

Not going to die under a mesquite tree, Molly Brock. Not going to get found one day by some silly housewife and her ass. Going to walk home.

A buzz in her ear.

Bee. First bee of the morning. Buzz off bee.

Molly moving around to another branch, pulling it down and away from the tree, beginning to tie her second baby blue bow.

"Oh, god."

Molly Brock backing up, slowly, and with intense care, one step, two. Another buzz in her ear. In both ears. In front of her face, not more than three feet away, a beehive. A beehive like a sack of shining white laundry hanging from a mesquite branch, a beehive so heavy, so loaded at the bottom with golden honey, the branch it hung from had split, might crash to the ground at any moment. And when it did, it would take the hive with it, and when the hive hit the ground, it would burst like an avocado with golden flesh—and out would pour unutterable sweetness and unutterable horror.

From inside the hive, an ominous buzzing. Molly backing into Brewster.

"Move, Brue. Please."

Brewster shaking his head, a bee in his ear. Molly pushing him, shoving him out from under the tree. More morning bees in the air, more crawling out of the awakening hive. And the buzzing growing louder.

Is this how the man died? Crawled under the tree to get out of the sun only to meet up with a million bees. African bees.

Maybe. Maybe not.

But not you. And not Brue. You're walking away from this. Slowly, one step at a time. No slapping at bees. No making them angry. Tiptoe away.

Twenty feet from the tree, Molly ran. And made Brewster run with her.

21

Hours later, Molly and Brewster had come on a view that stopped at least Molly in her tracks.

Down below, a valley like a deep yellow mixing bowl, and in the bottom of the bowl golden teddy-bear cholla glowing like birthday candles, along with hundreds of old saguaro, each with arms enough to beat egg whites. Rising on every side of the bowled walls, rocks like stiff meringue. Tall towering reds. Vaults of saffron yellow. Indian purple arches. Like chocolate sprinkles, little brown towhees chased each other up and down the whipped sides of colored rock.

Over her head, a red tailed hawk rode in the oven of the sun.

A secret valley, Molly. Hidden away, untouched, pure, delicious... or it would be if it weren't for the homemade dune buggy and the two men way down there doing something to that other man. Or boy. It could be a boy.

Instinctively crouching, at the same time pulling down Brewster's nose in case he felt like saying something, she hunkered back on her heels and watched. Two men, one small and one fat, pushing the third boyish man back

and forth between them. The third man was clutching
something large and bulky to his chest.

A bag of some sort. Backpack, probably.

Fat and Small were shoving Backpack harder and
harder. Hard enough now to hurt him. Fat got a grip on the
strap of the bag and was yanking him back and forth with
it, trying to pull it away from him. But Backpack wouldn't
let go. So Small hit him with something, and whatever it
was, it was hard enough to knock him down—but he still
wouldn't let go of the bag. Hands balled into fists, Fat stood
over him as he lay on the ground, while Small strode back
to the dune buggy, rummaged around behind the driver's
seat.

"What's going on, Brue? What are they doing?"

Small stopped poking around in the dune buggy, and
came away carrying what looked like a stick.

"Oh, heck, Brue. It's not a stick. It's a rifle."

Think fast, Molly. If you were Lassiter, what would
you do? You'd stand up, of course, and fire a warning
shot. Close and accurate. Then, when you got their full
attention, you'd stare them down over the bore of your
own rifle and tell them to back away fast, hands in the air.
And that's exactly what they'd do—if you were Lassiter in
black leather, glowing in the sun. And if you had a rifle.
Which you don't. So? You threw rocks once, you could
throw rocks again. But first, they're too far away. And last,
all they have to do is shoot you and you'd stop throwing
rocks. You could yell—but who are they? Backpack could
be a drug runner. His bag could be full of drugs. They could
all be drug demons and you could be up here watching a
drug war between demon drug dealers. Or, you could be
a witness to three corrupt cops arguing over their share of
a shady deal. Or, they're terrorists and you've stumbled
onto a terrorist cell's hole-in-the-wall and that's a bag of
high explosives. So, just as three crazed terrorists go off to
blow something up, one of them has a better idea and now
they're bickering over who gets to wear the dynamite. Or,
who the heck knows? Fundamentally, and as usual, you
could get your ass kicked. Or worse. Much worse.

Small had now reached Backpack. He aimed the rifle at the very center of his forehead. Backpack flat on his back on the ground, still hugging the bag to his chest, but lying still, very still. Small was saying something, though Molly couldn't hear what. Fat was pacing back and forth, listening. Backpack must have said something or done something—or maybe because he would not let go of the bag—Fat suddenly rushed forward and kicked him, hard, in the ribs.

Molly rocked back and forth on her heels. "We have to do something, Brewster. We can't just sit up here and watch this. Whoever he is, what if they actually killed him?"

Fat kicked Backpack again, this time square in the head, sending some sort of flat hat flying into a cholla cactus.

That's it. That's enough.

Molly stood straight up. She raised her arms. "Hey! You!" The little valley rang with her voice. And immediately, she got their full attention, both the small and the fat. They looked up from the motionless Backpack. Even from up here, she could tell they were thoroughly surprised to see a woman in pink overalls with her own personal donkey.

Whipping off Charity's brown hat, she waved it at someone behind her, though there was no one behind her—but how could these three know that? "Larry! Curly! Moe! Hurry up!" Then she strode down the hillside, as purposeful and confident as if Curly and Larry and Moe would follow on behind her, and behind them, the U.S. Calvary.

Fat broke first. Aiming a last kick at the man on the ground, he ran broken-field for the dune buggy. No more than a single second later, Small followed suit, but not before grabbing up the backpack. Leaping into the dune buggy, Fat driving, they backed up in a dusty skitter of sand and gravel, then careened off down the valley, vanishing into the cholla and ironwood and jojoba bushes, leaving deep tracks like wounds in the desert's tender skin.

If Molly Brock weren't already sweating like a horse in the desert heat, she would have broken out in a sweat. What if they'd held their ground? What if they'd laughed—

and then simply shot you? What if? What if? They didn't. They're gone.

How bad off is Backpack—and what in the world is in the bag?

Backpack's name was Ellis Harrison. He was a citizen of the British Isles, born in England's West Country in the City of Bristol. He was a student at the University of Arizona. He was one year younger than Peter Jr. Judging by the photo on his student I.D., the fat man's kick to his head hadn't done him any good, but even at the best of times he had no chin to speak of. He made up for it in nose.

So you know his name and you know his age. You know he's a student and probably not a terrorist, though he may be a drug dealer. What do you do now? The boy needs help. The boy needs more than your help.

"Jesus, Brewster, his eye is full of blood."

Leaning over, she put her hands on either side of the pale broken face and turned it towards her. "Ellis Harrison? Hello? Can you hear me?"

The boy's one clear eye found and focused on her. His blood flecked mouth, as white lipped as the skin of his face was ashen pale, opened and closed, then opened. Out came one painful word at a time. "Did... they... get... bag?"

"I'm sorry, but, yes, they—"

"Wankers." And with that, Ellis Harrison, perhaps as lost in the desert as she, fell into what looked like a swoon.

Molly quickly cleared the ground under an ironwood tree—check for beehives, first—then dragged the boy into its shade. Ground was hot. She made him a bed of her bed and placed him on it. That had to be at least a few degrees cooler. Using precious water, she tended to the mess the fat man had made of the skin and bone over his eye.

Not much of a nurse, are you Molly Nightingale? You think cuts around the eyes bleed more than cuts in other places. You think the bone of the brow is thick and strong. Even so, you think that a severe blow can cause the brain to swell. You think that's serious. But you have no idea what the blood in his eye means. And you have no idea what to do about any of it. Is he brain damaged? Any minute, will he have some of sort of seizure and die? You have to get him to a doctor. But how? Was that his dune buggy? If it wasn't, how did he get himself this far out in the desert? If it was his dune buggy, how did Fat and Small get out here?

There must be another car.

There was no other car. Only the deep destructive tracks of the dune buggy coming up, and the deeper, more destructive tracks of the dune buggy fleeing back down.

Too hot to be out and about. We can't travel in heat like this. He shouldn't be moved in it. So, whatever you have to do must wait for the cool of the waning day. Ignoring the faint whiff of skunk, Molly and Brewster rested under the desert ironwood tree just as they would have done if there were no boy.

But there is a boy, and he might be mortally wounded. He certainly looks mortally wounded. And if that's true, then the only thing that stands between him and death is Mrs. Peter Warner, no nurse and a very errant housewife.

And there was Brewster.

"Can you carry him, Brue?"

Brewster, who usually had something to say about everything, had nothing to say to this.

"If you carry him, it'll hurt you." Molly looked at the boy, at Brewster's panniers, at Brewster's small back. "But if you don't carry him, who will?"

Around and around and around you go, and where does it get you? Brewster was never packing out the dead man. But the boy's alive. Brue *has* to carry the boy — even if it kills him. Old woman said a donkey his height and weight could carry — tops — one hundred and twenty-five pounds. Burdened at his top weight, how long could a little donkey keep going? How many miles? How many days? But Ellis Harrison of Bristol, England, doesn't weigh one hundred and twenty-five pounds. He weighs a lot more than that. Maybe thirty pounds more.

Molly looked at Brewster backed as far under the barbed ironwood tree and out of the worst of the heat as he could get. One eye opened and one eye closed, Brewster looked back.

No animal is worth more than a human. No animal's life comes first. If an animal has to die to save a man or a woman, no matter who or what that man or woman is, then so be it. Right, Molly Brock? For god's sake, what if this poor kid were your own son? What if he were Peter Jr.?

The answer that rose instantly to mind was not only denied speech, it was denied thought—but not nearly fast enough to keep Molly from seeing it for what it was.

You are a monster, Mrs. Warner, and no kind of mother. Is it in the blood, do you think? Passed on from one non-Mother to the next? What kind of mom would pause for even a split second? Of course you'd sacrifice a donkey for your son. You'd sacrifice yourself for your son. And far better you than Brewster.

But... but... this is Brewster. He's proved your friend and your companion and your confidant. You've told Brewster things you've never told anyone. Brewster is a living creature. He's as conscious as you are and he walks through the world as himself. He trusts you.

So what? Here's this young man, a boy, somebody's son, and who is he? You don't know him from Adam. What is he doing here? What was in his backpack? Even so, even so—no matter who he is or what fresh hell is in his bag, if it comes right down to it, who gets to live? Your own species, of course. And who gets to die? A donkey. Only a donkey. Little Brue.

Right, Molly? Right?

Slumped, Molly sat in the hot shade and tended the boy.

22

Ellis Harrison came to life like the birth of the cosmos. From flat out on the ground, he bolted upright, and yelled, "Bloody hell! My bloody therapod, the bloody buggers!"

Molly and Brewster, both dozing, woke up with duplicate snorts of surprise to find the boy holding his head and going, "Oeeeooow!"

Molly instantly a mother. "Are you all right?"

At this, the boy noticed her. Noticed Brewster. Noticed where he was.

"You jokin'? How could I be all right? Fuckin' twonks said I looked like Ringo Starr and then they took my fuckin' bones. I told them they were bones. I said, since when does gold look like a bone? And they said — and I bleedin' paraphrase — since when does anyone with half a fuckin' brain carry bones around in a backpack in a hot fuckin' desert? And I said, since someone with a fuck lot more brains than you'll ever see is a fuckin' paleontologist, you fuckwads. So the puny bloke hit me. And the fat bloke kicked me."

Brewster said, "Awww EEE!"

Ellis Harrison struggled to his feet. "Get out of my way. I'm getting those bones back. Where's my hat?"

For shame, Molly, for shame. You see that the poor boy's alive. That it doesn't look like he'll die too soon. And the first thing you think is that Brewster's safe. And the second thing you think is that no one is safe.

"They've got a rifle. You're going after them when they've got a rifle?"

The boy stared at her with one blue and white eye and one blue and red eye. "You bet your sweet arse I'm going after them. Those are theropod bones they took off me. You think I'm letting them get away with a new carnivore? They stole my bloody doctorate. What kind of head start do they have?"

"At least half an hour."

"Right. That's it then. Tossers both so fuckin' pissed, by now, they've probably crashed into a fuckin' rock."

Bone hunter was on his feet, snatching his flat cloth hat off cholla spines, lurching towards the deep-cut tracks of the dune buggy. A few wobbly steps on his way, he turned to look back at Molly and Brewster. "Buggers are halfway vicious. You coming? I could use some help." And then he charged off after the small man and the fat man down below somewhere in their fat-tired dune buggy.

Unhooking the cowboy's dark green mummy bag from an ironwood barb, Molly looked at a yawning Brewster. "Well, Brue? Since he's headed in our fucking direction anyway, we might as well follow him."

Molly watching the bouncing bone hunter's hat appearing and reappearing through the tangle of desert thorn and bloom. Boy's moving too fast in this heat—what's a theropod? Something to do with bones. Me and Brue, we find sad Mexican bones and him, the kid, he finds what?

"My god, Brue—the kid's found a dinosaur!"

But what's he think he'll do when he catches up with "the bloody buggers"? Boy must leap like a gazelle—he's gone.

Walking as fast as they usually did, moving past cholla and ironwood, rocky outcrops and massive saguaro, Molly and Brue followed the tracks of the dune buggy. The bone hunter was following the tracks, so she and Brewster had to be following the bone hunter. Wherever he was.

Found him.

Boy was crouched behind a rock layered like a huge yellow onion.

"Shush," he said, yanking her down beside him. Brewster had already stopped, lured by a big palo verde. "They're right over there. Stupid gits. They drove into a hole."

Molly rose up a bit, just enough to see round the onion-peel rock. Sure enough, Small and Fat sitting in the shade of their overturned dune buggy sharing a Bud Ice between them. Scattered on the ground all around, everything they'd had in the dune buggy, meaning a beer cooler and a lot more bottles of cheap beer, full or empty or shattered on rocks. This also meant the rifle and the bone hunter's backpack. The backpack was between the fat man and the yellow rock she and Ellis were hunkered behind. Firmly secured by its thick canvas straps, whatever had been in it was still in it. The rifle had fallen closer to the small man. All he had to do to reach it was scoot forward a bit and stretch out his hand.

Molly leaned over to whisper in the bone hunter's ear. "So now what?"

"Buggered if I know. Any good ideas?"

"They could get drunker. They could pass out in this heat."

"They could at that. We'll wait."

It took Fat fifteen minutes to slump over in a sodden stupor. But Small went on drinking and muttering to himself. Whatever he said wasn't audible to Molly, but the intent was obvious. Small had grasped that it was hot. He'd also grasped that the last two 40 oz. bottles of Bud Ice had flown into the matted mess of a collapsed jumping cholla, dead cholla branches tumbled and tangled into an interwoven thicket of bristling spines. Molly could see him thinking about this.

He's wondering how to get the bottles out of the cholla. Like me and my purse, he thinks he needs a stick to reach in and dig them out. But there are no sticks. So he's wondering what he can use as a poker. Ah. He sees the rifle. The rifle will do. He'll use the rifle.

Small can't walk, he's too drunk to walk, so he crawls for the rifle. Gets a good grip on the stock. On his knees over the gun, he notices the backpack.

Now he's thinking: what's in that backpack? Must be something really valuable if it belongs to Ringo Starr. Must be a fortune for the stupid Beatle to hold on so tight. Gotta be gold. Or maybe it's silver. Rather have gold, but silver's good too. Lot you can buy with a lot of silver. So go look in the backpack. But wait a minute—what about your beer? You need more beer so you can enjoy what's in the backpack more.

Small turns back for the bottles. On his hands and knees straight towards the fearsome tumble of spiky cholla branches, rifle in his hand getting dragged through the sand and the ants and the dried dung. In the desert, there's always dried dung.

A sudden voice in her ear. Intent on Small, Molly jumped inside her roomy, linseed and oil-paint smeared, pink overalls.

"Don't take this the wrong way Missus, but you're the strangest looking prospector I've ever seen."

The bone hunter had made himself comfortable behind the rock. Or at least as comfortable as someone who'd had his head recently kicked in can get. "By your reaction, I have to assume you are not a prospector. So what are you?"

"I'm hiking."

The boy looked at Molly, in dabbled pink, at Brewster, at the stuff packed in Brewster's panniers. Like the cowboy, the bone hunter wasn't stupid. Stupid was on the other side of the rock poking a loaded rifle into a mess of barbed cactus, stock first. "Right. You're a hiker. And I'm looking for petrified wood, but I was hoping for dinosaurs. So blow me if I don't find one, an actual bipedal predator. Whole new species, a fuckin' huge blighter, which will be named after me." Reminded of his bones, Ellis poked his head round the rock again. "And it's in that backpack."

Small was leaning far out over the dead cholla patch, the rifle extended as far as it would go. Even so, he was missing the last bottle of beer by a good three inches. So he was trying to extend the rifle's reach just a little bit farther by extending himself just a little... bit... farther...

Leaping out from behind the onion-peel rock, Ellis Harrison yelled, "Fall in the bleedin' Briar Patch, you friggin' twat!"

Small, caught completely off-balance, did just that— and Ellis raced for his backback, scooped it up with one hand, then turned and bolted back for the rock, shouting, "Leg it!"

Molly snatched up Brewster's rope lead, and legged it.

Behind her, the sound of the bone hunter running as fast as he could. Behind them both, the sound of snap and crackling jumping cholla—and a small man, shrieking.

Back where they'd come from, Ellis Harrison, student paleontologist, pointed up at a wall of red rock. "Before those two plonkers, I was going that way—I'm still going that way."

Molly pointed towards a pass in the little yellow valley. "Brewster and I are going that way."

Backpack on his back, the precious theropod bones in the backpack, a perfectly formed dark purple egg over his eyebrow, and the blue of his eye embedded in red, the boy put the gift of half of Molly's aspirin supply in his pocket, then hitched up his trousers. "Guess that's it then."

Molly had hold of one of Brewster's warm and hairy ears, was thoughtlessly bending it this way and that way. Interesting, Molly. You admire this foul-mouthed English boy. Fierce, passionate, determined. A quarter of a world away from home and out here in all this heat looking for dinosaurs. Don't you wish Peter Jr. was out here looking for bones? Even more fervently, don't you wish Shelley was out here looking for bones? Or doing practically anything but what she's doing, or was doing last time you saw her. Yet even though you admire the boy, and even though there was a time you pined for company, now you can't wait to be alone. With Brewster.

She said, "Guess it is."

"I'll be off then."

"Me too."

Ellis Harrison going one way, Molly Brock the other. In minutes they'd lost sight of each other. Suddenly, there came the echoing British voice of the bone hunter. "What's your name?"

Molly stopped, looked back, couldn't see him. Yelled, "Molly Brock!"

"B... r... o... c... k?"

"Yes! Why?"

"Owe you one. Dedicating my doctorate to you."

23

Apricot house ought to be over this last rise. Or the rise after that. Soon see the cantaloupe mall. See PetSmart and Ross Dress for Less and McDonalds and Dollar Tree and Home Depot and Walmart and Costco and Starbucks. See all the banks and the car lots and the gas stations and the cineplexes. Getting dark now, but you'll make it by morning — for sure. This, Molly Brock, is your last night in the desert.

In her breast, panic bloomed like a cactus flower.

Suddenly you're frightened. Mouth's gone dry. Bowels are loose. Flesh crawling. Knees are spinning. Heart racing. And why not? Why shouldn't you be scared? For god's sake, woman, you're going home. If you go home — what fresh hell awaits?

Brewster stood with his head in a brittlebush while Molly used his bony flank to lean on, shading her eyes and gazing up at the last of the sun disappearing behind a volcanic cliff. Charity's hat on her head, mysteriously vanished old man's shoestrings holding up her saggy baggy jeans, Paula's baby oil on her lips, Cowboy's sunflower seed between her teeth, what she was looking at were rhyolite tuffs from volcanic eruptions, but what she saw were bread loafs and sugar cones and rock candy.

Funny what you can get used to. Funny what you can make yours. You've gotten used to this life. You're beginning to know how to do this. You sleep and you walk and you talk to your donkey while the world unfolds in glory before you. Sun and all the birds by day. Moon and stars and all the critters at night. Where will it all go if you go home? Where will you go? On a couch again, watching daytime soaps on TV?

A second huge shock of panic catherine wheeled in her chest. It got worse, it got so bad Molly gripped Brewster's panniers, scrambling for her brown leather bag. Where are they? Please god, tell me you didn't throw away your pills. Grateful hand closing over the plastic container at the bottom of her bag.

Take one, Molly, take two. Take five. In fifteen minutes, in no more than twenty minutes — you're an expert; you know it's never any more than twenty minutes — this horrid hell will stop. You'll be gaga, but so? The panic will stop. You walked away from it. You chose to die because of it. But you didn't die. You lived and you thought you beat it and you thought it was over. You thought it would always be over. No more panic for you, Mrs. Warner. No more calls from Peter's father who's been doing a little arranging, pulling a few strings, calling in a few markers. Who's been talking to Peter over a game of golf, over another woman's phone, discussing what to do about you. For your own good.

Molly sank down on the sand, no matter the spines, no matter the bugs, no matter the desiccated dung, no matter the heat.

But here it is again, just like old times again, and it feels just as bad as it always did, always does, and it feels so bad you want to run and to scream and cry: why Me? Why now? Why ever?

Unopened bottle in her hand, she held on to Brewster's leg (warm leg, bony leg, patient leg) and vomited chewed up sunflower seeds into a patch of fluff grass.

Stop it. Losing water.

She vomited until she gagged. Vomited until there was nothing left to vomit up. After that she vomited because vomiting was better than panicking. And when she was through vomiting, she was so unspeakably down-to-the-bone exhausted, she hadn't the energy left to panic.

Molly crawled away from the mess she'd made in the fluff grass and lay on her side, panting and shaking and avoiding any thought at all.

As for feeling — won't feel. Feeling hurts.

She's nineteen years old and she's just getting out of Peter's car in the driveway of the big white house in Laurel Canyon. She can't take her eyes off the house. First time she's seen it. It's like Katherine Hepburn's house in *The Philadelphia Story*.

She's come to meet his family.

"Hold on," he says, "let's see how you look."

She twirls for him, making the skirt of her new blue dress flare. She's an art student by now. Art students don't wear dresses. Art students wear black. But the blue dress was bought just for this one moment — to make an entrance at this house. Her mother had picked it out at the Burbank JC Pennys, chosen the shoes to match, combed her hair this morning, said blue brought out the blue of her eyes. Not to mention complimenting the blue eye shadow.

He smiles at her. Peter has a winning smile. He's slender now, like a dancer — though later he'll put on muscle, bulk out. He'll get wider. Bigger. Much bigger.

He pats her hand. "You look perfect. They'll love you."

Looking up at the wonderful house, she feels like Jimmy Stewart, half cynical, more than half in love, but she wants to feel like Hepburn. She wants to belong here. She looks at Peter Warner. Does he feel like Cary Grant? She hopes so.

Earlier, he'd said, "Don't tell them you want to act. Dad's up to here with girls who want to act."

"I don't want to act. I want to paint."

"Don't tell them that either."

"So who do I tell them I am?"

"Tell them you're my girl."

Now, in the driveway of his parent's house, he stands straighter. "Come on, little girl," he says, "it's showtime."

Sometime later, she drank half her water. But she did not take the pills. Tucked up and trembling in the warm green and orange mummy bag and looking up at the cold blue stars, Molly Brock made a pact with herself. Just get home. When you get home again you'll know what to do. But for now count the stars and breathe in the desert and listen to the sneak of the night—and stop this bloody nonsense.

In the morning, her apricot house wasn't over the next rise. No *bajada* leading down to an estate of apricot houses. No cantaloupe mall, no suburban roads, no cars, no bars, no scars, no haze of pollution, no city tumbled like trash over the desert basin. There was nothing up and over the next rise but more Arizona Upland desert, more saguaro, more cholla, more greasewood, more rocks, more heat—and one extraordinary baked clay house of pale lavender gray hung from the side of a bruise-red rock like the panniers on Brewster's back.

"Jesus, Brue. Will you look at that house. Have you ever seen a house like that?"

"Awww EEE. Awww EEE."

"Neither have I. Whose is it, do you think?"

Brewster either had no idea or didn't care. It was morning, they'd walked awhile—he wanted his water.

The closer they came to the house on the rock, the larger it seemed. And where is the road that leads to it and where is the front door? No windows, no doors, no chimneys or porches or decks. It's like a cliff dwelling. It's like the ancient Pueblo Indian houses that were tucked into deep shadowed crevices and under rocky overhangs with no way up or down but ropes.

Forced to climb down before they could climb up, Molly and Brewster came round a huge ocotillo growing out of a tangle of cholla and palo verde, each ocotillo whip tipped with the bright red flags of its flowers.

Good grief, even out here some people have money, real money.

From where she stood, the baked clay house was a series of delicately colored terraces, each rising above the other, and each terrace walled, and on each wall designs in darker clay than the clay of the terraces and walls.

Bet this house has been in *House Beautiful* or *Town & Country* more than once. Bet it's been used in a movie. Bet the owner is famous, or at least well known for being the owner of this house. Bet they'll chase me off if I ask for water. Might be hours yet before I get home—bet I'll ask anyway. Ah, there's the driveway and it leads to a road cut through the rock.

No one chased her off. Climbing up from the wrong side, Molly and Brewster had to make their way round to the driveway in full sight of anyone inside. No one shouted or waved or shot at them. Must be security cameras or Doberman Pinschers or—like the house in Laurel Canyon—those little red laser beams that sound an alarm when they're broken. Must be at *least* razor wire.

Nothing happened. Not even when Brewster's little hooves quick tapped across the dark purple brick of the first and lowest terrace as he trotted towards a pool in the shape of a star. Bronze statue of a man standing at the edge of the pool. Molly following Brue over, squinted in the sun to read the plaque at its base.

Plaque said: Wyatt Earp.

"Damn, Brue, it's a life-size statue of Wyatt Earp. Pool must be his badge."

Old voice, older than Charity's voice, older than her father's became before he died, suddenly saying, "Was a time I knew him. Knew him well. Played him once too. A fine time in a man's life, to be—just for a moment—Wyatt Earp."

Molly turned to see a little old man in a wheelchair.

Her first thought? It's E.T. E.T. didn't go home. E.T. stayed. I'm in Steven Spielberg's house and he lives here with E.T.

Old man's head and shoulders covered in a fine shawl of Shetland wool, old man's body covered in a shapeless dove gray robe. Not a tooth in his old man's mouth, he was smiling at her. And behind him stood Geronimo.

Or Chief Broom, Molly. It could be a very old Chief Broom.

In a soft breathy voice, old man said, "Allow me to introduce myself. I am, or rather I was, Ray Keene. And this here is Oley, the only son of Leino Coloradas, my once-upon-a-time faithful Indian companion. Leino is now sadly departed from this world. No, no. Don't tell us who you are. I figure we know who you are. Oley? How about you asking Margarita to set us two extra places for lunch?"

24

Not everything is wrong in our bravely baggy and sadly saggy new world, Molly Brock. Here you are, sitting at a table that's a slab of polished mesquite as big as a roller rink. Table's in a dining room made entirely of glass. The glass is molded to the natural, still living, rock face.

Did the table come, you think, from the Copper Crown?

Beyond the glass, seemingly untouched and seemingly forever: her heart-stopping desert. Desert includes a good view of Brewster eating something out of a wooden bucket held in the hand of a young Mexican girl.

Inside the glass — air conditioning!

The one flat wall of the air-conditioned vaulted glass dining room hung with framed movie posters. Not one of them was something she'd ever seen, or even heard of. *Under Arizona Skies. Two Gun Man. The Road to Hell's Bells. Six White Horses.* A couple of dozen others. And on each movie poster a young cowboy with cholla blond hair, ardent of eye and firm of jaw. Beside him or behind him — and always drawn smaller — the sidekick, the foil, Leino his faithful Indian companion.

At the end of the mesquite slab, Ray Keene, a thin scrape of white hair left on his freckled head and barely able to see over the edge of the table. On his right, Oley: gaunt and gray, tall in his chair. On his left—you: desert dusted from head to foot, desert browned, and eating a very credible Caesar's Salad while drinking a bottle of Dos Equis.

Heaven. This is heaven. Old man is gumming his mush, the son of his faithful Indian companion isn't eating anything, but he could if he wanted to, Brewster is eating whatever Brewster's eating—and you've just used your first real toilet in a month, one that didn't need pulling a chain.

Propped in his wheelchair, old man worked his food around in his mouth as he looked out the window at Brewster. And you look at him. Never saw anyone older. How does it feel being as old as he must be?

At long last swallowing, old man's voice came out as a shouted whisper. "Once there was old Bill Hart. Then there was young Tom Mix. And then there was me, Ray Keene. Compared to Hart, I wasn't much more'n a boy. Bill's horse was a gallant little pinto called Fritz, Tom's was Tony the Wonder Horse, and mine was a big dappled gray called Buddy. Buddy was a hateful beast, stupid and pig-headed. But he was mighty fine to look at and he could rear with the best of 'em. Buddy had a friend in a little lady burro called Titch. Never have forgot Titch, as lovable a creature as God ever made. I hope you christened that burro, young lady, threw a good name over 'im."

Molly only slightly ill at ease. Young lady? Odd to be called a young lady. Long time since young made any sense at all. Meantime, you are not going to tell the old man why you called him Brewster. You wish you hadn't. From now on, it's Brue.

"He's Brue."

"Brue." Old man rolled that around in his mouth like his mush. "Brue the burro. You like that, Oley? I have to say I like it just fine. But please, take pity on an old man— have some more of this Mexican beer. These days I don't add up to much more than that ripe old fellow in one of Mr. Raymond Chandler's books. What was his name? I

don't remember his name. But he lived in a Retirement
Home for Orchids and when Philip Marlowe came to call,
he took great pleasure in seeing Marlowe do what he could
no longer do. If only you took pleasure in a good smoke!
Oley does not smoke nor does he drink."

Oley grimaced. "Nasty."

"Taken to extremes, don't it seem to you most of man's
pleasures are brutish?"

"Speak for yourself, white man."

After lunch, Oley wheeling Ray around. Slowly,
slowly... time was no object.

Showing off the house to Molly Brock, Ray, like Marley's
ghost, lifting no more than one bent finger to point here and
to point there.

Look, Molly, a phone. A landline. It's been weeks since
you've seen one. You could ask to make a call. Old man
would let you make a local call. But not now. Not this
minute. And then again, maybe not at all. After all, you'll
be home in a few hours, no need to call first. Probably
nobody there anyway. And if someone is, it would probably
cause—speaking of nasty—one hell of a surprise.

Old man was saying, "It was a downright joy to build
this house. I was flush then, famous as all get out. I was
like Cagney when he stood on top of the world."

Oley said, "*White Heat.*"

"Exactly. See that picture over the mantle? That's Lola
Valdez, may she rest in one piece. Miraculous, wasn't she?
Why she married me I don't guess I'll ever know, but why
I married her is right up there for all to see. About that
time I had a full crop of long blond hair and Oley's father
and I had a new feature picture out every few weeks. I was
idolized by millions of white folks and even some black
folks and some yellow folks. Oley just naturally assures me
his father had his own loyal fans among the red folks."

"The Dinah," said Oley.

"Like I said, the Apache red folks. But the best thing
of all to the young man I was, was to call Wyatt Earp my
friend. Mr. Earp stood right on this very spot and he said:
'Ray, a man could spend his entire life right here and never
want for a better view.' So I bought the land and I built my

house and I said: 'Mr. Earp, anytime you want to see this view you can come here and settle down. There'll always be a room for you.' But he could only come the once. Tragedy of his life was that cold pudding of a wife. She gambled all his money away. She lied to him and she treated him bad. But would he abandon her? Never! No more loyal a man, never a more gentlemanly gentleman than Wyatt Earp. Unless it was Leino Coloradas. Or his son, young Oley here."

"Ask me," said Oley to a window, "Man was stubborn. Makes you stupid."

"I heard that."

By now, they'd reached a wide door of dark and glossy wood in a wall of amber stucco.

As Oley swung open the carved door, Ray said, "These are the rooms I prepared for Mr. Earp—and now they're yours."

Molly, full of Dos Equis and Caesar salad, listening and looking and trying to imagine this shrunken old man riding the range with his two guns blazing and his faithful Indian companion alongside him, trying to picture him walking with Wyatt Earp down the lawless streets of a lawless town, trying even to imagine the blond hair, blinked and said, "Mine?"

"Yep. Yours. And there's a stall for Brue good enough for Seabiscuit. Good enough for his grandpap, Man O' War. I'm hoping you'll stay. Oley here is hoping you'll stay. Truth is, we sure could use the company."

Molly heard this as she stood in the doorway of a beautiful suite of rooms in sienna reds and butter yellows. High ceilinged, high and wide windowed, there was a private bath, a large fireplace in the bedroom, a larger fireplace in the sitting room, and a small fireplace in the bathroom. In the bedroom, there was a bed as big as the mesquite dining table. And throughout, scattered on the shining floor of deep red tile, vivid carpets from far-flung looms. Brewster's panniers sat neatly in front of the carved mesquite wardrobe.

"But I can't stay."

"Why, that's plain nonsense. Lots of room here. Leino and I were forgotten a long time ago. The gun operas of Ray Keene and Leino Coloradas, his brave Indian friend, rotted away in their cans. I hear tell no one even tried to save them, not even the best of 'em in which I had the very great privilege of playing Wyatt Earp."

Oley muttering. If the old man didn't hear him, Molly did. "Bet your ass my father did not play Holliday."

Molly still looking at Wyatt Earp's rooms. Rooms are as neat as a firing pin. They smell of furniture polish and flowers. Someone's placed flowers on the mantles, on the bureau; there's a bowl of small pink sweetheart roses on the coffee table. Were they waiting for a guest? Did they know one was coming? Is all this for me?

Molly shuddered from top to bottom. But of course they aren't waiting for you, Mrs. Saggy Baggy Suburban Golfing Twonk. They're waiting for Wyatt Earp. They're waiting for Doc Holliday. They're waiting for Crazy Horse. They might even be waiting for Lassiter. Or Jesus. But no one's waiting for you.

She peeked round the bathroom door. Huge bath sunk in the tiled floor like a natural stone depression, a desert *tinaja* catching the summer rain.

Everyone's waiting for a hero to rescue them from life. Everyone's always waiting for a hero. No getting round it—you're waiting for a hero too.

Old man and Oley right on her heels, old man bouncing his rubber tires off the doorjamb.

"'Bout nineteen and forty, Tom Mix died in a car wreck right here in the state of Arizona, got his head taken off by his own damn suitcase flying off the back seat shelf. Leino went in '40 too, as stupid a death for a man as Tom's. Bad year for friends, that year. Bill Hart passed away old in '46. And Wyatt was done for by conjugal neglect over eighty some years ago. But me, I'm more'n a hundred. I've outlived my friends and I've outlived my enemies and I've outlived my family and I've outlived my sidekick and I've outlived my time. Can't be too long before Ray Keene himself rides off to that Last Roundup in the Sky. Oley, son of Leino, ain't no spring chicken neither."

Oley, tucking in the old man's woolen shawl, said, "When my time comes, I walk away into the desert." Aha. You knew it. Some people get totally fed up or totally freaked out or totally overwhelmed and do something stupid. But some, the very rare ones, have dignity. All an Apache had to say was: this is a good day to die—and then walk away. No fuss, no muss. More than you could do, Molly Brock. For which I suppose you should thank goodness. Or ineptitude. Or blind luck. Or the grudging kindness of bald-headed, semi-silent strangers.

Old man squeezing Oley's hand and shaking with silent laughter. "You should of been in pictures. Always was one for the melodrama. Just be careful is all I ask. Fall in a soft place and mind the snakes. As for you—"

Molly stepping back from the bathroom door. "No, really—thank you, but you don't understand. I can't stay here."

Old man fixing her with an old eye, old but shrewd. "You think so? Must be two weeks ago now, police were mighty damn sure they'd spotted you walking the shoulder of the Old Nogales Road. And if your face isn't already on a milk carton, you're bound to be on posters on every telephone pole in town. But they won't find you out here. Nobody comes out here."

Molly staring back at Ray Keene. *They won't find you here.* How does that sound, Molly Brock? It sounds just like—more heaven.

Old man's old head pushing out from his soft white shawl, urging his chair forward. "Come on, Oley. An old man misses his nap, that old man gets a mite cranky."

Molly watching them go. Oh the hell with it. Where's the harm? You'll go home rested and you'll go home clean—but you'll go home. Tomorrow.

Very first thing, soon as the door clicked shut, Molly took a shower in Wyatt Earp's bathroom. Then she crawled naked into Wyatt Earp's feather bed, pulled up Wyatt Earp's covers, and fell deeply asleep.

25

On the morning of the twenty-ninth day since walking away, Molly found an electric hair clipper under the sink in Wyatt Earp's bathroom.

Molly holding the clipper and staring into the bathroom mirror.

Well? Will you or won't you? Le Crap isn't working. Desert sun sucked it dry. Desert wind's blown it drier. Dried hair's sticking out every which way, all over everywhere. Dark roots are half an inch long. Ends are split more ways than a bad deal. You either curl this mess, Molly Brock, or you buzz it off. After that—like an Indian walking away—no muss, no fuss. But here's the down side. No hair. What will you look like with no hair? If you're lucky, it's Sigourney Weaver in *Aliens*.

Trying to run her fingers through her hair, getting stuck, hand coming away with torn and brittle strands. And if you're unlucky? It's the old woman. It's Charity.

Slumping one shoulder and raising the other, Molly held the clipper like Wyatt would hold a gun, looked herself straight in the eye.

"You got to ask yourself—you feelin' lucky?"

Molly buzzed off her hair.

Over a long afternoon on her twenty-ninth day, she learned how to handle a knife.

"Even a true blue born genuine hero can't trust to nerve alone," said Ray.

Molly said, "I'm not a hero."

Ray watched Oley open a case of knives. Ray saying, "My choice of weapon was a gun. And two guns was even better. But Leino preferred the knife. A knife is silent and it's swift, not to mention how it never runs out of ammo. 'Course, with a knife, you only got the one chance—so you got to be good. I reckon a woman like you would do well knowing a knife. Oley here learned from his dad, now you'll learn from Oley. Let's begin."

"I'm not a hero."

"We'll use us the living room. Room's always been too big for much of anything else and it ain't too likely you'll break anything."

"Ray, what do I want with knives?"

Oley, turning away from a large board he'd propped against a wall, holding out a knife, handle first, said, "This was one of my father's knives. It is a good knife. Benchmade. It will serve you well."

Molly took the knife. Looked down at it in her hand. Had no idea what she was looking at. Knives were for kitchens, for chopping and mincing and slicing and dicing. This wasn't a kitchen knife. It was meant for stabbing and cutting and gutting and throwing. Looked over at Ray in his chair. Light in his eyes like the light on the knife: focused and bright.

What the hell. He's a sweetie. And he's so old. Where's the harm if it makes him happy? Basically, a good guest does not deny her hosts their small pleasures.

Molly took her place by Oley, held the knife as he told her to hold it. Threw the knife as he told her to throw it. Wow, never did that before. Or that.

"Show me that again, Oley. Let me try it again."

Along towards evening, Oley said she showed promise. A lot of promise. Which was hardly surprising for a good tennis player and an ace pitcher.

After supper on her twenty-ninth day, Molly watched her first movie with Ray and Oley: *Shane*. Alan Ladd's fringed and lonesome stranger. The evening after that, it was Dustin Hoffman in *Little Big Man* growing as old as Ray Keene was old. Then Henry Fonda playing Ray's old friend Wyatt Earp in *My Darling Clementine*, John Wayne running from the law in *Stagecoach*, and Gary Cooper standing alone in *High Noon*.

Five nights of heroes and movies and popcorn, though without teeth, no popcorn for Ray. And every day a lesson with Oley. And twice or more every day, a walk with Brue and a walk and a talk with Ray.

On the morning of her sixth day in the baked clay house, she woke up from a wild and wooly dream about Lassiter.

Or maybe it was Cowboy Tom? Come to that, it could have been Ray Keene when Ray was young and cranking out a moving picture every two weeks. Dream fading so fast, it might even have been Wyatt Earp. Whoever it was who'd starred in the theater of her dreaming mind, he and she'd done everything together. Him on his horse, a big black, and her on hers, a strawberry roan. They cleaned up Dodge, rustled Mexican cattle, ran a saloon in Tombstone, homesteaded a spread in Wyoming and made a movie of the whole thing—in total silence.

In another borrowed bed, stretching and yawning and reaching out to hold the fleeing dream, she realized that at times she'd been a woman and at times she'd been a man and at times she'd had no idea which she was but at no time had it mattered one way or the other.

But maybe it mattered and maybe it didn't that she was always the sidekick.

Another day of sun, another day of light, another day of air conditioning and living in a work of art. Another day of stepping into a shower bigger than her bedroom in the apricot house.

Old woman could see all this precious Mother Light water swirl down this Mr. Hate drain, old woman would smack my saggy baggy butt.

Taking a shower, getting dressed, having breakfast with Ray in a room full of cacti. Looking out over a desert full of more and bigger cacti, watching a movie at night—that's your life now, Molly Brock. Old man is sweet and old man is funny. Seems like he hasn't forgotten a thing, not a date or a name or what it felt like or why it was happening or what happened next. Old man called someone as soon as you told him about the body you found, did whatever had to be done to ensure it was taken proper care of. Old man called someone else at the University of Arizona to make sure they still had a student called Ellis Harrison.

Molly washing her hair, gently running the palm of her hand over the soft sudsy stubble.

You still have more hair than that old man. Who can still see far out over the desert and pick out a silky-flycatcher eating berries in the mistletoe. Old man can hear every word spoken across the largest room, gets most of the answers right on the TV game shows, is an Alexandrian library of old movie memorabilia... and if he doesn't have a world class collection of cacti, you don't know who does.

Molly's hand reaching for the soap—damn. You've fallen in love with an old man, Molly Brock. You've given your heart to a man as old as Bob Hope, as irascible as Groucho Marx, as wry as George Burns, and as ugly as E.T. You want to tuck in his shawl and wheel his chair around and brush his three remaining hairs and listen to him forever.

Right on time, Mother in her head again. "Excuse me, but—WHAT! Are you sick? Are you kidding? You stop that right this minute, you hear!"

Molly lathering up. "Hi, mom. Long time, no jeer."

"In love with an old fart like that? He's falling apart! He's so beyond old, he's disgusting! All that hair in his nose! And not a tooth in his mouth, and his lips caved in like that. *Harold & Maude* was a stupid movie, stupid! Old people widdle in their pants. Old people smell. What could you be thinking, Molly? You catch me growing old, just shoot me."

"Jesus, mother. What are you talking about? Not *that* way."

"Stop it. The thought makes me sick. You make me sick. He makes me sick. Old makes me sick. Physically sick."

Norma Brock, Mrs. Lindsay Brock, dyed her hair red until she was seventy seven. Erect in a scaffold of corsets, sausaged into stockings, she painted her face until she looked like a mortician's test dummy. Shoot her? If only.

"Hold on a sec. He's rich. He's *really* old. He can't last long. Grab the old fart, Molly. Divorce Peter. You know I've always thought Peter Warner was a jackass."

"You never thought any such thing. You loved that white house as much as I do."

"I don't know *where* you get your ideas."

Molly shook her wet head, water slipping off her sleek skull.

Get out of my head. Go away. Play bridge, sink a putt, toil away on your celestial stair master, and leave me the bloody fuck alone as a certain paleontologist would say. If you shake your head hard enough, will your mother fall the fuck out? How can you love someone you hate so much? *Do* you love her? *Did* you? Don't know, do you? All you know is you're supposed to love your mother. And your mother is supposed to love you. Do know you love that old man. As for Oley, truth is, you love them both. Truth is, you love it here. So how will you leave when the time comes? Hasn't the time come and gone? When are you going home? No. Stop. Don't think about that now. Think about that tomorrow, Scarlett Brock.

Stepping out of her shower, Molly rubbing herself down. Slim again. Almost as slim as the young girl she'd once been. Not as firm, and not as juicy, a bit saggy baggy here and there, but what the hell — she was doing a lot of walking, wasn't she? Walking was good exercise. And then there was all the knife throwing.

A knock on her door and she was wrapped in a borrowed robe as fast as she could say Cowboy Tom.

"Yes?"

Margarita's husband Jorge. Come to give her Ray Keene's regards and to tell her that for an hour or so this morning Mr. Keene and Mr. Coloradas would be attending to personal business with a Mr. Mace of the Law Firm of Mace & Dickman, and could Jorge be of use showing her a perhaps interesting room no one had bothered with for thirty years?

26

All the dust bunnies found nowhere else in the house were caged in the room Jorge unlocked and left her to, all the spinning motes and nose-clogging must collected during the long silent years of neglect.

This is where the old man keeps Ray Keene, cowboy movie star. It's where Leino Coloradas, Indian movie star, sleeps. You think Wyatt Earp's in here?

Under a dome of dusty glass, a life-size waxworks manikin of Ray Keene in his Ray Keene outfit: ten-gallon hat and six-shooters in their tooled leather holsters, his trademark neckerchief of "Ray Keene" white stars on a black field. Nearby, as in life, a glass-domed manikin of the faithful Leino in buckskin leathers, his favorite knife in a buckskin sheath on his hip.

Molly peering through the glass. Lights coming on for the first time in years, and you coming this close to catching Cowboy and Indian blink in stuffed surprise.

On the walls, more posters because there were more Ray Keene and Leino Coloradas movies than the dining room wall could hold.

In pride of place, two huge oils.

Same painter, good technician. Cowboy Tom would say they were "serviceable." You'd say they reminded you of Dorian Gray — in reverse. One of Leino and his appaloosa Pie, and one of Ray and the dappled gray, Buddy. Old man was handsome, corn-fed and golden. Leino was even more handsome, a wild dark thing.

Standing in front of the paintings, staring, Molly trying to peel the years away, trying to see them as they were, feel them as they were.

Makes you want to weep. Mr. Hate sucking the goodness out of people — sucking all their juice until what was once a grape, collapses into the Time of the Raisin. And you too, Molly dear, you as well. There's no escaping Mr. Hate. He's there, in your bones. He's loose in your blood, humming through your wiring. He's stretching out your skin, crumpling it up like tissue paper. And no use screaming, no use calling for help. Wyatt Earp isn't around to outdraw Mr. Hate. No hero coming to rescue you — except maybe Mr. Death.

Molly is eleven years old. She'll be in the seventh grade in the fall. But right now it's June and the children of summer are outside, running in the sun. In a week Molly will go to Aunt Evelyn's as she does every summer, but until then, Molly is home, alone. She's inside, drawing.

There's a sound in the kitchen.

Molly looking up from her sketch of a horse. Norma is playing bridge at her woman's club. Her dad is at work — what's that?

Silence.

Nothing. It's nothing.

Molly wants to be an artist. Since she was four, she's drawn her pictures. Norma says they're nice. But she never looks at them. Lindsay says they're very good. Her dad says they look like what they're supposed to be. He would look at them, but he never has time. Molly keeps drawing. She has boxes of paper she's drawn on in her closet, under the bed.

There's that sound in the kitchen again.

Better go see what it is. Mom killed all the mice. Couldn't be a mouse.

It isn't a mouse. It's a man. There's a man standing near Norma's sink drinking Norma's water in one of Norma's good glasses.

"Who are you?"

The man puts his finger to his lips, and says, "Sssssh."

Molly just stands there staring at him as he walks towards her, smiling.

Back up, Molly. Run. But it's your house. This is your house. What is he doing here?

"This is my house," she says. "That's my mother's glass."

Man keeps coming. He's wearing a shirt with his name over the pocket. "Cliff," it says, and under that, "Security." His smile is bigger now. She can see his teeth. "Cliff" has lots of teeth. He doesn't make her feel secure.

He's five feet away, four and a half feet, four — before she turns and runs from him.

Molly slams out the front door and down the walk past the oleander bushes and up the path to Mr. and Mrs. Howe's house. Mr. Howe is out front, swearing at the lawn mower. His lawn mower is broken again.

Mr. Howe tells Molly to go into his house, and to stay there. He tells Mrs. Howe to call the police. He doesn't go into the Brock house, but he stands outside trying to see in the front windows.

When the police come, "Cliff" is still in Molly's house. They find him sitting on the couch in the den, bent double, laughing at a rerun of *I Love Lucy* in black and white on the color TV.

Molly doesn't remember who said it or when, but she learns later that Cliff, whose real name wasn't Cliff, had walked away from a State Hospital. Norma called it the Loony Bin. The Nut House. The Booby Hatch. The place where they locked up all the crazy people.

When she asked her father about it, Lindsay Brock said, "You wouldn't want to go there, Molly. When people go there, they never get out again. Ever."

Trailing her fingers over dusty cabinets and dusty cases, picking up Ray Keene and Leino Coloradas playing cards and lunch boxes and comic books. All alone, little Molly Brock playing with a Ray Keene doll, taking the little guns out of the little holsters. The Leino doll had a tiny knife. Leino had real beads on his fringed leather shirt. What's under Leino's little leather skirt?

Old man, behind her, softly lisping, "Life, ain't it a kick in the pants?"

Molly forever spinning round to find someone sneaking up on her. What was left of Ray Keene had driven his own chair around his own house and into this neglected room to find her playing with his forgotten toys. And Molly, in her own Time of The Raisin, sighed, saying, "And what does it all come to?"

Old man bumped her hard with his foot rest.

Bloody ouch! Was that on purpose?

"What's it all come to? What kind of stupid question is that? Life is life. It ain't coming to anything — it's already there. You could be fifty, sixty, seventy or more, I'd figure you for young. When you were born, I'm betting I was already getting on to old." Ray watching with interest as she hopped about, rubbing her shin. "Stop that. You're making me dizzy. Was a time I could wrestle Buddy and win, now I need help back to my room."

Molly behind his chair, and guiding it. Ray under his shawl and talking.

"You ain't the only one ever walked away. Not by a long shot. First time for me, I was twenty years old and still living right where I was born which is Bisbee, Arizona, and I'd never been anywhere but Bisbee, Arizona. Slow down."

Molly slowed down.

"Then one morning early in the Spring I'm baking my fifth batch of hot cross buns when I happen to catch a glimpse of my own face reflected in the glass of the bakery window. 'Bout burnt my buns when I all of a sudden realized I didn't know who the hell I was looking at. Staring straight at a red-faced, overweight, prime fool of a fellow, and damned if I knew who it was. That did it. I about broke off the knob of the Bisbee Bakery and Bread Products oven turning it off, ran up the two hundred and three steps to where I lived, and wrote Eileen a goodbye note."

"Eileen?"

"First wife of four. By god, but Eileen was a lovely girl. Long neck and long legs and grip like a boa — but not one loyal bone in her body. Over eighty years ago, this was. Eighty years! Eight zero. Even I have trouble believing that. To this day I reckon if anyone back then'd heard tell about Ray Keene, big ol' cowboy movie star, abandoning his teenage bride in a shack a body could only reach by a nearly perpendicular two-hundred-step staircase, well, let's put it this way — me and my friend Fatty Arbuckle, we'd a both been on the bread line. Even knowing Eileen was already contemplating exchanging me for an Arizona Ranger… nope, not even that would of cut any ice with Joe Public."

Molly helping him climb into his big soft four-poster bed, pulling up the covers as far as his grizzled chin, settling him in for the first of his thrice-daily naps.

"Eileen Wadeson was the heart of my heart, my sweetie, my boyhood's honey bunned angel."

Old man's eyes crossed in remembered rapture. "When I was a young Bisbee buck, I wanted to please that girl in every way I could — and I wasn't the only one. Trouble was, I also had a hankering to be an actor and I'd taken to infesting the Lyric Theater and, brother—that did not please her at all. Eileen wanted me to become a baker like her father. And I swear I tried. I tried every day but Tuesday for two whole years, and two years is a dickens of a long time when a man is young. Often thought I'd of made a damn good baker, probably a lot better than the actor I became."

Old man winding down, getting tired as he patted Molly's arm. "Thirty-three years old when I walked away from Hollywood. Got as far as Australia. Stumbled onto an opal mine. Walked away from that a rich man." For a moment he seemed to fall asleep. Molly, sure he had, was staring fondly down at him, wondering at how fragile his wrists, how sunken his eyes and his cheeks and his lips. Old man's eyes snapped open. "And now that I am so damnably old, I reckon it's time to walk away from this life."

Molly starting. God, no. I've just found you, old man. You can't walk away again.

Ray smiling up from the depths of his goosedown pillow. Age had made his face so small, all that was left was the toothless smile. "You remind me of Lola. First thing I thought when I saw you."

With one shaky finger, the old man touching the back of her hand. Tapping it with the curve of his old man's nail. "Old as I am, I don't wet my pants and I don't drool and I can still feed myself. I also got all of my money and half of my wits. If I've done nothing else, I've learned one certain thing in my very long life."

Molly leaning down close, for if there was one thing she wanted to hear, it was something certain.

Old man whispered, "Every time I walked away, I always found there was somewhere to go."

27

Molly woke early on her seventh day in Ray's house. On this day, the once Bisbee baker — born again as the silent cowboy movie star Ray Keene, born again as the man who discovered an Australian opal mine, born again as too old to enlist in the U.S. Army so volunteering instead to work behind enemy lines "gathering information," born again as R. Keene, romance novelist, born yet again as the old man, too old to give a fuck — was turning one hundred and one years old.

With nothing else to offer, Molly's gift was preparing everything from canapés to the contents of Brue's feedbag.

Some time back, Cowboy Tom had asked if Mrs. Peter Warner could cook — but he'd never asked if she could cook well. The answer would have been: Cook? You, Tom, are looking at a Mother Light angel, an ardent English bone hunter, a New York cowboy-artist of a cook... and after the ketchup-loving Peter, the toothless Ray Keene might be her supreme challenge.

For soup, she would make a mushroom consommé with morels. For the main course, she planned the perfect gum food: Shrimp & Spinach Dumpling with an Asian dipping sauce. Very yummy, this, though you might want to make two versions: mild for Ray, and less mild for everyone else. For something essentially green that required absolutely no chewing, her special guacamole with pears and pomegranate seeds. The seeds and the mushrooms would slide right down. Perhaps even Oley will eat what you cook — fussy eater, Oley.

And for something to stick Ray's birthday candles into: soft and rich and splendid: a Chocolate Ganache Cake with White-Coffee Foam.

Hurry up. Get dressed. So much to do. The black sweatshirt with the red quote from Longfellow, I think. And your best pair of jeans since they are your only pair of jeans.

The seat of her jeans came nowhere near her butt. Even her shoes felt roomy.

If you've ever thought fat was a matter of "hormones," you can forget all that now. Amazing how fast you lose weight when you don't eat. The pounds fall off. Look! You have bones in your hands again, bones in your feet. Best of all, you have bones in your face. No time for preening. There's food to prepare. A cake to bake. A table to set. And since he's invited, there's Brue to curry and fuss over.

Molly bustling about in Margarita's kitchen, as unique and beautiful as all the rest of the house was beautiful and unique. Margarita hauling out colored bowls and shining pans and intriguing utensils with a great clatter. Margarita and her daughter Elvia laughing.

Hope Oley remembers the candles. How to get one hundred and one candles on a single cake? It'll be meltdown. Maybe you'd better settle for a candle a decade?

No keeping a secret, and no keeping the old man out of the kitchen.

Old man's so old, there's no one left to come to his party. Only Margarita and Elvia and Jorge and Oley and Brue and me. When he was Ray Keene and on top of the world, how many had come? When he was the Opal King? When he was B. Keene writing books like *All I Have Is Yours* and *The Breathless Coquette*? Four wives yet no child. No children to produce grandchildren making great grandchildren. Nothing but Leino's son, old now, with no children of his own. How sad it will all stop here, Molly Brock, in this house. And who will remember?

You, that's who will remember.

Folding the cream into the chocolate for ganache, she said, "Ray, have you ever played golf?"

Ray, his finger in the cake batter, blinked. "Golf? I tried it once. With my good friend, Bing. Couldn't see the attraction. Mark Twain said golf was a good walk spoiled."

Knew it. Knew Ray Keene was no saggy baggy golfer demon, no fuckin' bloody twonk.

Hours later. House was quiet. Night was quiet. Even Brue out in his adobe stable was quiet. Molly, propped up by all the pillows on Wyatt Earp's bed, quietly reading a B. Keene romance: *The Lady and The Buckaroo*.

Note to self. Books are worth all the stars in the sky. Convert TV room into a library. Buy books. Begin with Zane Grey and B. Keene. Build from there.

Laying the book aside, staring out the window at a saguaro with an owl on top.

His dinner went well, didn't it? Oh yes, Ray's dinner went more than well. Ten times better than Peter's birthday parties where you, you mad housewife you, would try so hard. You invited everyone you could think of, made a huge meal of it — and Peter always complained: so and so didn't come, so and so's present was lame, didn't you think it was lame, Moll? And such and such and so and so and so... sew buttons on his underwear. Ray's party also went a hundred times better than Shelley's and Peter Jr.'s. Theirs always seemed to end in tears.

Owl on the saguaro took off, floating away on great round wings.

Old man's party was full of laughter. Old man gummed all your food. Old man's old eyes watered as he listened to Margarita and Elvia sing a song Jorge wrote called *Nuestro Buen Amigo*. Smile all over his wrinkled face when you did the knife tricks Oley's taught you. Old man positively trembled when Oley slowly and with solemn ceremony took a hand-rolled Honduras cigar called *La Luna African*

Fuerte from his shirt pocket, rolled it around in his fingers, sniffed it, clipped it with a gadget he also took from his pocket, then lit it with a butane lighter. This last came out of his pocket as well. Which explains the mysterious trip he took to town this morning in Ray's 1954 soundless silver Cadillac Eldorado.

Puffing and sucking until its thick tip glowed with heat, Oley blew out the soft gray smoke in curls and coils and wreaths of spicy aroma that enveloped Ray's blissful head as he watched his birthday movie.

Old man had to be patted on the back when Stan Laurel, handing the villainess in *Way Out West* the deed to a gold mine, said: "Now you've got a mine, I'm sure you'll make a great gold digger."

Middle of the night, moon outside the window like the edge of a coin, and she read because she couldn't sleep. Twelve days ago she'd lain beside the cowboy under these same desert skies miles to the south deciding it was time to go home.

And here you are again. As much as you feel at home in Ray's house, it isn't your house. Much as you've fallen in love with Ray Keene and Oley Coloradas, and as much as you wish they were family, they aren't. No matter what the old man said, she couldn't stay a guest forever. Sooner or later, she and Brue were bound to wear out their welcome.

Well, maybe not Brue — but you, Molly Brock, have to face the inevitable. It's time to go home. Again.

With this thought, she braced herself. Prepared for the sickening sweep and swoop of panic. But it did not come. No wheel of nerves in her chest. No uneasy flight of black and broken thoughts. No hideous whoops of nausea. But there was an electric pricking over her cheeks and the backs of her hands. Up and down her spine, there came a wave of prescient gloom.

Before it could become more, Molly rose from the bed, slipped into the gray jersey robe Margarita had left in the wardrobe, and paced through Ray's house. Touched the books and the paintings and the walls, pale by the light of the stars.

And in this way, kept calm.

"Your aunt was invited. She could have come."

"She was invited, Peter. She's always invited. But she's never welcome."

Peter already turning away, an arm around the broad shoulders of Peter Jr., a hand out to greet his brothers, his brothers-in-law, his uncle, his father's accountant, hugs for his mother, his own aunts, his three sisters, their kids, all crowded round the long white table at the deep end of the pool, same table used every year for the holiday buffet.

Thanksgiving at Mr. & Mrs. Stanley Warners.

Molly the last to arrive. No Shelley this year. Or the year before. Or the year before that. Shelley had vanished into East L.A. again. No one will ask Peter where Shelley is. By now, no one mentions Shelley at all. Shelley is the family secret, the skeleton, the failure.

Peter's dad, Stan, is the family patriarch. This allows him to hide in his study taking phone calls no matter what everyone else is celebrating. That way, they can't get at him.

And he can't get at you, Mrs. Molly, not quite right wife of the oldest son. But right enough to come on to when no one's looking. And what did Peter say when you finally told him, when you finally plucked up the courage after the third time in as many years? He said he was proud of you. The old man's choosy, he said, he has taste. And what did you say? You don't even remember what you said. But whatever it was, it wasn't much. You never said much, did you, Brock?

Molly's Aunt Evelyn isn't considered family. If she were, she'd be the family eccentric.

She's odd. She says odd things. She makes them all nervous. They make her nervous. She brings strange gifts at Christmas. Vegetables. Things she knits. Rocks she's found on the beach. Feathers. They smile when they look at her presents. Oh my, how nice, they say. They say thank you. They get rid of them as fast as they can. They never know what to get her. Stemware. Monogrammed guest towels. Fancy soap. Aunt Evelyn doesn't fit into the white house on Laurel Canyon.

And neither do you, Molly Brock. How long have you known it?

Is the house on fire?

Molly, more and more quickly following the smell of smoke, found herself in the corridor outside Ray's open bedroom door, found Oley sitting erect in a chair and smoking a cigar in the dark.

"One cigar and now you've a taste for it?"

"Nasty. But I will smoke until he dies."

"You bought that many cigars?"

"He will die tonight."

Oh god. By the pricking of my thumbs. Heart racing, Molly was across the old man's bedroom and kneeling by his side. Old man barely breathing, old man looking ghastly in the soft pink night-light—yet he was alive. And awake.

"Greetings, fair wanderer." No more than a whisper, Molly's ear almost to his sunken mouth to hear him. "Any time now, I shall see Lola." Old man's eyes widening. "And perhaps Wyatt will be good enough to show up as well."

Molly holding his hand. Only bones, a slight bundle of old bones. Tell him what you feel, Molly. Why don't we tell each other what we feel? For fear they don't feel the same?

"I love you, Ray Keene."

Old man's hand moved in her own, the slightest squeeze. "And you, you are my last flame."

Molly Brock, the once Mrs. Peter Warner, burst into tears.

"I'm getting wet here," wheezed Ray Keene. "Oley, fetch the lady a hankie."

A big hand smelling of cigar coming over her shoulder. In the hand, a box of tissues.

One hour later, Ray Keene died holding Molly's hand.

28

If up to Oley, the husk of Ray Keene would have been laid out on a bier and the bier left on a high hot place for the turkey vultures. Oley said, "A man makes his own way, has his own medicine — this is my way. I would wish for my father's spirit to return to the White Painted Woman who is our Mother."

But no matter how he worded it, the State of Arizona made a terrible fuss — therefore, on the third day after Ray Keene's one hundred and first birthday, Oley and Molly Brock placed the urn of his cremated remains in one of Brue's panniers, and walked out into the desert. Oley chose a place below the final terrace where Wyatt Earp kept his vigil by a pool shaped like a star, and there he and Molly poured the old man's ashes into a hole at the foot of a saguaro half his age.

Standing back with Margarita and Jorge and Elvia and an absurdly suited and painfully young lawyer called Steve Faulder representing Mace & Dickman — arrived first thing this morning: already too hot, a little pot belly, toothpaste in the corners of his tiny mouth, Faulder couldn't look at Molly with her hair cropped close to her skull — Oley gazed out over a desert shivering with heat, and said, "I have buried the father of my heart. I have done the last thing."

Molly, only a guest, and trying to gauge her proper place behind everyone else, kept a tight hold on a restless Brue, and a tighter hold on her tears. He was old. Ray was terribly old, much older than most men ever get. Let him go.

Oley reached out for the young lawyer's hand. Engulfed it with his own. "I thank you for coming here. I ask you to thank Mr. Mace and Mr. Dickman. They have done what my father wanted." A nod for Elvia and Margarita and Jorge, a smile for Molly. "I am going now."

Of them all, only Steve Faulder asked, "Going, Mr. Coloradas? Where are you going?"

"It is a good day to die."

"Excuse me. But... die? You can't die."

"I can die."

"But why? Are you upset? Is it grief? Do you need a grief counselor? I know one. I could call her."

"As much as my heart is broken, it is not grief. I have lived many years and done many things. I am a man, and a man must die as he has lived. A cancer like my cancer will not let me die as I have lived."

Molly's knees buckling. Cancer! Cancer is why Oley is so thin. Cancer is why he does not eat. Cancer is why he holds himself so tightly. He is in pain. He's dying. Did Ray know?

Molly's father rushing into Molly's mind. In a hospital and pinned to the bed, tubed and tied and monitored and drugged—not a father but a diagnosis. A patient with pancreatic cancer, a "thing." But before that, Lindsay Brock had pleaded with them. He'd begged them to leave him in peace: "Let me go, let me go!" He told them it hurt, it hurt more than they could know. He told them they were hurting him, they were shaming him. Mother rushing about. Norma hush-hushing him. Saying to one and to all: "Never mind what he says, he's not in his right mind."

They all listened to Norma.

Lawyer almost hopping in place, seeking agreement in Jorge's face, in Margarita's, even in Molly's. "But if you're sick, Mr. Coloradas, you should be in a hospital. These days there's so much they can do—"

"When I was ready to be born, I was born. Now that I am a man and I am ready to die, I will die."

"No. Wait." Faulder reaching for an inside pocket in his suit jacket, slipping out a cell phone. "You're not in your right mind. I'm calling a doctor."

Oley dismissed him by turning away, his eyes seeking out the high place he would have chosen for Ray. Then Oley Coloradas, son of Leino Coloradas, walking away into the shimmering heat, his stride long and his footing firm.

Molly restraining Brue from going with him. Molly watching him walk away.

He isn't like you were, Molly. Oley won't just walk until he dies. Oley will jump. Oley will fly away. He'll choose a place so high that before his body hits the ground, his spirit will soar.

Cell phone at his ear, Faulder was asking for a Dr. Peiser. "A conference? Drag her out of it. And do it quick, it's urgent!"

That is, his spirit would soar, but not if this saggy baggy son of Mr. Hate has anything to say about it. Bet he plays golf. Bet he plays golf in the desert.

Faulder, waiting for whoever Dr. Peiser was, glancing round at Jorge, a rash of self-important anxiety rouging his face. "Soon as I talk to the doc, I'm calling the cops. Or you could call the cops. Why're you just standing there?"

Jorge just standing there. Faulder looking at his phone, still no doctor on the line—and Oley rapidly becoming a mirage. Quickly hanging up to redial. "Fine. I'll call 'em. Right now."

Molly thinking: no phone, no call. So who's in the majors when it comes to pitching cell phones? You are, fair wanderer.

As smooth as a sidewinder over sand, Molly plucked the phone out of his hand, a powerful twist of the wrist, and in three neat pieces, Faulder's little cell phone bounced off a rock twenty feet below.

A furious and embarrassed attorney-at-law spinning to confront whoever, and whatever, she was.

For a relative beginner, he spoke outraged lawyerese fluently. "As an official representative of the law firm of Mace & Dickman, who as you certainly know handles the Ray Keene estate, I'm ordering you off this property — right this minute." Then, spinning back, he hurried after Oley, calling out, "No! Wait! I can help."

On her thirty-seventh day of walking away, Mrs. Warner could have gone home, or to a cop station, in a cop car. Thanks to Oley's illegal death, there were enough in the driveway to choose from. Instead, she and Brue climbed a faint path that began behind the little stable and went straight up through a cleft in the sheer rock. Eventually it led, Jorge assured her, to the road that would take them back to the city. Another minute, and they would be out of sight of the house and its terraces and the overheated lawyer standing in front of the three car garage explaining everything to an officer of the law.

His explanation, no doubt, includes you, good golly Miss Molly. How you showed up from nowhere. How you have no hair and no visible means of support and how you have made yourself at home. How you hindered him from saving Oley's life. Oops, here comes a TV news truck.

"Move it, Brue."

"Awww EEEE!"

"And shut up."

An hour later, they'd come to the top of the ridge of standing-on-end rocks above Ray's land. Off to the northeast — finally — high and low, good and bad, in beauty and in horror: the city. It was still there, still going about its business, still getting bigger and louder and messier and dirtier and meaner by the day, and still full of people she did not know and never wanted to know.

And that goes double for the saggy baggy golfer demons and for all the bloody dune buggy wankers and for anyone related to Paula of the Copper Crown Mining Company. Triple for whoever it was who allowed every Ray Keene & Fanta Coloradas movie ever made to rot in their cans.

Somewhere off to her right, still hidden by the spiny shoulder of a steep *bajada*, was the Calle de Flores mall.

And near the cantaloupe mall, her apricot house. She'd be in it by sunset without fail.

And who will be there to meet you? Hope they've taken their Valium.

Directly below her, just as Jorge had said it would be, the paved road to and from Ray's house. Seldom used except by Oley in the Cadillac Eldorado, or Jorge in his truck, now there was one cop car heading down towards the city, and two heading up towards the house, and these were followed by a wailing ambulance. Behind the one cop car, Steve Faulder's SUV: red, almost new sticker on the back bumper that said: *I fought the law and the law won.*

"Better have a seat, Brue. We might be here for some time."

29

The day you walked away, this is the place you were looking for, Brock. High up on the side of a mountain and all around a desert so strange and so beautiful, it's a privilege just to breathe its air.

Somewhere "nice." With a good view.

A month ago you might have died here. Who knows where you'll be a month from now. One thing you do know — if it's up to you, you'll be alive. And glad of it.

On her head, Charity's hat. On her hip, one of Leino's knives in one of Leino's buckskin sheathes. In Brue's panniers, everything they'd arrived at Ray's with, plus Margarita's hastily gathered offerings as soon as she'd heard the cops were coming.

"Go now," she'd said, "the police, they will take you away, they will question you. But come back. Mr. Keene, for many years he took care of us. He would want to take care of you. He would want you to stay here with us."

"Thank you, Margarita, but Oley knew when to die. And I should know when to go home."

"We will miss you."

On the mountain now and looking out over the city, light hand on Brue's lead rope, Molly sat on Cowboy Tom's

pillow. No need for it tonight, no real need for it ever
again—your pretty little house has plenty of pillows—but
no need to ruin it. She'd spread out black plastic underneath.
Also in the panniers, a copy of *Be Mine Tonight* by B. Keene.
Picture of the author on the back. Nice looking middle
aged woman in a twin-set and pearls. Who was she, do you
think? His mother? Publisher? Agent? Eileen, the Beauty
of Bisbee? Wish you'd asked when there was still time.

The plan now was to drink a bottle of Ray's Evian water
and to read a Ray book until things settled down on Ray's
road—and then she'd go home. Things had finally become
as simple as that.

As simple as that? If only. For what happens then?

Molly opened her book. Page one, first sentence.
Couldn't see it for the tears.

You're crying. When did you start crying?

Didn't see the horned toad that looked like a Japanese
Samurai on the hot red rock beside her. Didn't feel the blast
of the sun which made sweat trickle down the skin of her
back and her belly. Wasn't aware that Brue had come to the
end of his rope and was testing a cholla fruit with tender
lips. Molly suddenly crying for the dead man of Mexico
walking towards hope. For the terrible loss of Ray. For the
loss of Oley. For Shelley. Molly finally crying for herself.

What happens then is this. You find Shelley and tell
her you love her. Tell her she's all grown up now, but if she
needs you, you're there. Then you call Peter Jr. and tell him
you love him. You do love him even if you don't actually
like him. Wish him well and let him be what he is. Then, if
Peter doesn't happen to be home, you go looking for him.
You'll tell him he and his father don't have to "help" you
anymore. You'll tell him you want a divorce. Nothing
nasty, nothing greedy. No intent to hurt or to punish or to
gouge for the apricot house or for money. Only a clean and
honest parting of the ways which have already been very
parted for over a month. Over a month? Longer. Much
longer. Tell him you'll put it in writing. And then? Well,
then—who the hell knows? But whatever it is, it will not be
more of the same.

Mother instantly slamming into her head. As usual. "But what about the house in Laurel Canyon? You'll never see the house again."

Fuck off, mom.

"Of course, you do realize, Miss Crisco, you will have to get a job."

Molly jumped where she sat.

That's right! A job! But who would hire you? To do what? You took art in college, for fuck's sake. You haven't had a job in years. You've turned into one of those good women who volunteer for things. You're one of those very nice women who do unrecognized but very important things and never get paid for them. Like raising children and sheltering the homeless and protecting the abused and campaigning for clean air, clean water, wholesome food, less money for war and more for education. Unlike bankers, crooked politicians, corporations, and Charity's saggy baggies, you're the glue of the world. When did that happen? When did you stop being different and unusual and become one of "them." One of who?

Oh hell. Oh my god. Oh bloody bleedin' poop.

"Knock it off. Stop crying. You'll cope."

First page of Ray's book, first sentence. "When Roger came home from the war, more than his leg was missing."

Molly is sixteen. She's spending her last summer at Aunt Evelyn's farm, not that she knows it. Aunt Evelyn probably knows it, but then Aunt Evelyn isn't sixteen and confused.

A month ago, Molly met Antonio. Antonio is eighteen, half Jewish and half Mexican. He plays the guitar. He writes his own songs and he sings them, out loud, anywhere. Antonio looks like Jim Morrison, only ten times more soulful and twenty times less vain.

She's in love. Love, she's in the midst of discovering, hurts. And one of the most hurtful things about being in love is being apart. Another of the most hurtful things about being in love is being together.

Norma hates Antonio. Enough said. It's summer. The children of summer are doing what they always do. When

they are sixteen, what they do is group together and feel
different and unusual. Molly is on the farm again. Antonio
is not.

Molly is lying in a hammock strung from the porch to
an avocado tree. Her aunt is sitting on an upended stump
drinking a beer. No glass. No beer opener. Overalls and a
man's shirt. Hair piled on her head in a messy bun. Molly
thinks her mother's sister looks like a young and slender
Ma Kettle. She thinks her mother Norma looks like Joan
Crawford after Crawford was embalmed, but before she
died. The only person she's ever said this to is Antonio.
Antonio said she was funny. "You make me laugh, Molly.
I really love that about you."

Molly can't think of anything but Antonio, or more
precisely, can't think of anything but how she feels about
Antonio, but Evelyn can think of everything and anything —
and always does. For the moment, she isn't talking. Molly,
in a rush of young anguish that feels like true love, cries out,
"I hate her."

"If you're speaking about my sister, I know how you
feel."

Molly surprised. Looking at her aunt. "You do?"

"Yep. Hated her all my life. Love her too."

"You can't love someone you hate."

"'Course you can. Happens all the time. Poor Norma.
Poor thing can't help herself. It's how she's made. You got
to let her be."

"But she hates everybody. She hates me."

"Hates you? She doesn't hate you. It's just she can't see
you through herself."

Molly doesn't know what to say to that. Out of a
hopeless love, she was hoping to talk about hate, how it
feels, she wants to chew on it like gum. Make shapes out
of it. Savor her hatred. Aunt Evelyn has changed that. But
into what?

"Come on. We'll make something. Today I feel like an
artist."

Evelyn off her log, wiping the seat of her pants, throwing
her empty in a big bucket of empties.

By the end of the day, Molly and her aunt have painted a wall in the kitchen. Between the pantry and the fridge, there is now a half opened door and beyond the door, a glimpse into a deep green jungle. Molly thinks what they have done is wonderful, but she still wants to go home. Or rather, get back to Burbank to see Antonio. Savor her turmoil. It's hers. It's who she is at sixteen.

Before dawn, Molly is out of bed and on the road. She's running back to Burbank.

Three days later, Antonio has packed everything he owns into an old duffle bag. He's taking a bus to New York City to sing. He will be a songwriter, a singer, a poet. Stars in his eyes, he asks Molly to go with him.

Molly tries. Even though she has run away, she still phones Aunt Evelyn for advice and Aunt Evelyn says, "Think of it, Molly — New York City!"

She phones her dad. And he understands. He really does. His voice is a husk of understanding. "I just want my little girl to be happy. But you're so young. And New York is such a hard place. It's full of hard people. And what would you do there? You haven't finished high school. How would you take care of yourself?"

"Antonio will take care of me."

"As a folksinger?"

"I can get a job."

"Doing what? What can you do?"

Molly doesn't know what she can do. And Lindsay, hearing this in her voice, says, "Wait à while. If the boy loves you and you love him, it will last. Do what's in your heart. But honestly Molly, I've worked so hard to send you to college. I've been counting on it."

Molly doesn't go with Antonio. She doesn't ask her mother for advice. But her mother somehow knows something. She says, "If you're thinking of doing anything with that Jew boy, Molly Brock, you'll do it over my dead body. Good grief! Isn't he a Mexican too?"

Molly meets Peter Warner in college. It's not love at first sight. It doesn't feel like it did with Antonio. It doesn't hurt. But it's very nice. For one thing, he has a great car, a white Thunderbird with portholes. The top comes off.

And that house. Which belongs to his mom and dad but will one day be his.

Oh no. Can't blame Norma, Molly. Peter was your choice and your choice was who you were right up until you walked away.

30

Nothing up or down for over two hours now. The news truck was long gone, trailing after the ambulance that must have held Oley's body — taking it away, burning it, burying it, hiding it.

And Oley, where is he really? You know where he is, Molly Brock. He's where he wants to be. Oley's with Ray and Ray is with Lola Valdez. And Lola and Ray and Oley are with Leino Coloradas who lives with his mother, the White Painted Woman. And they all ride with Wyatt Earp. And they all ride with Doc Holliday. Every one of them heroes. Every one of them Ghost Riders in the Sky.

She'd counted the departing cop cars. Enough of them gone to make all of them gone.

If she were to go back now, turn Brue's nose around and walk back the way she'd come, there could only be Jorge and Margarita and Elvia in Ray's beautiful house.

Go on. Do it. Turn around and go back. Give yourself just one more night. Go back and say goodbye in quiet and in peace. Molly resettling Brue's panniers, setting her face towards the road. No. Can't. Get behind me, Sweet Mother Light Temptation. Have to go face whatever there is to face — at "home."

"Here we go, Brue. If no one arrests us, we'll be there by dark."

Straight over the side and down the loose stones of the path to Ray's black-topped road, then following that road down until it met up with a larger road, a four-lane that ran directly towards the heart of the city, picking up traffic as it went.

Can't go there, can't use the wider, faster, straighter, four lane. A woman and her ass could get her ass kicked walking that one; people and their cars go too fast, see too little, stop too late—best to cut over the trackless *bajada* somewhere off Ray's lonely road.

It was best to go back just as she'd walked away, straight through the Sonoran desert.

But first she had to travel along the shoulder of the little-used road she was on as it cut through a small desert basin before skirting the last cholla'd *bajada* before trash and suburbia.

Four days before walking away, Mrs. Warner snorted awake in the middle of *General Hospital*. Two doctors stood at the foot of a hospital bed. One said to the other: "She won't make it. It's fatal." All of them: two doctors, the patient, and three of the patient's worried friends, looked as young as Shelley, as vain as Peter Jr., as air brushed and too-perfect as the faces on hair dye boxes, and as vacant as—you are, Mrs.

Mrs. Warner fell off the couch trying to reach the remote.

"I see you're enjoying yourself."

Peter. He's home.

Mrs. Warner climbing back up off the carpet, using a table leg for support. Valium doesn't leave you much room for grace. Her wandering husband already off to the kitchen. The kitchen! When's the last time you cleaned the kitchen?

Propped against the wall, she's straightening her hair, retying her robe. It's—a glance at the kitchen clock—ten minutes after three and she's still in her bathrobe.

Ten minutes after three? What's Peter doing here?

Peter with a salami in his hand. In his other hand, cheese. "Isn't there any bread in the house? Where's the bread?"

"Have to go shopping... "

"Yeah? Like a lot of other things you have to do."

"I'm sorry, honey, I was... "

Peter slamming the salami down on the kitchen table. "What's the matter with you? What's got into you? This isn't like you."

Something in his voice made her spine sag. Is there pity in his voice? If there's pity in his voice, maybe you can tell him about the panic, about getting old, about being lonely, about Shelley, about Peter Jr. and your mother and his mother, about his father. About him. "I don't know. I don't know what's the matter with me."

Peter coming closer, leaning down to peer into her eyes. "You sick? You want to see a doctor?"

Do you want to see a doctor? You've already seen a doctor — that's where you got all the pills.

"No. I'll be all right."

Peter standing straight again. He was always a big man. Now he was a very big man. "Damn well hope so. Damn well getting sick of this." Picking up the salami again, slamming it down for a second time. "I'm going out to eat. I'd invite you along, but how long could it take you to look good?"

Peter back out the door.

Molly leaning on the wall, watching him go. Poor thing. He's as lost as you are, Mrs. Warner. Only difference is, you know it.

So close to home now. Old woman's hat brim shading her face, Molly sleep walking for the past hour. Nose to the ground, Brue sleep walking too. Two or three cars, all that had passed. And a Pima County maintenance truck. None gave her a second look.

You're day-dreaming about Ray. Broiling in the sun and thinking about that old man. Old man took in Oley when Oley was thirteen. Poor kid saw his father die, killed on Sunset Boulevard by a beer barrel. Barrel was part of a delivery, got away from the delivery man, rolled down the boulevard, people leaping out of the way. Crushed Leino against a wall.

Old man wasn't an old man then. Old man was in the prime of his life between careers and between wives, living in his beautiful house with the ghost of Wyatt Earp. Couldn't happen now. A single man raising a child. Girl or boy. Now everyone would suspect Ray's motives. Nowadays they'd wonder if he was a pervert.

Sad Times at U.S. High.

This is how Norma Brock died.

Sitting at the kitchen table in the little house in Burbank. Frozen dinner cooking in the microwave, a game of solitaire spread out in front of her. Just about to place a black eight on a red nine, she'd fallen forward and died. If it weren't for the corset, she might have smashed her nose. Instead, she fell only so far and then stayed there. Eyes open and staring at the cards.

Coroner said she sat like that for over a week before the mailman noticed the smell.

Peter Warner and Mrs. Peter Warner were with their kids in Hawaii.

Norma's sister, Evelyn, took care of everything.

The Warners flew home for the funeral. Norma's entire Bridge Club came. It was a respectable turnout.

More than you'd ever get, Molly Brock.

Norma's only child felt empty. She sat in her pew waiting to feel something. She never did.

Brue stumbling over a rock. Molly stumbling over the same rock. Both of them waking up. Brue pricking up his ears, then laying them down. Brue snorting and shaking his little white beard. Brue growing skittish. Molly growing concerned he was skittish.

"What's that, Brue?"

Up ahead, a huge angry swarm of something, or a vast, dark, low-lying cloud, or the thick dust thrown up by a fleet of tractors, or the black smoke from an enormous dump fire, or an oncoming wall of exploded debris. Or none of these. But whatever it was or wasn't, it was headed straight for them.

Brue planting all four feet, not budging another inch.

Suddenly, from the side, a sharp gust of crosswind so strong Molly was pushed against a braying Brue who lost his footing and went down on his bony knees. At the same moment, a hundred or so feet farther along the road, a giant saguaro with as many arms as the dancing Kali went down, whumping smack! into a wash. And then—nothing. There was nothing because the swarm or cloud or dust or smoke was on them, thick enough to choke, thick enough to blind.

Oh my bloody christ—it's a haboob. It's a sand storm. And it's fucking huge!

Molly struggling to rip her tee shirt in two, to tie half of it around Brue's tossing head to protect his eyes, then struggling to cover her own eyes and nose and mouth with the other half.

Got to get out of this, but where? Nowhere to hide.

Hugging Brue's head, taking one terrible step at a time along the black top, feeling her way, Molly inched towards the fallen saguaro. Only knew the saguaro was there, because it was very much there before the haboob hit. Thorns ripping into her jeans, catching at her denim jacket, raking along her cheek. Must have lost Ray's road, no cacti in the middle of Ray's road. My god—we're not on the road, Brue!

Brue hee-hawing with woe. Brue leaning on her legs, stepping on her feet. Eyes squeezed shut, Molly crashing through a cholla, opening her mouth to scream her pain and dismay, only to get a mouthful of cloying grit and dust. Spitting and choking. No breath. No light. No hat—hat was gone with the wind. The skin of her face and her hands stinging with driven sand and all around—inside her head and out—a sound like a jet engine revving up. And up. And up.

Deafening, terrifying. We should lie down, nowhere to go but down. Get to the big cacti. Hide under the cacti. Get under the worst of it.

She found the fallen giant by stumbling into it. Ignoring the thorns, ignoring the disturbed bug life. It was all there was of shelter.

Twisting Brue's head to force him down; Brue raising it higher. Tugging down hard on his halter, leaning on his neck; Brue pulling away. Brue suddenly rearing into the haboob, half a tee shirt torn from his head, panniers torn from his back, both instantly gone in the dark of the hellish yellow dust. And then — Brue gone too. Little donkey letting out a last Awww EEEE! and lost in the twisting roaring haboob.

Molly screaming, "Brue!"

31

All the world was gone, swallowed in a sulfur yellow wall of shrieking sand.

Molly far under the fallen saguaro, tucked away in its arms, trying to avoid its spines — but what was pain compared to being swept away? Or ground away.

A breathless minute passing. Two. Three. Her eyes tight shut against the wounding grit, Molly Brock, riding her panic. Letting it buck, but holding on.

You are not afraid of fear. You will not get the heebie jeebies. You will not become helpless with panic. You will get out of this — and when you do, you will find Brue and get him out of this with you.

Molly talking aloud to herself, close to chanting, not hearing a word over the wail of the wind.

Wild burros live in the Sonoran desert. They live here year round, year in and year out. You never hear of any of them dying in a haboob. You never hear of people dying in a haboob. Haboobs are only wind in a desert. They never last long. If wild burros don't die and people don't die, then Brue won't die. No — he — won't.

But the wind can die, slowly, slowly, and with it the haboob. Sand and grit drifting back down, covering the

small desert basin and everything in it with a thick coating
of fine dry dust.

The world gone quiet. Molly curled in on herself in the
arms of the cactus. And the heat rising.

A woman who's had a few panic attacks can take a little
fear. A woman who's had a few babies can take a little pain.
And a woman who's had a few hot flashes can take a little
heat.

Molly uncurling herself. Pulling away from the spines.
Ripping her jacket, her jeans, herself. Came the call of a
single bird. One tentative chirp. Desert rousing itself.

But here's the thing: you can't take losing Brue. If you
lose your companion, you have nothing left but fear and
heat and pain and your life, Molly Brock.

Molly, crawling out from under the giant saguaro.

Two hundred summers and two hundred winters and
nothing in all that time had stopped its climb to the sky. Until
now. Cactus stood here when the Spanish came calling.
Cactus kept growing when Mexico moved in. Cactus was
old when Wyatt rode by. But it was ephemera to the desert.
Desert raised it up and the desert knocked it down—all fifty
green and pleated feet of it, not counting the spiny arms.

No thought for the tears in her clothes, for the punctures
in her own skin, Molly Brock was penniless and pannierless,
and she stood in the middle of Ray's road, bleeding, her
ears ringing, her skin stinging, her eyes watered with red
tears.

A few more miles and you're home. It's just over the
same *bajada* it was just over before the haboob hit, no more
than a long hot walk in the settling air. Clearing her throat
of grit, spitting out sand. But not without Brue. Find him,
Molly Brock, you fair and resourceful desert wanderer
you.

Molly turning in place, all three hundred and sixty
degrees—but no little brown donkey with a little white
beard and a big white belly anywhere. Molly stepping out
one way, then another.

Stop! Think about this. Use your head. A haboob
isn't a hurricane. It isn't a tornado. A haboob couldn't lift

up an entire three hundred pound burro in Pima County and slam him down over in Cochise County. A haboob is a dust storm. Nasty — but not deadly. The most it could do was... my god. Look! Those are my overalls.

If those were her pink overalls stuck in the branches of an ironwood tree, and her overalls had been in Brewster's panniers — then where were the panniers?

Catch in her throat, sharp pain in her heart. "Where's Brue?"

Molly now far from the road, calling over and over. "Brue! Brue!"

She found Charity's hat in the greasewood. Old woman's old brown hat blessedly back on her head, she found her brown leather Gucci bag. Poor purse had been through hell in the last month, one whole side looked like someone had tobogganed down Highway Ten on it, but oddly — what had been inside it was still inside it.

She found a lot of black plastic, but the way things in the desert were trash wise, she couldn't be sure it was her black plastic. She found her enameled cup and one of her candles. And then she found the Mexican panniers. They'd blown into a huge prickly pear, a monstrous thing, complex with pads and spines, growing on the edge of an arroyo, much like the arroyo she'd once fallen into, long long ago. Cowboy's green and orange mummy bag was still in one of the panniers, his pillow still in the other.

She found all these things. Even more, she'd found all the things that had been thrown away, blown away, run away, from everyone else, and yet she hadn't found Brue.

You haven't found Brue. It's been an hour, maybe more than an hour — where is he!

Shaking with nerves, Molly threw back her head and screamed, "Brue!"

Came back a faint, "Aw ee."

Molly Brock almost fell into an arroyo a second time. Was that real? Please god or manitou, whoever you are — make it real. "Brue?"

Nothing.

"Where are you, Brue?"

Nothing. But she'd heard him. She was sure of it. Who else could it be?

Molly dropped to her knees, then onto her belly, wriggling to the edge of the arroyo so that she might look down, and oh lord, there he was, fifteen or so feet below: your very own donkey.

Brue was standing on his hind legs but his front legs were dangling in the air.

Why's that? And why is his head twisted up and his neck bent sideways?

In horror, Molly suddenly understood. In falling, Brue's rope halter had snagged on a root just as her purse had once snagged on a root. If the drop had been farther, the arroyo deeper, little donkey would have snapped his neck. As it was, poor Brue couldn't lower his head or his front legs, couldn't straighten his neck.

Look at the ground all around him—churned up and dug into. He's been hanging here, balanced on his back legs, struggling to get loose.

Molly scrambling to her feet. "I'm coming, Brue. I'm coming."

Brue's eyes rolled back in his head as he pulled up on the halter, his hind legs digging for purchase, his front legs feebly kicking the air. Got to get down there, got to get down there right this second! There's something about the roll of his eye. Something about the way his lips are pulled back from his big orange teeth and the way his flanks flutter and tremble.

No doubt about it—Brue's slowly choking to death.

Like her first arroyo, this one was straight up and down. Like her first arroyo, the roots of ironwood and palo verde grew from its walls of dry red dirt. No time this time to run along the edge looking for an easy way down. No use jumping in. This time she'd probably kill herself. Nothing for it but to swing down, or climb down, or scramble down, using the roots to cling to. Too bad if her back throbbed with saguaro punctures, if she banged up her knees or twisted her shoulder or gouged more holes in her hide on the way down.

Dropping those things she'd found looking for Brue by the prickly pear, but making sure of her hat and the last bottle of water tucked in a pocket, Molly was over the side and working her way down the tangle of roots. A ragged cut in the side of her hand opened wider and bled. She pulled a muscle in her back. She scraped her ankle when her foot slipped off a root and banged into a protruding rock. But she scrambled down and she did it fast.

Knife out of its sheath, she sliced through the rope of Brue's halter even faster... and Brue came down on his front legs with a hard dry cough but without a bray.

Her arm around his neck, her sand-blasted cheek to his, she felt Brue's legs wobble, front and back.

She let him lean his full weight against her hip. She let him drink half of their water. And then, when he'd shook his scrub-brush mane and flipped his toilet-brush tail and shuddered in his skin—a cloud of hot yellow dust engulfing them both—Brue said, "Awwww EEEEE."

It was louder and brassier and longer, and hearing it, Molly kissed his soft hairy nose.

At this, whatever was keeping her up and moving, simply slipped away. You need a rest, Molly Brock. Brue needs a rest. Sun's high and blazing, getting like the oven in Ray's Bisbee bakery down here.

Before the last of their long walk home, they would have one more nap in the dappled one hundred degree shade of a palo verde tree.

32

The morning she walked away, Mrs. Warner had a hair appointment.

Waking on the couch—you fell asleep on the couch again—she told the time by the TV. *Good Morning America* was saying good-bye. Bye bye.

Mrs. Warner stumbling off the couch and into the bathroom. Can't be late for Henri, getting an appointment with Henri was like catching the head waiter's eye at the Regent Beverly Wiltshire. After her hair, she'd go shopping. Told Peter she'd do some shopping. What did he say he wanted? Bread. And when did he say he wanted bread? Hard to tell. Time just kept slipping by, slipping by.

Maybe you're taking too many pills, Mrs. Warner?

After her hair, and after Safeway, there was something else. What was it? Cleaners? No. Bank? No. Oh right. The Jeep Cherokee. A service, it needed a service.

Home phone rang.

Halfway to the bathroom, Mrs. Warner froze. Who could that be? Who calls here? No one calls here. Landline on its third ring.

What if it's important? What if it's about Shelley! If it's about Shelley, you'll be sick, can't take any more news about Shelley. Maybe it's Shelley herself. Calling you. Hi Mom!

Mrs. Warner scooping up the receiver. "Yes?"

"Hello. This is your long distance carrier. We were wondering if—"

Mrs. Warner slammed down the phone.

Hand reaching for the knob of the bathroom door, home phone rings again.

Ignore it.

Mrs. Warner throwing cold water in her face—wake up, wake up—and the phone ringing. On the fifth ring, the machine picked up. Her own voice saying, "Hello, you have reached the Warners. No one can come to the phone right now. Please leave a message at the tone."

Beeeep.

"Molly? You there?"

Oh my goodness. It's Stan! Why's Peter's dad calling? Molly on the verge of running, until she remembered she's here, and he's—not here. He's on the phone.

"You're probably there, Molly. Listen, I've only got a minute here. I've been talking to Peter and we both think things have gone far enough. It's time something was done. So I've made a few calls, talked to a few people, pulled a couple of strings. I've got an appointment for you with a doctor at this place I know—very expensive, very exclusive, out near Palm Springs—for the day after tomorrow. Peter's driving you there. He'll be home tomorrow night. So you pack a few things. Joanna and I'll be out to visit in a few weeks. In Palm Springs. You'll love it. And I can get in a little golf."

Click.

Mrs. Warner cold all over. Her teeth chattering, she stared at the phone.

Where were you going? Yes. Chez Henri. Then Safeway. Then the car. Then—nothing nothing nothing. Her days were full of nothing.

She replayed the message. Listened to her father-in-law's voice, the one he used for little kids. Stan hated little kids. "Things have gone far enough. This place I know. Get in a little golf."

Not her mother, but her father's voice in her ear: The place he knows? You'll never get out, *never*.

"Take a shower. Wake up. Get out."

There was a time Molly couldn't have climbed up out of the arroyo. That time was long past. By now, Molly could make a credible showing in the Boston Marathon. But no matter what Molly could do or couldn't do, Brue could not hoist himself up the arroyo's red walls — and she couldn't carry him. They'd have to do what she'd done before: walk along the bottom until they found a way out.

But first, she'd have to climb up for her purse and everything in it. Not leaving that out here for someone to find. Pack it in, pack it out.

Molly went back up the way she'd come down almost as fast. No retrieving the panniers, they were too much a part of the prickly pear, but Cowboy Tom's mummy bag and his pillow came away easily enough. Without the panniers, the mummy bag would have to hold whatever she and Brue now owned. Which included a cup, but did not include a lot of water.

No matter. All the water we need is at home. Must be five in the afternoon. We'll be there by dark.

Molly and Brue walking again.

Overhead, a turkey vulture floated by, its pale green chicken legs trailing below it. Darting past her nose, a dragonfly with dry whispery wings, snatching little black ants from the green bark of the palo verde. A rattlesnake coiled on an outcrop of yellow rock, its black tongue tasting the oven-hot air as they passed. Snake no longer causing even a stutter of Molly's heart. But Molly pulling Brue away from the fat dusty leaves of *Datura*, then having to pull him away from its tender flower, fatal at the heart.

"You eat that, Brue, you're a goner."

And the walls of the arroyo becoming higher, not lower.

"Maybe we should have gone the other way?"

Brue not answering, just plodding along, his nose touching Molly's hip. No matter how fast or how slow she went, he kept his soft warm hairy nose on her hip.

The red walls of the arroyo got higher still as the fiery ball of the sun slid down the sky.

"You think we're sleeping out here again, Brue?"

Are you doing this on purpose, Molly Brock? Are you making this happen? If it's not one thing, it's another — so who said you can't go home again? Or step in the same river twice? Or draw a straight line. Or walk a few simple miles from Ray's house to Mr. Peter Warner's house. You and Brue, you're going to walk this desert forever? Damn. You'd think you didn't want to go home.

"The hell with it. We'll walk in the dark."

The old man had said, "Every time I walked away, I always found there was somewhere to go."

Hope you found somewhere to go, old man. Hope you're young again. Where are you going, Molly Brock?

"Dunno."

Walking with Brue by the light of the rising moon, Molly began to sing a song Antonio wrote back when she was so much smaller.

Might be in a little trouble here. No water left. Brue needs water. Who are you kidding? You need water, you singing cowgirl you.

They'd come out of the arroyo an hour back, found a wide place where their arroyo met another arroyo, and this second arroyo fading away into a shallow wash. Now she and Brue were weaving through an endless stand of cholla and barrel cactus and prickly pear and creosote, the land flat under their feet, the air black and still.

Read somewhere that long ago someone said this land was so poor, "You couldn't even raise hell on it." Love this land. Nothing wrong with this land a little water couldn't make a little better. Remember something else. General William Tecumseh Sherman was once told Arizona could be heaven — all it needed was more water and a better class of people. And he said, "That's all hell needs."

Stars and the swollen moon lighting their way.

"Look up, Brue. The stars are trembling. Oh my! Shooting star."

Brue's nose still on her hip, he nipped her.

"Ouch! Why'd you do that?"

"Awww EEEE."

"What's that supposed to mean?"

Brue stepping on her toe, butting her hip. Molly grabbing hold of his mane to keep her balance.

"What the hell, Brue — oh shit."

Directly in their way, a five-strand barbed wire fence. And beyond that, a one-story building spitting image of the cardboard box fast-food takeaway comes in. And beyond that, a water tower, white, stained, leaning a little. Beyond that, a jumble of shapes in the dark. Could be more buildings, could be rocks, could be a junk yard. All this by the side of a lonely road — a road!

There were three pickup trucks in the parking lot out front of the flat building: one of them rusted, one up on tires big enough for the back end of an agribusiness tractor, and the third no more than a year old, sleek and black and shiny — and shot full of holes.

Of course it's a bar. What else would it be? It's one of those places you and Peter'd be driving by on your way to somewhere like a shopping mall or a "recreation area," and Peter would sneer at it and call it a "pecker pit." But Cowboy Tom would say it was a painting by Edward Hopper.

Place is certainly bleak enough, lonely enough.

One door with a small round window in it, both door and window painted black. By moonlight, rest of the building could be any color, but was probably a shade of old plywood since plywood made up most of its front wall. No other windows, no steps, no porch, nothing to mar its lines but a cement watering trough from the days the customers showed up on horseback.

And one neon sign.

Held high above the roof on a scaffold of rickety sticks, it was a gorgeous snowblue in the hot black of the starry starry night. The sign said: *Road Rash*. And under that: *BABES*.

33

On her side of the fence, Molly stood as still as a bobcat at a rat's hole.

You found a road—and that's good. You found a water tower—that's even better. But you also found "civilization"—and that's good and that's bad.

Brue had eased himself close to a fence post, was lining up his rump for a good scratch. Molly pulled him away. "Too loud, Brue."

First time you've been really afraid. Like in deep-down afraid. That is, aside from your panic attacks. But panic attacks are all about the fear of Fear, and this is all about the fear of something to be afraid of. Look around you, Molly Brock. This is about the fear of the kind of people, of men, who park their pickups out in front of a place like this. It's about being a wee bit concerned when one of the trucks has been shot up for some reason. A rusted-out 1934 Ford with Arkansas plates is romantic when it's shot full of old lead. But a brand new pickup truck someone's been taking aim at in this day and this age is—well, it's not nice, is it? Question is: why would anyone shoot at a pickup truck? And the answer is: they wouldn't. Not exactly. A better question is: why was someone shooting at the driver of the pickup truck? But the real question is: is there water in that watering trough? Brue needs water. You need water. Too bad about the men and the bullet holes and this being a pecker pit all by itself out here at the back of beyond and you being all by yourself — you're going in.

"Water, here we come."

No trouble getting round the barbed wire fence. A mere walk to the road and a simple going round the end of it. No trouble with the parked pickups. Their owners were safely tucked away inside a bar called *Road Rash*. And easy enough to stroll on over to the trough for a drink. The trouble was — no water in the trough. Dead bees — large bees, African bees? — but no water.

"Not really surprising, is it, Brue?"

Brue hanging his head over the side of the cement tub, sniffing for long gone water, moving the husks of the dead bees around, tail hanging down, ears flopping over.

Molly leading Brue out back of the bar. Tying what was left of his halter lead to a bit of the plumbing. Rummaging around in her purse before stuffing it back in the sleeping bag.

"Keep quiet and wait for me. When have I ever failed you?"

Here you go. You're going to walk into a bar called *Road Rash*. And not just any bar called *Road Rash*. You're going to walk into this bar on the edge of nowhere. You're going to walk in and order a drink even though you haven't got a dime to your name. Why not? You still have plastic, haven't you? You bet you do. You just slipped it into your back pocket along with your driver's license. But you're not ordering an Evian water. Or even a martini with a twist. You'll order a beer served in its bottle. Any beer. And you'll ask the bartender to fill your two containers with water. Then you'll drink up, and you'll leave quickly and quietly — no foolish chatter. Remember, you're the Compleat Silent Stranger and just passing through. Mean no harm to man nor beast. So what if your face is rasped. If your hand is throbbing. If your ankle is killing you. Too bad you have dried blood all over your jeans and all over your jacket and you lost your toothbrush in a haboob and they're bound to think you're a dyke your hair's so short. Quit stalling. Walk through the door. Walk tall. And do it—right now.

Molly pushing open the scuffed black door with the round black window getting hit with the sound of Johnny Cash singing *A Boy Called Sue*. Also getting hit with the sour smell of beer and the fug of cigarettes and ripe body odor. Eyes already watering from the combo two steps in.

Fah. Nothing PC about this place. Good god almighty. Fluorescent strip lights and no air conditioning. Bet nobody gets too far whining around here about secondhand smoke. Screw the law. Everybody smoking. Almost makes you want to light up.

"Everybody" was the four men sitting at the bar, though none of them near each other. "Everybody" was also the bartender. But no "babes." Only babe around here is you, babe—such as you are.

No dramatic posing in the door, Molly taking a step in. Two steps.

Double shit. It's the Clantons. If it's not the Clantons, it's Ma Barker's boys. And if it's not the Clantons or Ma Barker's boys, it's as good as. But go on, belly up to the bar, Molly Earp. You ain't come for no trouble. Downright peaceable, you are. Hell, all you come for is water for you and a little more water for your trusty ass.

When Molly Brock walked in, the bartender had been smoking an unfiltered butt and watching the TV. By the looks of it, stock car racing. But nobody on the TV actually racing yet, just interminably talking about it, not that anyone could hear what they were saying over Johnny Cash. Bartender dragging his eyes away to look her over, from head to foot and back again, but going heavy on the in-between.

Bartender barely tall enough to see over his bar. But it didn't make him short. It made him loud. "Well hello, momma."

Molly walked toward the bar.

Times like these, you'd burst into chatter, wouldn't you, Mrs. Warner? Chitchat away, bright and snappy and normal. You'd be one little pig, hoping by a wall of words to keep the wolf at bay. But not anymore. Nope. Would the old woman babble? Or the cowboy? Not on your life. Would the bone hunter? Bone hunter wouldn't chatter; he'd orate. Dazzle and confuse the wankers with a flood of Brit and profanity. As for Ray Keene, old man was like Jesus — he'd disarm 'em all with a passel of tall tales. Oley? Oley wouldn't come in here in the first place. Oley would dance a rain dance and have all the water he wanted. Peter now, Peter would babble. But you, Brock, are not Peter. And it's been an eternity since you've been Mrs. Peter Warner.

Big and bulky man puts down his cigarette, turns sideways on his stool, head like a glazed ham, cross-hatched with hair. He said, "Turn the juke down, Lloyd. Ain't sure, but I think we got us a lady in here."

Lloyd was the man with a face full of acne scars closest to the jukebox. Practically yanked the juke's plug out of the wall, cheap construction board wall practically coming with it. "Good. I got to hear that asshole do any more what he calls 'singing,' one of us ain't livin' much longer."

Molly at the bar now, choosing the widest empty space which put her between Lloyd and a quiet kid with a ponytail, and almost missing the bar rail with her upraised foot. Someone in a dump like this doesn't like Johnny Cash? Isn't Johnny Cash god to these guys?

Then for one long second, nothing but the sound of stock cars revving their engines. Until the man at the end of the room suddenly slapping the top of the bar with the flat of his hand, and saying, "How'm I gonna dance with the bald lady if they's no music, Lloyd?"

And the big and bulky man plugs his ciggie in his mouth and is off his stool and over to the door, opening it a crack and peeking out.

Oh dear. Here's trouble. Ham-headed man's checking to see who you're with. Won't see a thing. No car. No friend. No back-up. Won't even see Brue. Not that you'd want him to see Brue.

Man at the end of the bar with more to say. "Rev 'er back up, Billy, and punch me up some Dolly."

Don't look at him. Don't. Have to look.

A thin man, but wiry. Muscles like ropes wound round his arms. Muscles like cords holding up his narrow head. Teeth going every which way. Hair greased back and stained tee shirt stuck to his skin with sweat. Fluorescent light shining out of his eyes.

Looks like a skinned rat sitting there staring and slowly peeling the label off his beer bottle. Got four other stripped bottles in front of him. He sees you looking. Nods his head in greeting, tips his latest bottle your way. What a gentleman. So you give him a look like—Me? Dance with you? As Shelley and her pals would say: like, in your dreams. And you keep waiting for Billy the bartender, who is, unfortunately, "punching up some Dolly." But remember who the Clanton gang is here, and who's Molly Earp. The Earp family don't turn tail and run—hell no. The Earp family can outgun the Clanton family any day of the week.

The last man at the bar was the kid with the ponytail. Nursing a Mexican beer, flicking a dead bee off the bar top, keeping his eyes on the TV.

Though maybe not his mind. You think there's something about that ponytail. You think that it's so... attentive. Could be that one's waiting to see how it goes. Isn't going to make any move of his own, too young to have the moxie, but'll be happy enough to race his engine when the starter gun goes off—so to speak. Or maybe not.

Judge not lest ye be judged.

Molly setting her plastic jugs on the bar. "Fill these up with water, Billy. And gimme—"

You're not going to order a beer, are you? A beer'll take too much time to drink. And time's one of the last things you want to spend in this bar.

"—a tequila, neat."

Rat man sliding off his stool and coming at her from one direction, ham-headed man coming from the other. Lloyd's pitted chin quivering with interest. Short Billy slopping the tequila, his pouring hand shaking so much.

Only the kid seeming distant and apart from what was going to happen.

Molly in the middle, turning to face them, taking what comfort she could in the knife tucked up her patched denim sleeve now slipping down handle-first into her hand.

Molly with her back to the *Road Rash* bar, turned slightly to keep Billy the bartender in sight as well as all the action out here on the floor. Good to see that Billy'd already filled one plastic jug, was now holding the second under the tap. Only man she couldn't see was the kid, but banking on him not joining in—not yet anyway.

She said, "I won't dance. Don't ask me."

A few feet away and still coming, a straight-faced rat man. "A course you dance. I ever saw me a dancing woman, I'm seeing her this very minute."

Knife was in her hand now, but hidden at her side. Knife in her right hand, festering cut on her left. Going to be tricky picking up a shot glass and throwing tequila down your neck, Molly Earp. But you got to do it. Got to do it for the Lassiter look of it, for the *High Noon* hell of it. Got to do it so that you're telling these nice men you aren't to be trifled with. And when you're doing it, got to look the ratty son-of-a-bitch in his wandering eye the whole time. She scooped up the shot glass with her wounded hand, knocked back the drink—wow, whoa! Billy made this himself, in his bathtub—then slammed the glass back down on the bar, upside down. Saw that last bit in an Indiana Jones movie.

"Let me put it this way: I won't dance with you."

Ham-headed man laughed, smoke pouring out of his nose. Pitted Lloyd laughed. Very Little Billy the bartender laughed. And surprise of surprises, the rat man laughed. All this laughing was making her ill. Here's another insight to add to your dance card, Brock. Hell is other people.

"Fair enough. Name's Nick. If you won't dance, maybe you'll let me buy you that drink?"

Man was close enough now to smell him, to share the air with him, to look into his bloodshot eyes.

What do you see in there? You see hate? You see fear or loathing? Maybe a little lust, but what's a little lust when it's keeping its hands to itself? A woman needs to see a little lust now and then, makes her feel—how about powerful? Grounded. You also see a little anxiety. But then—who likes being rejected? So. No, can't say as you see hate or fear. Seems to me, Molly, you've seen too many movies, read too many Zane Greys. Nick's a little drunk. A little lonely. Poor fella just wants to dance.

Molly said, "I've changed my mind."

Working the knife back up her sleeve, she let Nick spin her round the worn and sticky linoleum as Dolly sang: *Why'd You Come In Here Lookin' Like That?* And found that Nick was to dancing what Tom was to painting what Ellis was to finding bones what she was to cooking—pretty damn good.

34

"You tired, Brue? You want to catch a little sleep or you want to push on?"

Nothing from Brue. Molly would have to decide all by herself.

Brue and Molly maybe half a mile from Billy's *Road Rash* no-BABE bar and keeping well away from the potted two-lane blacktop. Two reasons. First reason: don't want to step in roadkill. Second reason: don't want to be roadkill. But staying close enough to follow the road. This road actually goes to town, no doubt about it. Nick said so. Nick also said he'd drive you home. And you said, "Thanks, but no thanks. Nice night for a walk." And he said, "Catch me walkin' around out there day or night, it's due to I went nuts. But whatever pops your corn." And then Nick and the big and bulky ham-headed man whose name never got mentioned and Lloyd wished you well and went back to doing what they do: drinking at Billy's bar. And the whole time, the kid watched TV.

"I'm tired too. But it's downright galling — you've been out here so long, Brock, you're starting to sound like Yosemite Sam — to quit so close to home."

For answer, Brue yawned, buck teeth shining by the light of the up-and-coming moon.

Lights lit up the road fifty feet behind them. Car coming. Headlights picked out a cluster of five white crosses on a curve. Old curve, new crosses. Hope whoever it is slows down. Sure is Dead Man's Curve.

"Keep still, Brue. Wait 'til it passes."

Molly and Brue standing amidst the cholla and the greasewood and the trash in the hot dead of night. Ten feet farther into the desert stretched a graveyard of junked cars and trucks and buses and assorted RUM, meaning "rusted unidentified machinery." Junk silent and still. Lumpen with mystery. Molly meaning to go on when the car had passed by. Or to bed down in all this discarded metal. She hadn't yet decided which. Headlights caught up with her now. Too late to duck down out of sight.

Brue doesn't do any ducking.

Car's awful slow. Car's too slow.

It wasn't a car—it was a pickup truck. It was a sleek black pickup like a hole in the night and it was so slow Molly could have out-walked it. From the corner of her eye, she watched it pull over to the side of the road, its tires crackling in the grit and cholla debris, bumper coming to rest inches from the first white cross.

The driver's side door opening, man getting out and walking towards her, pickup engine idling, pickup door left open.

You know who it is, don't you, Brock? Not Nick. Not Billy. Not Lloyd. Not even the nameless ham-headed man. It's the kid.

No hiding Leino's knife this time, no keeping it sheathed. This time it was in plain sight, Molly holding it as Oley had taught her to hold it, moon glinting off its blade. And she waited.

Kid stopping a prudent distance away, both hands hidden in the pockets of his windbreaker. Backlit by truck lights, can't see his ponytail, can't see his face. But you know it's him, the kid from *Road Rash*. And you know he can see your face. Keep your face blank. Like Lassiter. Like Wyatt. Like a mask.

He said, "What you got there?"

"Knife."

"Knife, huh? What you planning on doing with a knife?"

"That all depends on what you're planning on doing."

"I'm planning on having some fun."

"That's what I thought."

"I can have fun where you get hurt, or I can have fun where all you get is a little mussed. You decide."

"Seems to me I'm the one with the knife."

"That's true. But I'm the one who's probably crazy, and you never know with crazy people. Maybe you can cut 'em and they don't bleed. Or maybe they have their own knife. Or just maybe, they got a gun." Kid pulling his hands out of his pockets, making Molly's knees buckle, making her fingers squeeze the blade of the knife — easy now, easy. Don't let him spook you. Kid balling his empty fists, tapping one on top of the other. "One potato. Two potato. Scissors, rock, gun, knife. Gun beats a knife."

And all the while, the kid slowly circling round Molly and Brue, and all the while Molly turning to keep him in front of her.

Oh hell. Oh damn. Oh... klahoma. Dozens of books, dozens of lonesome silent strangers, a hundred sticky moments, Zane never mentioned how Lassiter wanted to throw up, to beg for his life, to throw his apron over his head and run away screaming.

She said, "If you've got a gun, then shoot me. Otherwise, fuck off."

"You got balls. I give you that."

Enough of the old Mrs. Warner left to say, "Thank you."

Kid reaching around behind his back. As if he keeps his gun shoved down his waistband back there. Like a movie cop. Or a movie baddie. Or like a goon in the New Jersey Chapter of the Cosa Nostra. He keeps his gun where he's seen a hundred border town Cartel honchos keep their guns. Any second now, you — you're going to die. You're finally going to die. But first you're going to have a very bad time.

Molly ground her teeth, was oblivious to the blood dripping from her hand, saw nothing but the kid, his face now lit by his headlights. How old? Twenty. Twenty-one? Younger than Peter Jr. Young as Billy the Kid when Pat Garrett shot him in the doorway of a darkened bedroom. Unlike Billy, this kid is good looking. Even grinning like a lit pumpkin, he's a good looking kid. A kid who drives the almost new pickup, the one with the bullet holes. Why's he doing this? What's it do for him? You know what it does for you, Brock—it terrifies you. So, that's probably why he's doing it. To feed on your terror.

Mother in her head. "You see, Crisco? You see what you've done? A crybaby like you out here all alone. I could have told you right from the beginning how it would end. But would you listen to me? No. Not you. You never listen to me. You should have let them lock you up. You should have let them put you away. But oh no, you had to try and die. You happy now?"

Shut up! Shut up!

Tears welling up, nose already stuffy. Won't cry. Will not cry. But oh, how this saddens you. How it makes you grieve. Just when you were just beginning to like yourself a little. Just beginning to think well of yourself.

Now Shelley in her ear. Shelley drunk and ranting. Shelley drunk and weeping. Drunk and falling off the bed and trying to explain herself. Slowed and stupid and slurred.

"Like all you feel is unhappy, Mom? Like all you feel is sad? I mean—fucking what? You wanna know how I feel? Like this totally pisses me off. Who is this fucking asshole? Who the fuck is he? This is so not fun. This is so not cool. This isn't what I'd want to be doing on my last night in the desert. So, like, Jesus H. Christ, Mom—kick him in the balls."

Molly taking a step back. The kid taking a step forward.

God dammit. You walked away to die, Brock. And you lived. You've been walking back home ever since. And will you get there? Will you ever fucking get there? Not looking too bloody likely just now. God dammit to hell!

Can't you ever, just once, bloody have what you bloody fucking want? Pissed off? You're fucking furious.

Molly feeling the blue chill of the blade in her hand. Moving her desert-thinned, desert-hardened body to keep it protected from his. Knees slightly bent, up slightly on the balls of her feet, breathing in and breathing out.

This is stupid. The kid is stupid. And scary. You're so scared of him, scared of what he'll do. But you're not panicking. He wants to see that fear. Fear's what he wants from you. Fear makes him feel powerful, and you, Brock, aren't going to give him that power. For one thing, you know how to hold a knife. And for a second thing, you know how to throw one. Oley taught you and Leino Coloradas taught Oley. You're not going meekly. Or quietly. You're goddamn Molly Brock, and you can take care of yourself. Probably.

Molly has stopped backing up.

Seconds to decide. Is he reaching for a gun? If he's reaching for a gun, maybe you could beat him to it. Scissors, rock, gun, knife. Knife beats a gun. Like James Coburn in *The Magnificent Seven*, you could stick him now before he has a chance to shoot you.

Molly holding the knife by the tip of its thin blade, fingers part of the steel, balancing it.

But what if he isn't reaching for a gun? What if he's only faking you out—and you knife an unarmed man?

Kid moving forward, his arm coming away from his body.

What's in his hand? Can't see, can't. So, yes. Yes, you could knife an unarmed man. He flat out said he means to harm you. So you can flat out throw the fucking knife. So throw the fucking knife, Brock. And do it. Now.

Letting loose of Brue's rope, flipping the knife from blade to grip in her hand, Molly turned—and ran. Straight for the silence and the shadows of the junked cars and trucks and buses, diving behind not the first and not the second but the third—and this one, not in a row, but an abrupt turn to the left and down.

Running and dodging and hearing Ray say, "With a knife, you only got the one chance, so you got to choose your moment real careful."

If you'd thrown the knife, you'd be defenseless. You missed or you did not miss, and unless you killed him instantly, he would have your knife and you would have — nothing. This way you still have your knife.

Comes his voice cold on her ear. "Hey, dancer! Wait for me!"

Steeling stars and wheeling bats and a pink coracle moon under a black sail of sky. Heart in her mouth, blood hot behind her eyes, Molly peeking over the husk of a Chevy Impala. In every dark direction: busted windows, hollow headlights, rusted engines. Metal bones, metal flesh. Brue, as she'd hoped, had trotted away, was standing in front of a gutted Bookmobile, one long ear straight up, one long ear at a right angle to his head, and for some donkey reason or other, silent. But the boy was just where he was, something in his hand lit by the light of half a moon, nothing more than an edged flicker in the loony dark.

Is it a gun? A knife? A pipe bomb? A comb and brush set?

Whatever it was, boy standing there as if he were standing anywhere, doing something — doing what? — to whatever it was he held in his hand.

Whatever he's doing, he's calm, Brock. He's calm and he's easy and he's taking his time. The boy needs you to be terrified. The boy's counting on it. Like any good predator counts on the terror of its prey.

Molly slipping the knife into its sheath, sliding back down the Impala's corroded flank, sitting back on her heels, sucking in air, slowly blowing it out, slowing the beat of her heart.

Terror confuses, immobilizes, empties your mind as well as your gut. Terror gets you killed. On instinct alone, Molly scooping up dirt, never mind thorns, glass, stinging bugs, dried whatever, rubbing it into her sweating bleeding hands. Dear Mr. Darwin, please explain frozen fear in the face of danger. How has this helped in the advancement of the species? Any species?

Long ago, back when you were Mrs. Peter, shaken from hours and hours of lonely panic, head in the toilet, skin chilled with sweated fear, you used to wonder at the use of panic. What good is it? What does it serve? Now that you are Molly Brock, head down and skin chilled with sweated fear, you have a better question. Not what, but who does it serve? You know the answer now. Panic does not serve that which panics; panic serves the predator.

Are you prey, Molly Brock? Is that what this night has come to? Or is it this month in this desert? Or is it, perhaps, what your whole life has led to?

And then, for one eternal moment, Molly pretended this wasn't happening, pretended she could change reality by ignoring it—drifting away into a golden afternoon in 1934 when Bonnie Parker sat on the running board of her brand new Ford, machine gun babied in her cradling arms, posing for her picture.

"Go on, snap it Clyde. I can't be this beautiful forever."

Kid called out, "This is fun. I'm havin' a good time. You havin' a good time?"

Hot night. Toenail moon. Dead cars. The hunter and the hunted. Am I having a good time? It's been worse. Huge black bug, buzzing and clicking, booms by her head. Molly ducking. Turning on a whirring wing, it comes back. Molly ducking again. It comes back. Enough! She swatted it out of the air, the sound of its fat little body hitting the Chevy. Blat!

Fuck this, Brock. What does a predator least expect while it's hunting? To become prey. So get up. Get moving. Blindside the fucker.

35

Bent over, almost but not quite crawling, Molly slipped quickly away from the Chevy Impala, aiming for something that once worked a farm, but was now a flimsy sculpture in rust. Allowed herself only the briefest moment to look back, to check on the kid.

Where is he?

Backlit by his own headlights, up now to the first junked car, headed towards the second. The path he took might or might not lead him to the Chevy, but it would not take him to the combine harvester or the baler or whatever it was she now hid behind. For that he would have to double back, go off at an acute angle.

Lead him in farther. Get him tangled up in this junk. Get him turned round. Think what Lassiter might do. Lassiter would consider the terrain. He'd use whatever came to hand.

Molly felt in the unseen dirt for something, anything, with weight, with heft. A rock, a bolt, a beer can, scrap of corroded metal—what's this? Fingers closing round an ancient spring. Part of an ancient car seat. No hesitating. Do it now. Standing, she pitched it deeper into the desert, aiming for an ocotillo, hoping she'd miss everything other than bare ground for the rightful sound of things, hoping to fool the kid, make him go towards that sound intent on chasing her. But Molly not depending on it. Crouching before it landed.

Came a distant dull thud. Kid halfway between the second hulk and the Chevy, stopped. Listened. Began walking towards the ocotillo.

Yes! That way you poor, pathetic, good-looking deviant.

Molly down behind the farm machinery truck so soon as she'd released the spring, sucking the edge of her hand. Palm was slick with blood. No matter. Up again.

Where is he now? Shit. Can't see him. Oh god. Oh god.

From somewhere behind her, Brue brayed. "Eee awww!"

From somewhere ahead, the sound of the kid spinning on his boot heel in dry sand.

Scared him, Brue did. A donkey scared him. Not so cool as he thinks, the horrid little predator, heartless little prick.

Molly just then noticing she was closer to the kid's pickup truck than he was. An idling pickup truck at the edge of the road. A pickup truck that had to have its keys in it.

Okay! Finally. Here's something for your side. The kid's not as smart as he thinks he is. Kid's made a few assumptions. Assumes you're a Mrs. Nobody. Assumes you're just another dumb bitch. Assumes you'll panic. Assumes this and assumes that... and it's made him cocky. Made him stupid in that very special way only a cock can be stupid.

Running flat out, she could make it to the truck before he could. If she didn't trip over a bit of car or crash into a bus or get caught in a prickly pear. If she didn't twist her ankle or go the wrong way, or do any other dumb girly thing dumb girlies do. The kind of dimwitted something that's always happening to silly helpless women in movies so the hero can save them.

Except there's no hero here. There's only you, Brock. Only you—and Brue.

Shit! Fuck! There's Brue. You might be able to escape in the pickup, but Brue can't. Molly could just make him out by the Bookmobile. What's he doing over there? Eating? Sleeping? Looks like he's just waiting for you, waiting to go home with you. But you, here you are with a way out—and you're going to risk your life for a donkey?

In answer, Molly dropping to the desert floor, crawling away from the harvester, working her way to a high shouldered school bus, a pale glow in the moonlight. Lot of the bus left, seats still in it, tires all there, every one of them flat, windows all accounted for. There's still a door and it looks like it still opens and closes. Molly headed for the door.

You're a fool for not leaving Brue. Even so—you're not leaving him. You get away, take the kid's truck, the kid could take it out on Brue. Can't have that. Can't live with that. Lived with things like that for years, small betrayals, little murders, can't do it anymore. But you get in that bus, Brock, you hide in there, and you're trapped. Even so, even so—it's sooo tempting. Crawl in and hunker down in a seat. Don't move. Maybe the kid won't see you. Maybe he'll give up and go away.

Molly as she crawled looking back, her heart leaping in sudden hope. He's leaving. He's giving up. You're not worth it. He's had enough.

Kid was walking back to the idling pickup. Kid was already out of the junked cars. Throwing something into the bed of the pickup, kid climbing into the driver's seat.

Watching him go, Molly bloomed. Every muscle relaxing, singing: Thank you! Thank you!

No spending the night here, Brock. Not another minute in the desert for you. The second the kid's tail lights disappear in the dark, you and Brue are walking all the way home. It's less than an hour away. Only a little more if you have to go round something. It's only over the hill. Soon as the kid leaves, you leave just as soon. Any minute now, any second.

Kid in the pickup, just sitting there.

He'll go. He'll leave. Even the best predator misses now and then. He's just messing with something. Probably choosing a CD to drive home to. Probably going to crank up the sound and shred the hot desert night with some blasted crudity of spoiled youth.

Molly using the moment to move around behind the bus. Hearing, as she'd hoped, music.

Not rap, not crude and not loud. What is it? It's *White Rabbit*. It's Grace Slick singing *White Rabbit*.

Once tucked behind the bus, looking round again.

Oh Jesus. Oh Christ. Kid's getting out of the pickup. He's turned off the headlights, turned off the engine, shut the door of the pickup, but opened the window so you can hear Slick. And he's coming back.

Kid slowly walking the wrong way, moving between cars, calling out in the dark, "Hey, dancer, you like this old song? Don't it make you wanna dance?"

Kid wouldn't be walking the wrong way for long. Sooner or later, he was going to find her. What to do? You could make a break for it, race him back to the *Road Rash*. It's an idea, though not a great idea. You might be fit for a marathon, but so could he. He could be a lot fitter and a lot faster than you. You could do what a rabbit does, a little brown rabbit: hide, keep still, and hope your number isn't up. But that makes you prey again, Brock. Just when you have to be the predator. So act like a predator. You can't overpower him. You probably can't outrun him. How long are the odds on waiting him out? Not good enough.

No more time to think. No more time to sit on her heels, rocking with nerves. No more time. Molly shoving her hands in her pockets. Found the bootlaces she'd put there back when she rode with Ray and Oley. Bootlaces, Molly. What can you do with the old woman's mysteriously missing old man's bootlaces?

Heart thumping, she crept back round to the front of the bus. Looking at the door, at the latch someone had once welded to the frame. Sneaking inside, moving slowly down the aisle. Windows rusted shut, two open a crack, but not budging up or down.

It'll do. It'll have to do. What's that?

On the back seat of the bus, hanging from the hand grip, suckered to the back of the back seat, was a white sack, a very large, pleated, white sack. Half empty or half full, like a hot water bottle made of gauze. Or maybe like tripe in a butcher's shop. Molly poked it. Dry. Crumbly. Poked it again, and from within came an ominous buzz.

Oh fuck. Oh god. Bees again. Big bees. Explains the bees in the dry water trough. Explains the bee in the bar. Get back from the bees. Bees wake up, find you on their bus, you could be just another dead Mexican under a mesquite tree.

Swiftly, heart thumping, Molly taking off her jacket. Leaving it on a seat with her hat. Out the bus door again. Quick quick quiet. Got to find a cactus, a barrel cactus. A small one, just the size of your head. Got to find dead cholla.

Besides heat, besides hunger and thirst and death, if there were two things the desert could give her, and give her in abundance, it was barrel cactus and cholla. *White Rabbit*—as bent sinister as it had always been—and the kid calling out for you: "Wanna dance? Let's dance, come on out and dance!" Molly quickly and quietly gathering dead cholla branches, taking them back to the bus. Picking up a dented can, its label flowered with rust. Once a can of Penzoil. Long empty. Taking that back to the bus. Unsheathing her knife to cut a small barrel cactus from its mooring.

Pick it up, who cares if it stabs you, hooks you, who cares how much it hurts, how much you'll bleed. You're already bleeding. The kid catches you, you're going to know what bleeding means.

Molly in the bus, crouched down below the windows, keeping away from the hive—a little buzz from the bees, sleepy bees, sleep—stuffing crushed cholla into her jacket, padding out the arms, the torso, wincing at the small inevitable sounds. Thanks for the music, Little Kid Krazy. If music's all I can hear besides a bee turning over in its sleep, music's all you can hear. Place the empty can on a seat towards the back of the bus, sitting the stuffed denim jacket on top of the can. Taking a moment to peek over the window sill. Kid's not too far away, but far enough. He's looking at Brue, not at you. Thinking Brue must know where you are, thinking Brue can smell you. Quickly balancing the barrel cactus on the neck of the jacket, putting the old woman's hat on the cactus, then shoving it all down as if it were Mrs. Peter "the Dancer" Warner slumped and hiding in the seat. Mrs. Warner trying not to be seen in the desert dark at the back of the bus. Mrs. Rabbit Warner hiding from Coyote.

Scramble back out of the bus. Fast.

Where to wait? Somewhere close enough, but not too close. There! Between the Bookmobile and the VW beetle. Who could junk a beetle? Never mind.

Molly stilling her heart by stilling her mind. Repeating a mantra: there's always someplace to go, always someplace to go. If you die here this night, even then — there'll be someplace to go.

"Not having a lot of fun here, dancer. Getting tired of this shit. Come on out now, we'll do just fine. You make me find you, you're gonna regret it."

Molly making the slightest noise. A small thump on the Beetles back bumper with the heel of her shoe, loud enough to be heard over Grace Slick. Immediately, the kid turned her way.

One step towards her, then another, and another, all the while saying, "I met this other dancer once." Like he's talking to a friend, talking to someone who can hear him, who wants to hear him. "This other dancer had long black hair, hair down to her butt. I got that hair in a baggie. I got the baggie in a box so it doesn't get dirty."

Another saggy baggy, Brock. The saggiest of them all.

"You already lost your hair, so what am I gonna take from you?"

Moving back a foot, Molly reaching out to push at a rusted gear in the rusted Beetle. Small sharp squeak. Just enough to be the rabbit making a final fatal mistake.

Molly dropping down and crawling behind the Bookmobile. Brue sensing her, catching her scent, wagging his ears, flipping his tasseled tail. Shush, Brue.

The kid quickly coming to stand near the door of the bus. From under the belly of the Bookmobile, Molly could see his boots, his pant legs. *White Rabbit* over and done with, Molly could hear him breathing. He's wondering if you're dumb enough to be on the bus. He thinks you're dumb enough. But he remembers the knife. He's wondering if he'd be as dumb as you if he got on the bus.

Molly's hand in her pocket, willing the kid onto the bus.

Go on. Go get her, Krazy Kid. She's just another bitch, just another ho like the rappers rap. Chanted hate, chanted bile, chanted whine, strutted whine, lockstep whine. Monotonous penile whine. She's your mother, your sister, your lover, your child. Like your religion tells you, she's there for your use. Go on. Kill her. If you kill her, you'll feel better. You don't know why, you just will. Only way you can feel better is by making a woman, the female who scares you, feel worse. Much worse.

She's not hiding on the bus. She's on the bus and waiting for you. She wants to dance.

Kid getting on the bus. Slowly, carefully, watching and listening and straining every Krazy Kid nerve to feel his own terrible need — but getting on the bus.

And as the kid did what he could not stop himself doing, Molly did what she must force herself to do. Take those few steps from behind the Bookmobile out over open ground to the bus. She had to shine by the light of the moon for one long horrid moment.

Wait until he gets past the fifth row of seats, far enough in so it takes too long to turn and run out, but not so far in he sees what's in the seat, Molly. Don't let him get a good look at the dummy in the back of the bus.

Don't let him see the hive.

Now!

Molly running for the school bus, meaning to slam the door, to close the welded latch, meaning to tie it with the old man's bootlaces. Meaning to trap the kid in there, then to grab Brue and run away, flee into the night.

Brue, hearing her come, brayed, "EEE AWWW!"

The kid, hearing Brue, did two things at once. Saw her. And turned to run for the door.

Beat him to it, Brock. Move. Folded door pulled shut. Now for the latch. Old latch squealing with rust; old latch wouldn't move. Molly screaming out loud: "Close, goddammit, close!"

Kid two strides from the door, kid's eyes wild with surprise, wider with hate.

Molly balling her bleeding fist, to use it like a hammer, hammering on the latch. "Let me *do* this!"

Molly's hand throbbing with pain, something breaking inside, but she hits out again, and the latch comes loose, slams into place, old man's bootlaces slipped through the metal loop. Only threaded once before the kid whams into the door from the inside. Laces stretched taut—but holding.

Kid slamming again, putting his shoulder into it, folded door bulging out, pressing on the latch. Laces barely holding. Won't hold a third time. Molly's fingers shaking, fingers like cactus pads, awkward, fumbling. Molly's whole body shaking as she wound the laces through the loop, over and over. And over.

Kid slamming into the door, over and over.

Just above her head, Kid Krazy at the door, one palm pressed against the glass. A little more light, a palmist could read his fortune. Kid's lips pulled back from his teeth. He's yelling at you. He wants you to let him out. He's calling you names, Molly Brock, you bad bad prey animal you.

Molly taking this one single moment to look into his face. Pony tail's come loose. Spittle on his chin. Teeth need straightening. Not to mention brushing. Whoa. Is that a pimple on his nose? Is that a bee on his shoulder? Are there more bees coming? And more bees?

Molly couldn't smile. Too shocked to smile. But she could still talk.

Comes out as a whisper. "Molly Dancer beats the Beehive Kid."

36

Molly and Brue on the *bajada* above the Calle Des Flores mall, Brue leaning on her hip, Molly trying not to lean on a young unarmed saguaro, front page of a newspaper blown against her ankle, trash under her feet, hand aching like a tooth.

Below them, everything slick with heat, weighed down with heat, nothing moving but a handful of early Sunday morning cars. No one would walk. No one would go out in this heat. Saggy baggies are all in the mall, safe from the dying desert. Sounds drifting up from Burning Jail Road. Dog — little dog, Mrs. Demon Golfer Perez and her Pomeranian, dog like a hairy golf ball with teeth, both dog and woman Peter's always saying he'd like to putt straight back to Pomerania — yapping in the A/C behind a closed window. A phone ringing somewhere. A short sharp shout, man's voice, angry.

Not Peter. You'd know if it was Peter.

No mended jacket, no old woman's hat, her good hand gripping the base of Brue's bushy mane, Molly looked down at the apricot house.

You're back, Brock. This is your house. Go on down there. Move. There's a phone in the house. You need a

phone so you can call the cops. Give them the license plate
number of a dead black pickup truck. Tell them the kid
might not, but then again he might, be sitting — or lying — in
a school bus in the junk yard half a mile from the *Road Rash*.
But just in case he'd charmed the bees, that you slashed
only two of his tires, one to slow him down, two to slow
him way down.

Molly lifted a foot, set it down, was on her way.

There's a bathtub down there. And wine. There's a bed
and books and air conditioning. What else is there? Well,
there's always Peter.

Molly stopped, though Brue didn't. Molly getting
pulled down the hill.

What the hell. Today, tomorrow. Bound to see Peter.
Accept it.

Peter wasn't there. He had been, and recently, but he
wasn't there now. House was lived in, house was a mess.
Not your mess. His mess. The mess a man makes living
alone. And he's sure to be living alone. Even if she wanted
to come, was eager to come, wouldn't do to move in the
woman from Dry River Street. Not if the police suspected
him of anything. Like the killing of his wife.

"Hello, dear! I'm home!"

Molly stood in her own kitchen, what had been her
kitchen, the kitchen she'd cleaned for a year now, cooked
in, had solitary cups of tea in, stared out the window of,
panicked in — her kitchen. It didn't feel like her kitchen. It
didn't feel like anyone's kitchen. It felt like the cave a bear
hid in, somewhere a great shaggy smelly beast brought
back bones to gnaw.

It's the kitchen of Yeats' Rough Beast. It's Grundel's
lair.

Sink full of dirty dishes, greasy counters buried in
dirty dishes, opened boxes and opened cans and burst
bags dragged from cupboards and left there, trash
can overflowing onto the floor, microwave door open,
microwave floor, ceiling, and walls splattered with hard-
baked fast food. The same old peanut butter you left — still
open and still on the counter.

Something's living in the peanut butter. Can't stay in here. Go somewhere else.

The bedroom.

Same sheets on the bed. Sheets have tales to tell, and you don't care to hear a single one of them. Whole room stinks.

The bathroom.

Jesus. Indescribable. Find the disinfectant. Find the tape and the bandages. Take care of your hand, and then get out of here.

Molly lifting her head for just this moment, staring into the mirror through the splattering of toothpaste and mouth wash. Get out. Get out of here before you start cleaning. If you clean, you're doomed.

The living room.

Molly sat on the couch. On the edge of the stained couch. What's he spilled here? What's that?

She perched on her once couch. Straight backed, knees together, feet together, hands on her thighs, prim with her desert skin and her desert hair and her desert heart. If she wanted to, she could turn on the TV. Maybe not the computer and maybe not the VCR, but she could work the TV.

Fuck the TV.

With all else, and all of it caked, coated, or matted, there was mail on the coffee table, a months worth of junk mail, bills, stuff for Mr. Peter Warner. Reaching for the phone — have to call the cops about the kid, have to do that much at least — her arm brushed the pile, knocked half of it onto the carpet. An envelope fallen from between the pages of a Walmart's sale flyer, a letter to her, addressed not to Mrs. Peter Warner, not even to Molly Warner, but to Molly Brock.

Peter hasn't opened it. He would, he always opened her mail. This one must have lost itself in the junk mail. It's from Mace & Dickman. Old man's lawyers. What could they want? For her to turn herself over to police for aiding and abetting a man to walk away? Forget that. The state didn't own Oley's life. If Oley Coloradas thought it was a good day to die, it was a good day to die.

Folding the letter in half, she stuffed it in the pocket of her pink overalls.

You're back, Brock. You're on the couch again. You can sit on it. You can lie on it. You can sleep on it. Can you still panic on it?

Only seven hours ago, eight at the most, Molly Anne Brock had faced Krazy the Kid in the dark — without panic. Now she was home, panic nibbled at the edge of her mind.

Can't breathe. Can't sit still.

Up and off the couch with the phone.

From outside, from behind the house, came Brue's bray. "Awww eeee! Awww eeee!"

Molly at the window, the one that looked out at the *bajada*. Looked away from the city, away from the street and the mall. Small yard encircled by a low wall of peach colored stone. Nothing in the yard but a gas barbecue, used once, faded to dust in the sun — and Brue. Brue had his front legs up on the wall and his long orange teeth clamped round a small hard orange that grew on the neighbor's orange tree.

You'd open the window and yell at him, but you can't open the window. Window's sealed. House keeps the desert out. House keeps life out. Got to get out of this house.

Molly standing dazed at the window. You're not home. This isn't home. It's never been home. It's a house. You used to sit in it. You used to watch TV in it. You used to clean it. But you never lived in it.

"So now what?"

Now you could sit down. You could fall down. But there's no place to land.

Back to the bedroom. Straight to the closet. Pulling out skirts and shirts and coats and shoes. So many, too many. Opening her dresser drawers. Don't need this and don't need that. None of it fits anyway. But that — that I could use. And this. Still has the yellow rag around his neck. You've kept him all these years, not leaving him now. So it's silly? So it's childish? Sew buttons on your underwear. Teddy comes too.

Out through the kitchen door into the garage. The Warners kept all their camping gear out here. Garage was spotless compared to the house. Molly digging through everything. Choosing this, choosing that.

And when it was all neatly piled in the empty space next to the Jeep Cherokee, the space Peter's Nissan Pathfinder would be pulling into at any time, Molly took a shower. Scrubbed the house off her skin.

Dressed in a pair of Shelley's old jeans—hot damn, you fit in a pair of Shelley's old jeans!—Molly opening the garage door.

Hurry up, Brock. Any minute now, someone will see you: "Missing Housewife Returns Bald!" They'll get their picture in the papers, get quoted expressing their surprise, get to say they knew all along that Mr. Peter Warner wouldn't murder his wife. Poor man, been all alone for a month, longer than a month, no one to take care of him, just sitting in his lonely house, grieving for his lost wife.

Last thing she did in the house was remember to call the police. Reporting a kid trapped in a junked bus in the old junk yard out near the *Road Rash* , she neglected to give her name.

"Brue!"

Brue, never obedient but always curious, trotted around the side of the apricot house, orange tree leaves in his mouth.

Molly woke on the morning of her fortieth day, bedded down somewhere up and over the *bajada* in a small canyon. She and Brue under an ironwood tree, a huge saguaro over the tree. She could make tea now, had a groundsheet, a small pup tent. She had maps.

Topographical map of America's Southwest spread on the ground, Brue stepping on it.

Molly pushing at him. "Get off, Brue."

Brue off, to be replaced by a strolling spider. Not as big as Puppet, but a tarantula just the same. Molly shooing it away with her bare hand. "You get off too."

Meaning to mark the map, calculate ways and means, Molly searched for a pencil. Got one here somewhere, brought a bit of everything.

In exasperation, searching her own pink pockets. Only to find the letter she'd put there the day before, the one addressed to Molly Brock.

"No harm looking now, is there, Brue?"

Tearing open the envelope. Single sheet of crisp white paper falling out, not handwritten, but typed under the letterhead of Mace & Dickman.

Brue got to the envelope before she could stop him, and ate it.

Molly, reading while he chewed.

Dear Ms. Brock,

This is to inform you that you are prominently named in the will of the recently deceased Ray Keene. If you would be so kind as to call our office at your earliest convenience, we can discuss the details.

Sincerely, John Mace

Molly turned the letter over. Nice white blank space. She refolded it, stuck it back in the pocket it came from. You never know. Could come in handy for lists. Things like that.

Now where the hell was the pencil?

"Time to be moving on, right Brue?"

Brue turning his nose to the south. Where there was nothing but desert. Which was everything.

To enjoy other titles by Ki Longfellow
visit www.eiobooks.com

or follow her online at:
www.kilongfellow.com

Walks Away Woman facts:
www.eiobooks.com/waw

For detective fiction try:
www.eiobooks.com/samrusso